Award-winning author **Karen Rock** is both sweet and spicy—at least when it comes to her writing! The author of both YA and adult contemporary books writes sexy suspense novels and small-town romances for Mills & Boon and Kensington Publishing. A strong believer in happily-ever-after, Karen loves creating unforgettable stories that leave her readers with a smile. When she's not writing, Karen is an avid reader who also loves cooking her grandmother's Italian recipes, baking and having the Adirondack Park wilderness as her backyard, where she lives with her husband, daughter, dog and cat, who keep her life interesting and complete. Learn more about her at karenrock.com or follow her on Twitter, @karenrock5.

Also by Karen Rock

Falling for a Rancher
Christmas at Cade Ranch
A Cowboy to Keep
Under an Adirondack Sky
His Kind of Cowgirl
A Heartwarming Thanksgiving
Thankful for You
Winter Wedding Bells
The Kiss
Raising the Stakes

WINNING THE COWBOY'S HEART

KAREN ROCK

MILLS & BOON

First Published in Great Britain 2019
by Mills & Boon, an imprint of HarperCollins*Publishers*
1 London Bridge Street, London, SE1 9GF

ISBN: 978-0-263-27233-8

0419

MIX
Paper from responsible sources
FSC www.fsc.org
FSC™ C007454

This book is produced from independently certified FSC™ paper to ensure responsible forest management.

For more information visit: www.harpercollins.co.uk/green

Printed and bound in Spain
by CPI, Barcelona

To star-crossed lovers the world over,
may your love be as boundless as the sea,
your happily-ever-afters deep and infinite.

CHAPTER ONE

"THANK YOU FOR coming out tonight, Carbondale!" Heath Loveland shouted into the mic at Silver Spurs, the town honky-tonk. A drumroll behind him, followed by a cymbal crash, punctuated his closing set's final remark. His bass player, Clint, hammered a quick, throbbing beat.

Heath loosened his sweaty grip on his Fender and peered into the throng of country-western-dressed locals, searching out his MIA fiancée. No surprise she hadn't shown. In fact, it would have been a surprise if she had, seeing as she disapproved of his gigging. "We hope you had a good time tonight."

Raucous hoots and hollers rose to the exposed-beam rafters in answer. Stamping feet vibrated the dusty wooden floor. Water streamed down condensation-covered windows while overhead fans stirred humid air reeking of beer, body odor and peanuts. Beneath Heath's Wranglers and black muscle shirt, sweat slicked his body.

A wide smile creased his face as he absorbed the room's electric energy. Playing for hyped crowds was like a hit of pure sunshine; it lit him up with the force of a solar blast. Hardworking folks watched his band, Outlaw Cowboys, to forget about life for a while, and he gave them that amnesia: a hat-raising, boot-stomping, tail-swishing night out.

"We love you!" a pair of cowgirls in Daisy Dukes screamed from the front row.

He tipped his black cowboy hat, earning him another ear-splitting screech, and ignored Clint's eye roll. Not a night went by that Clint didn't gripe about renaming their band the Heath Loveland Fan Club. Heck. Wasn't like Heath could do anything about it. They followed him from show to show. What's more, he'd never get involved with groupies, even if he wasn't already spoken for...though he supposed their attention figured into Kelsey's demand he quit gigging and "grow up," as she put it…

…and set a date for their wedding.

A heaviness clamped around his chest. He slid a finger along his damp T-shirt collar, stretching it from his steaming neck. She'd be fit to be tied if he told her about this morning's call from Nashville. And she'd never agree…

"Marry me, Heath!" an unfamiliar female voice hollered.

With a wink, he strummed a quick open-string scale, then cranked a tuning peg to sharpen his G, sending his hovering female fans into a tizzy of squeals and shrieks. "How about a little Johnny Cash to finish us out?"

"Yeah!" roared a pack of men near the bar. They raised their overflowing mugs.

Heath strummed the opening notes of "Folsom Prison Blues" and caught his bandmates' surprised expressions from the corner of his eye as they scrambled to catch up. Usually they closed with one of the band's originals. Yet this cover popped in his head and shot straight to his fingertips before he'd given it conscious thought.

He played close to the bridge for added twang as he growled out the opening verse. The gravelly words were dredged from a dark well inside him. Low and deep. He was stuck, trapped, he crooned, listening to the train going by without him. His chest ached. His eyes stung. Like every tune he performed, he experienced the song's pain, loss, regret, becoming the music, the notes pouring from him like an open wound.

He grabbed his Fender's headstock and bent it back, strumming low on the E string so the notes arced as they flew. When he hit the bridge, his foot stomped on his Boss compressor to give it lots of swells. Behind him, Remmy, his drummer, pounded a driving beat while Clint thrummed the deep *bow-wow-wow* bass line that vibrated your body, your organs, your cells even.

His gaze swept the stomping crowd as he sang and stopped dead on a pair of luminous brown eyes. It wasn't so much the shape that caught his attention, though they were enormous in her freckled face or the thick fringe of lashes surrounding them—it was their ferocious expression. A fierce hunger and an aching vulnerability directed not so much at him but at his music...which was him...the person few really saw.

Jewel Cade.

His new stepsister.

His fingers stumbled and missed the eight fret when he changed chords. Heat swamped his face. He tore his attention from Jewel and muted the strings with the side of his hand for the next seven bars before risking another glance.

Her magnetic eyes lifted from his guitar and clicked with his and in that moment, a strange sense of connection, a recognition, jolted through him. Despite the dim light, he spied her rapt expression. It softened her lean face, parted her full lips. She wasn't just listening to music, she was breathing it in, was sustained by it, just like him.

Music was his life support. Once taken off it, would he survive?

He ripped into his guitar solo, hammering the B7 chord, adding extra flourishes as he kicked up the tempo.

"Where's the fire?" Clint muttered close to Heath's ear, jamming beside him, but Heath only played harder.

He shredded the notes, alternating octaves, grabbing the horn of the guitar and pulling the top into his stomach to bend them. Sweat rolled down the sides of his face and his muscle shirt clung to his torso. His fingers slid along the neck from one fret to the next. He toggled while he plucked up one note, then stroked down another, fast and tight, picking like a madman. One, two...eight phrases later, and he peered up from his guitar in Jewel's direction. Was she impressed?

And why did he care about his new stepsister's opinion?

Disappointment washed over him. She was gone. He kept strumming, continued singing, but his earlier excitement faded. A few minutes later, he ended the song with a rowdy flourish to roof-raising applause. Heath and the rest of the band broke down their equipment, loaded it in Remmy's van and then sauntered back into Silver Spurs for some tall cool ones.

Clint signaled the bartender and ordered beer. "Who are you looking for?"

Heath quit craning his neck. "No one," he lied. He sought out Jewel's fire-engine-red hair for no good reason except the connection sparking between them. Had he just imagined it?

Not that he'd pursue her, even if he weren't already engaged. She wasn't even his type. He liked gals who wore makeup and nail polish, who fixed their hair pretty and smelled like flowers. Soft and sweet. Jewel, on the other hand, was scrawny and hard-edged, a prickly tomboy cowgirl who preferred horses to people and was as approachable as a cactus. Not to mention they were now family, and he was engaged to a woman he was supposed to love forever.

"Last call!" shouted the bartender to the mostly cleared honky-tonk. He slid them three cans of Bud.

"Has Kelsey made any of our shows?" Remmy asked.

"She's busy with work." Heath gulped his beer and scanned the room again.

Kelsey, a tireless volunteer and fund-raiser at the local animal shelter and food shelf, also helped at her father's ranching supply company, Hometown Ranching. When he and Kelsey married, she expected him to leave his family ranch, Loveland Hills, and join the business. He tugged at his limp collar again. Nothing against their enterprise, but working the open range left him free to sing to the cattle, compose songs by the campfire and gig in the local honky-tonks. He'd have to give it all up…

Once he agreed to a wedding date and said, "I do."

Their families expected him and Kelsey to marry, seeing as they were high school sweethearts and got engaged after graduation ten years ago. Kelsey was sweet and generous, his first love. So what was stopping him from setting a wedding date with her? It'd make everyone happy…

"Can we get your autograph?" A trio of gals shimmied close, wriggling in their boots and fringed skirts as they stared Heath up and down like he was the last steak at a family reunion.

He shot them a giggle-inducing smile and signed the backs of their phone covers with an offered Sharpie. They flicked their hair and batted eyelashes long enough to scare a daddy longlegs.

"Call me, sexy." One of them shoved a paper in his pocket before traipsing out the door, Silver Spurs's last customers.

Heath read a cell number on the note followed by a *<3 Jaimey* and crumpled it up.

"Did you make up your mind about Nashville?" Clint snagged the paper, drained his brew and chucked the can in the recycle bin behind the bar.

"Hey!" groused Kevin, Silver Spurs's owner. "Make yourselves useful and put up some chairs."

"You got it." Heath quit drinking, despite his dry, hoarse throat, and headed for tables grouped around a pool table.

"Do you ever say no?" Clint caught the dishrag Kevin hurled at him and wiped surfaces as Heath cleared.

"He's a people pleaser." One of the waitresses, June, held out her tray for the empties Heath collected. "My therapist says I'm one, too. Means you always make everyone else happy except yourself. That's why I owe five hundred bucks to Pampered Chef."

Clint slapped the dishrag on another table and swished it across the wet-ringed surface. "Are those pans solid gold?"

June laughed and her earrings, peeking from beneath a short pouf of strawberry-blond hair, danced. "My friends threw parties all month. I had to order from each or I'd offend them." She shifted her weight and sighed. "See? Can't say no, just like Heath. Though that's why we all love our heartbreaker." Her nails lightly scraped his cheek as she patted it. "Just remember: 'to please is a disease.'" She sashayed away.

"I've said no before." Heath diligently stacked Kevin's chairs, despite needing to get home for some shut-eye. In four hours, he'd be vaccinating calves alongside his brothers. He rubbed his gritty eyes, then hoisted another chair.

And what was wrong with wanting to make people happy?

"Like when?" Clint scooped peanut shells into a pail.

"Ummmmm…" Heath's brow creased as he searched out an example. "I didn't let Pete Stoughton borrow my bike."

"Dude, that was in eighth grade," Clint laughed.

"Still counts." Heath positioned the last chair and hustled back to his half-finished beer. The empty bar top met his eye. He bit back a request for another when Kevin pressed a hand to his back as he straightened from the mini fridge.

"What about Nashville? Are you saying no to that?" Clint tossed his dishrag into a bucket filled with cleaning fluid.

"Nashville?" Remmy ended what'd sounded like an argument on his cell phone and joined them. "What're you talking about?"

"Clint's been posting our videos on YouTube. Some Nashville person saw them and wants to give me a tryout."

Heath propped a hip against the bar, his tone casual, as if this wasn't the biggest thing that'd ever happened to him.

"Some Nashville person? It's Andrew Parsons!" Clint grabbed a cherry from the garnish bin and tossed it in his mouth.

Remmy's eyes bulged. "You're fooling, right?"

Heath shook his head and despite his best effort to act unruffled, the movement was jerky, tense.

"He owns Freedom Records." Remmy shoved his longish hair from his face. "They're the biggest country music company in America. Heath's gonna be famous."

Heath held up a hand. "Don't get ahead of yourself. It's only a tryout. A snowball in hell has a better chance than me earning a contract. I'm not sure if I'm even doing it."

Clint jabbed his index finger into Heath's chest. "You gotta do it, dude."

"You want me to leave the band?" Heath shoved his balled hands into his jeans pockets.

Clint shrugged. "Once you make it, you'll bring us with you."

Heath scuffed floor dust with his boot tip. "What's wrong with just gigging?"

"Nothing if you want to get paid in beer and pocket change and never have anyone except Carbondale hear your originals. You've got talent. Don't waste it." Clint ambled behind the bar and popped the tops off some longnecks when Kevin disappeared into the back room. "Wouldn't you like to make real money?"

Heath lifted the offered beer and sipped. Writing and performing music had never been about money. He understood the grasp music had over people, what they needed it for, how it got them through and the role he played. He lived his life in service to song. Freedom Records would help him reach more people, millions of lives to touch…

to move. He wanted the chance as badly as he wanted his next breath.

Remmy waved a hand. "Once he marries Kelsey, he'll be plenty rich."

Heath bristled. "Who's saying that?" Locals had accused Pa of marrying Heath's now-deceased mother for her money. The rumor mill revived last week when he married Joy Cade, the well-off widow and matriarch of their feuding neighbors, a rivalry that began over 130 ago with a suspicious death, vigilante justice and a priceless jewel theft.

Remmy chortled. "Just about everyone in Carbondale."

Clint nodded. "Quit being so sensitive."

Heath raised his bottle to cover his red face. His brothers had dubbed him "The Sensitive Cowboy" when he'd been the only one able to soothe their disturbed alcoholic mother with music. He'd been the family peacekeeper and her minder, keeping her from calamity until he'd made one selfish decision and it ended in tragedy. He bit the inside of his cheek hard enough to draw blood.

Clint cocked his head, studied Heath a long moment, then shoved his shoulder. "Lighten up, dude. And what was with that solo? Must have been one of them scouts in the audience."

"Yeah," Remmy chimed in. "That was triple time."

Jewel's magnetic brown eyes returned to Heath. "Just thought I'd shake things up." He donned his leather jacket.

Clint blocked Heath's path to the door. "So, are you going to Nashville?"

Heath fumbled with his zipper. "I have to talk to Kelsey first."

Remmy shrugged into a plaid jacket smelling faintly of hay, feed and manure. "If she loves you, she'll support you."

"Yeah, right," Clint scoffed, guffawing, then sobered when he met Heath's scowl.

Sure, Kelsey was a bit traditional. The only child of wealthy parents, she wanted the kind of respectable, conventional life she'd grown up with...white-collar parents who toiled at desks, not on microphones or in the saddle. People who sipped champagne at charity benefits rather than slugging beer in a stifling honky-tonk.

Kelsey was used to getting what she wanted, and she worked hard to get it. He'd always admired that about her, especially as she gave even more than she took. Before they'd graduated from high school, she'd fund-raised nonstop to create a college scholarship in his ma's name for students studying psychology with a focus on addiction.

Classic Kelsey. Sweet, generous and focused.

She always knew exactly what she wanted. Seeing as Heath didn't sweat the small stuff, he had no problem letting her have her way until recently. She'd given him an ultimatum: set a wedding date by the end of August or else.

Just a couple of months away...

"Promise you won't let this pass by because of everything going on at the ranch." Clint folded his arms over his chest.

Heath grimaced. With money issues dogging the ranch, as well as an unrelenting drought, Loveland Hills struggled. They'd secured an extension on their overdue mortgage until fall. If they kept their herd intact through the summer, despite dried-up watering holes and the Cades' refusal to let them access the Crystal River through their property, they had a final chance to earn enough at fall cattle auctions to prevent foreclosure.

"They can do without you for a week. Heck, I'll take off work to fill in for you," Clint offered.

Heath pulled off his hat and tossed back his damp hair. "Thanks, man."

Clint's mouth turned down in the corners. "I know you, buddy...if something comes up at the ranch, you'll bail."

"You'll never forgive yourself if you don't take a chance." Kevin called from behind the bar.

Heath's pulse kicked up as the idea of chasing his dream settled inside…like it had a right to be there. The image of Jewel Cade's rapt face returned to him. Usually she had a chip on her shoulder, a hard exterior and closed-off expression screaming "back off." Yet tonight, his music had transported even her, an exhilarating experience he wanted to repeat with millions of others. He drew in a long breath, then released it. "Okay. I'll do it."

Clint clapped Heath on the back, and Remmy shot him an approving nod.

"Don't forget us when you're a big shot," Remmy joked.

"This head ain't getting any bigger." Heath donned his hat, pulled the brim low and sauntered outside with his buddies.

After waving them off, he rounded the corner to the rear parking lot. A petite redhead, struggling to haul an enormous spare tire from beneath the bed of her dually, pulled him up short.

"Need a hand?"

His heart did a funny kind of flip when the woman turned, and deep brown eyes met his. Instantly, her surprised expression turned into a scowl.

Jewel Cade.

"Nope." She dug the heels of her boots into the gravel and heaved backward. Her biceps, revealed by a black tank top tucked into faded Wranglers, strained. With a cry, she fell on her butt, the spare tire still lodged beneath the rear bumper.

"Do you need to change it?" Heath eyed the dual-rear-wheel truck. She could easily get home on what she had.

"I'm. Not. Showing. Up. At. Home. With. A. Flat. Tire," she grunted, tugging harder.

Heath rubbed the back of his neck, puzzling out the

scrappy cowgirl. Why worry about going home with a flat? Her brothers, part of the hot-tempered, impulsive, mouthy Cade clan his family had feuded with for over a hundred years, ribbed her from time to time. Was she sensitive about how they'd react? It seemed improbable. Her impressive left hook kept them in line. Some called Jewel cocky, boastful and brash. Yet he'd glimpsed another side tonight, seen a vulnerable hunger that'd called to him.

"Oof!" She landed hard on her back again and stared up at the brilliant star-studded sky, winded. A warm June breeze ruffled the loose red strands from her braid and carried the scent of decaying pine needles, wet soil and wild honeysuckle.

He held out a hand, but she ignored it, shoved to her feet, and marched back to the spare with her jaw set. "If you keep gawking, I'll have to charge you for the show."

"I'm not—"

She angled her face his way, and her bow-shaped lips curved in a knowing smirk that infuriated and excited him. Her rosy mouth nearly blended with the freckles covering her face. She must have as many as the stars overhead, he marveled, taking in her slim nose and lean, angular cheeks. She was sort of cute beneath her frown, like Huckleberry Finn's younger sister, cowlicks and all. "Now you're just staring."

"No… I…" He shifted on his feet. Why did Jewel keep him off-balance and lingering? Heath eyed the empty parking lot and cocked his head at the distant yip of coyotes lurking on the forested slopes surrounding Silver Spurs. "Who are you with?"

"Me," she panted, the cords of her neck popping as she hauled on the wedged spare harder still.

"No one else?"

"Myself and I." Her sarcastic tone called a smile to his lips. "Something wrong with that?"

Since he'd only ever dated Kelsey, he had limited experience with women. Kelsey preferred he accompany her everywhere, and his sister, Sierra, was never without at least a four-legged friend. Jewel's dogged independence, her refusal to ask for help, to depend on someone, intrigued him and left him wondering. Did she have any friends? "No…it's just… I'm not leaving you here alone."

Jewel quit tugging to point out a twelve-gauge shotgun mounted on her pickup's gun rack. "I can handle myself."

No doubt, yet a desire to help kept Heath's stubborn feet planted. So much for being a people pleaser. By staying, he angered Jewel, something he usually avoided. But Jewel tapped a stubborn streak he didn't recognize. Stranger still, he was enjoying their test of wills. "Your mother wouldn't want me to—"

"Look," she cut him off, "just because our parents are hitched doesn't mean you and I are brother and sister now. You're still a Loveland, which makes you public enemy one."

He hooked his thumbs in his belt loops. "Just trying to be neighborly."

"If you want to be a good neighbor, stop suing my family for five million dollars."

His jaw clamped. "You owe us. A Cade judge revoked our easement across your property without just cause." Long ago, after the Cades jumped to the wrong conclusions and strung up Everett Loveland for the death of Maggie Cade and the disappearance of her priceless sapphire, the Cades sued to revoke an easement allowing Heath's family access to the Crystal River to water their herd. With their consistent water source gone, Loveland Hills fell on shaky financial ground that only worsened through the years as summers became drier and drier.

"A lie." When Jewel staggered backward again, he

stepped ahead of her, yanked out the tire and rolled it to the flat.

"Hey!" she protested, but he ignored her, grabbed up a nearby long-handled wrench and fitted the squared-off crank over the tire's bolts. Within minutes he'd whipped off the flat and heaved it over the top of her truck bed.

"Not bad for a Neanderthal," Jewel drawled behind him.

"Neanderthal?" When he turned, she'd already fitted the spare into place and stretched a hand out for the wrench. He passed it over, impressed as she secured the new wheel faster than he'd removed the old.

"Yeah," she grunted as she tightened the last bolt. "Primitive man."

"I'm not primitive."

She sat back on her haunches and eyed her tire change. "You practically clubbed me over the head to get the tire."

"I've never raised a hand to a lady."

Her gaze collided with his. "Don't get your panties in a twist. And I'm no lady. Or some damsel in distress. Play your hero act with your fiancée."

With that, she tossed the long wrench in her truck bed, hopped behind her wheel and started up her powerful engine. It throbbed, loud, in the night air. Before she left, she leaned out her window, her expression smug. "And you're welcome."

"For what?" Shouldn't she be thanking him?

"For protecting your fragile male ego. See you in court!" She shifted into gear, then raced off, her tires kicking up gravel.

He coughed on exhaust fumes and dust as he stared after her disappearing taillights. Aggravating, cocky, exasperating woman. Yet the wide smile reflected in his rearview mirror when he started his pickup belied his irritation. He reversed from his spot and cruised onto the road.

Why was he so amped?

He had plenty to worry about. The make-or-break Lovelands versus Cades trial began in August and tomorrow, he'd tell his family, and Kelsey, about his Nashville tryout. Would they support him? He cranked a George Strait tune and lustily sang along, a sense of buoyancy nearly lifting him from his hard seat.

The audition of a lifetime awaited him, but he suspected one saucy redhead might, oddly, have something to do with his mood, too. He'd moved Jewel while performing, her reaction strengthening his resolve to chase his dream.

His foot stomped on the gas and cool air drove through his windows. Potent anticipation lifted goose bumps on his arms. He had the world tucked in his pocket. For the first time in forever, a career in music seemed within reach and Heath aimed to go for it, no matter the cost.

CHAPTER TWO

JEWEL TORE OFF her hat and swiped her damp brow. Overhead, the midafternoon sun beat down, unrelenting in a cloudless blue sky. She peered at the calves she and her brothers had isolated from the herd this morning. Panicked bleats filled the dry air and mingled with their mothers' answering bellows. They hadn't been separated since calving season three months ago. The sooner she got them through the pen system she'd designed to lessen their stress, the better.

"Next!" she hollered to her brother Justin. With a *clang*, he opened the metal latch and released the next calf from the holding pen. It raced forward, encountered a secured gate, and jerked to a stop in the extended neck chute she'd convinced her brother and ranch manager, James, to purchase. The calf tossed its head and rolled its eyes. Air huffed through its flaring nostrils.

"Easy, girl." Jewel stroked the little one's soft gray side. The scent of disinfectant soap stung her nostrils. Earlier, her brother Jared and nephew Javi had cleaned the calves to prevent infection. "Easy now."

The calf settled as Jewel grabbed a syringe of Bovi-Shield while murmuring steadily, her tone soothing. She talked plenty tough to her rough-and-tumble older brothers, but when it came to animals, she took extra care to be gentle.

"Now you won't get a respiratory infection," she crooned, pinching the skin on the calf's neck and pulling it away from the muscle to tent it. She slipped the eighteen-gauge needle into the subcutaneous space to prevent skin lesions.

"See. Not so bad." She stroked the calf's quivering neck after pushing in the vaccine, then hustled to its other side.

"Now this booster will keep you from getting blackleg." She delivered the second neck injection. "You're doing great."

The calf snorted but otherwise remained still in the narrow chute, absorbing Jewel's voice, her calm as she circled back to the spot where she injected the third vaccine.

A large Brahman bellowed beyond the fence. Jewel compared the cow's and the calf's ear tags, noting their matching numbers.

"Almost done, Mama," she called to the pacing cow.

"Hold up a minute, Jewel." Her brother James sprayed the calf's shaved hindquarter with 99-percent alcohol for adhesion, pulled a poker with a brass number three from the cooler and pressed its cold tip to the area, freeze-branding it.

The calf twitched for a few seconds as Jewel continued petting it, then calmed as the temperature numbed its skin. A couple of years ago, they'd switched to freeze-branding after Jewel attended a cattle conference. It was more time-consuming than regular branding and took practice, but it reduced the calves' stress.

"Ready?" Jewel called once James grabbed the second poker.

"Go ahead." James pressed the number five into the now-docile calf's hip. Over the years, she and her brothers developed routines so ingrained they barely had to talk while performing them.

She tented the loose skin underneath the calf's shoulder and delivered the last vaccine. "There you go, Sunrise, no BVD for you," she murmured, low, so James didn't overhear her ritual of secretly naming the calves. No matter how long they had on this earth, every living thing deserved a name, to have an identity, to be someone, although it made sending them off to the fall beef auctions even harder.

She grimaced. Jewel Cade, sentimental…no one would believe it. All her life, she'd acted tough, chasing after her father's affection by trying to prove she was as good as his favored sons. That she could ride, shoot and brawl with the best of them. Yet he rarely paid her much mind except to complain she needed to wear dresses to Sunday services.

When he'd passed away, she doubled down on proving herself in the male-dominated ranching world, even if she ruffled a few feathers and agitated the status quo to do it. Her thick skin hid her sensitive side, a weakness counter to her goal to be Cade Ranch's range boss. She wanted to oversee cattle herding and husbandry, calling the shots the way she preferred, a job where she wouldn't be overruled or overlooked. James had yet to delegate the position, and she intended to convince him this summer to choose her over her brother Justin.

As for the Sunday dresses, she'd worn one to her father's funeral, hoping he'd see her from above in a way he'd never noticed her on earth.

Jewel ignored the painful throb of her heart and cranked down the release lever. Sunrise rushed headlong from the chute. The calf slowed when she spied the barn wall, swerved, then trotted into the final pen where the vaccinated animals awaited Jewel's final checkup.

"Good move in facing the exit to the barn." James added more alcohol solution to the cooler holding the pokers.

Jewel pressed her lips flat to hide her pleasure at James's rare praise. He needed to see her as a capable professional, not a little sister chasing her big brother's approval. "I didn't want them running for the gate and getting injured like last year. It's all part of the herd health, value-added market report I gave you last month."

James grunted, but otherwise didn't answer as he checked the cooler's temperature. For optimal freeze-branding, it had to be at minus 200 degrees.

Jewel hid her disappointment and grabbed her records book. Her stubby pencil flew as she jotted down the vaccines' lot numbers, treatment date and withdrawal period, her name as the one who administered them, and the vaccination method used.

James retrieved a couple of iced teas from another cooler. When she set down her log book, he tossed her one. "The neck extender chute's working out better, too. No bent needles or trapped fingers."

Jewel sipped her tea, then pressed the cool plastic mini jug against her steaming cheeks. Even her freckles would be burned tomorrow. "That's why you need to make me range boss."

"Now's not the time for that discussion."

"Then when is the time?" she demanded.

Instead of answering, James gulped his drink. When he finished, he mopped his face with a red kerchief. "How come we're not putting on nose flaps?" he asked, referring to the device used to wean calves.

She blew out a frustrated breath at his change of subject. Fine…she'd give him a little more rope, but not enough so he slipped away without giving her answers. "Weaning them after branding is stressful."

"Corralling them again is more work for us," he grumbled. "We should go back to separating them from their mothers."

Jewel bristled. "The most stressful part of weaning is losing social interaction. The calves were calmer when we started using nose flaps a couple of years ago."

James doffed his wide-brimmed rancher's hat, scooped some ice from the cooler and dumped it over his head. "Should never have sent you to that conference. It gave you too many ideas."

"Nothing wrong with new ideas," she charged. "The herd health program's been worth about three to six dollars per hundredweight over the past eighteen months. We've had less morbidity and behavioral stress—something you'd know if you bothered reading my report."

"I'll get to it. Next!" James called to Justin, and another calf barreled into the chute.

Jewel bit her lip and got back to work, ignoring the sting of being dismissed again. She had to convince James and wouldn't quit until she did.

"How come you look so tired?" James pressed one of the frozen pokers into the calf's side once it settled in the chute.

Jewel injected the blackleg booster. "Got in late." Her cheeks heated as she recalled tall, gorgeous, commanding Heath Loveland performing "Folsom Prison Blues." When he sang, his powerful voice carried her with him. It drummed inside her, beating her heart, stirring her blood. It was like he was made of music.

She concentrated on the calf's next shot.

"What were you doing?" James exchanged the first poker for the second.

"Went out." She gently pulled the needle from the calf's skin. "Good job, MooShu," she murmured near its ear.

"Where?"

"Silver Spurs." She kept her voice even around the skittish animal, despite her rising irritation at nosy James. He had to know every detail about the ranch and those who lived on it.

"Wasn't Heath Loveland's band playing last night?"

Jewel's hackles rose at the knowing sound in James's voice. "I guess so."

James narrowed his eyes at her. "Interesting..."

"What do you mean?" Her brothers loved tweaking her about her supposed crush on Heath Loveland, coming up with all kinds of crazy theories about her carrying a torch for him...when everyone knew she loved only three things in life: her enormous stallion, Bear; physically demanding ranch work; and her family.

James stowed the last poker in the cooler. "I don't mean anything. *Much*."

"I don't like Heath Loveland." She released the latch and the last calf of the day sprang away.

A groan built in the back of her throat. Last night, Heath saw her as weak, in need of help. Why hadn't she pushed back as hard as she would have battled her brothers?

Because you don't look at him like a brother...

Her old mixed-up feelings returned for the boy who'd once witnessed her most shameful moment. When her father had ignored her 4-H booth's blue-ribbon win, she'd cried. Heath, who'd had a display beside hers, had shielded her, preventing others from knowing she'd been hurt. She clenched her back teeth. Why was he always around when she was at her most vulnerable?

Even if she might—*might*—have had any kind of softness for Heath, he was taken, about to walk down the aisle soon, rumor had it. She'd never be interested in a guy involved with someone else. And even if he were free, she had no use for a boyfriend and never intended on marrying, would never sacrifice her independence to a man no matter how kind and sensitive he seemed. What she wanted most was respect, something she'd have if she became range boss. It'd prove, once and for all, she was worthy—just as good as or better than her cowboy brothers.

James began packing up the branding equipment and his silence on her supposed feelings for Heath nettled her. She blocked his way into the nearby barn. "I don't like Heath."

James shrugged. "It's your life. I'm not judging. Although, keep your distance until after the trial."

"Why's that?"

"You know how those Lovelands are." He stepped around her and disappeared in the cool dim of their stable.

She gathered her vaccination equipment and followed. "How are they?"

"They know how to sweet-talk a lady."

Her lungs expanded at the sweet aroma of freshly strewn hay. Bear, along with the other horses, picked up his head. He nickered a greeting. "I'm no—"

"You're still a woman. Heath's broken almost as many hearts in this county as Jared," James said, referring to their lady-killer brother who'd given up professional football to manage his legally blind wife's barrel-racing career.

Jewel dumped the syringes in a bucket full of sterilizing fluid. "He's taken."

James shrugged as he stowed the coolers inside the barn's cabinet. "Like all Lovelands, he can charm the birds from the trees, as Grandma would have said."

"Example?" Jewel challenged.

James opened his mouth, then shut it.

"Exactly. We can't blame the Lovelands for causing our feud anymore. Clyde Farthington killed Maggie Cade for her brooch and his jealousy over her secret love affair with Everett Loveland. Our ancestors jumped to the wrong conclusions when they found Everett beside Maggie's body and hanged him without giving him a trial."

"Cora's Tear was still found on their land," James insisted, referring to the priceless fifty-carat sapphire their ancestor had mined from the Yugo Gulch along with enough silver to buy their land and establish their ranch.

"Because Maggie hid it at her and Everett's meeting spot so Clyde wouldn't get his greedy hands on it, remember?" Jewel pulled off her gloves and washed her hands in a small stainless sink. "Besides, after Cole and Katlynn found Cora's Tear, they returned it to Ma."

"Fine," James grumbled. "But what about Boyd and Ma?"

Jewel recoiled, drying her hands on a stiff brown paper

towel. "You think Boyd only wants Ma for her money? That she has nothing else to offer? You married Sofia, and she had nothing."

James took Jewel's place at the sink. "That's different."

"Yeah, because at least Ma and Boyd were childhood sweethearts until her parents broke them up." Jewel lobbed the balled-up towel into a large plastic trash barrel.

"And who's going to pay for their monthlong honeymoon to Europe?" Without waiting for an answer, James forged on, soaping up his hands. "Ma."

"What if she *is* paying?" Jewel leaned over to scratch a barn cat's ears and imagined her mother at Loveland Hills, packing, laughing and talking with her new husband about how excited she was to be taking this trip tomorrow, the one she had dreamed about for a lifetime. "A woman can spend her money how she pleases." Though why waste it on a honeymoon? Jewel would never be as happy as her mother was being married; she just wasn't the girlie-wife type, as her father put it.

"I'm just saying." James paused to grab a paper towel. "Going to watch Heath Loveland perform is one thing. Just don't get romantically entangled like Ma. He'll try to persuade you to change your mind about the easement, convince you not to fight their court case when it was a fair judgment." James tossed away the paper towel and peered down at her. At six feet two inches, he had her by over a foot. "We're fighting this lawsuit, no matter how Ma feels. This is Cade land. Defend it.

"Heath is nothing to me." Though no denying, the deep blue of his eyes had rattled her last night. "And I've always defended our family and this ranch, which is why it's time you made me range boss."

"When I feel one of you has proven yourself, I'll make the call." James cranked the barn fans' lever. They blew with a loud, buzzing roar. "Until then—"

"You'll continue being a control freak who should delegate tasks to spend more time with your growing family?" Jewel's balled hands landed on her hips.

James stared at her for a moment, then shook his head, smiling. "Now you sound like Sofia."

She snorted. "Another woman you need to listen to more."

James laughed. "You do beat all."

"Just as long as I beat Justin." Jewel crossed to pet her stallion's broad black nose. "It's still between us, right?"

James nodded.

"He's already got extra work teaching ranching skills at Fresh Start," Jewel said, mentioning the rehab facility run by Justin's fiancée, former army chaplain Brielle Thompson. "But Cade Ranch…" She pointed at the rolling slopes leading up to Mount Sopris's peak. "It's all I have."

James squinted at her. "Maybe that's not a good thing."

"I'm not cut out for marriage or a family like the rest of you." Jewel buried her head in Bear's warm, velvety neck.

"How do you know?"

She closed her eyes, shutting out the rising memories of her father's criticism and dismissal. She didn't measure up to what women…wives…mothers were supposed to be. "Promise you'll decide who's range boss by summer's end."

James considered her, then nodded slowly. "I can live with that."

She blew out a relieved breath, pressed a quick kiss on Bear's nose and headed for the calves. A sense of contentment stole through her as she assessed the injection and branding sites for irritation. This was her world…and for her, there was nothing else.

Now she only had to convince James by the end of the summer, and she'd have everything she ever wanted.

"GOOD EVENING, CARBONDALE. Temperatures today peaked at ninety-eight degrees with humidity at twelve percent.

Severe drought conditions continue to expand across Colorado, and that means an elevated fire danger just about statewide," announced a local weatherman.

Heath dropped the ice cream scooper in the carton to crank up the radio's volume.

"A T-shaped swath of northern and central Colorado is listed as abnormally dry with record-breaking temperatures continuing into next week."

Heath swore under his breath and his sister, Sierra, groaned. She finger-combed her long blond hair into a ponytail and secured it with an elastic band. "We'll be lucky if we get through this summer without a major forest fire." As a wildlife veterinarian, weather extremes were her greatest fear.

"And without losing any cattle." Heath plopped vanilla ice cream into a bowl and passed it to his adopted brother, Daryl, who drizzled fudge topping on it.

"We've got to keep the herd intact." Daryl's light blue eyes gleamed beneath black brows.

"How come, Pa?" Daryl's eight-year-old daughter, Emma, twirled on the ranch house's bare wood floor in stocking feet.

"Nothing for you to worry about, darlin'." Daryl ruffled Emma's fine blond hair. He, Sierra and Heath exchanged silent, anxious glances. Any cattle loss put them closer to foreclosure. "Want sprinkles?"

Emma jumped. "Yes! Can I have a lot?"

"You got it, honey." Sierra held up two containers. "Chocolate or rainbow?"

"Rainbow." Emma pointed to the colorful bow around the bun she'd worn to dance class. "I want to match like Grandma Joy."

"Can I have chocolate?" Daryl's six-year-old son, Noah, scooted onto Sierra's lap. His thick black hair, exactly like his father's, swished across his round face. "And rainbow?"

"Anything you want," Sierra vowed.

"Don't spoil him," Daryl warned, all while pouring on heaps of fudge. The hypocrite.

"These are my only nieces and nephews so I'm spoiling them rotten." Noah giggled when Sierra tickled his side. "Maybe Heath and Kelsey will have babies soon, so I'll have more to spoil..."

An expectant silence fell as Heath wordlessly passed over another bowl. He still hadn't told Kelsey, or his family, about his Nashville tryout. When Pa and Cole finally got in from their fence inspection, he'd quit stalling and share his plans to drive to Tennessee next week. His stomach twisted. Would they be happy for him? Would Kelsey? Anticipation kept him up last night, imagining a future he'd never dared dream before, along with his fiery exchange with a certain redheaded cowgirl.

An *ungrateful* cowgirl.

"Can I be your flower girl when you get married this year, Uncle Heath? Huh? Can I?" Emma asked around a mouthful of ice cream.

Heath swallowed hard as he met Emma's expectant blue eyes. "If I do, you're the only flower girl I'd want."

"If?" Emma angled her face up to her father. "I thought Mama said you were setting a date or something..."

"Hush now and eat your dessert," Daryl urged, his tone gentle but firm.

"Is Mama coming?" Noah asked, his lips rimmed in sprinkles and chocolate.

A shadow darkened Daryl's eyes. "No. She's got another headache."

"She always says that." Emma dropped her cheek into her palm and sighed. "And she never wants to do anything except type on the computer. How come you don't sleep at home anymore, Pa?"

Daryl's face flushed, and concern for his brother spiked

inside Heath. Daryl and LeAnne's nine-year marriage had problems from the start. Lately, Heath woke to find Daryl sleeping on the ranch's sofa rather than in his family's cabin. They hadn't spoken about it since Daryl, like all Lovelands, valued his privacy, but his suffering was clear.

"The drought has dramatically expanded recently," the weather reporter droned on. "Thursday's drought monitor indicates that more than ninety-eight percent of the state is in a drought, up from only ten percent at the start of the year. That's a dramatic increase from just three months ago."

"How come it never rains?" Noah scooped the fudge circling his melting ice cream and dumped it back over the top.

"And it didn't snow at Christmas, either." Emma's face pinched. "Are we going to die like the polar bears? That's what Jenny says."

"Don't listen to foolish talk." Daryl accepted the bowl Heath passed him and dug in.

Heath eyed his niece's and nephew's wide, fearful eyes, clicked off the radio and slid a sundae toward Sierra. "We need to do a rain dance."

"I want to do a rain dance!" Noah hopped off Sierra's lap and clapped his hands. "What's a rain dance?"

Heath stowed away the ice cream carton. "It's a sacred ritual Native Americans do to ask for rain."

Noah's body practically vibrated with excitement. "Can we try?"

Heath shook his head. "Well, we can't do a real Native American rain dance, but we can do our own." He grabbed a small pot and a spoon and handed it to Emma, then passed over two boxes of elbow macaroni to Noah. "Line up behind me."

"She just pushed me!" Noah complained when the kids jostled for the spot directly behind Heath.

"Did not!" Emma cried.

"Did, too!"

"Enough!" barked Daryl, a hint of a humor lightening his tone. "Or the rain dance is canceled due to bad behavior."

"Sorry!" Emma and Noah squeaked.

"What do I do with these?" Noah held up the boxes. "They're heavy!"

"You shake them." Heath demonstrated, then handed a box back. "They'll make a rain sound to call the clouds."

"I'll take one." Daryl dropped his spoon in his bowl, snagged the box and lined up behind his son.

"What's mine do?" Emma gestured with her spoon.

"My guess is you're going to bang the pan so it makes a thunder sound to call to the sky." Travis, their brother and the local sheriff, stomped into the kitchen, doffing his tan hat.

Noah shivered. "I like thunderstorms, but only when Pa cuddles us."

"Hey, Ginger and I want in on this." Sierra joined the lineup behind Heath, their tabby curled in her arms.

"The more the merrier. Ready for the rain dance?" Heath glanced back and grinned at the sight of his niece's and nephew's expectant faces. What was so bad about pleasing people? A moment ago, they'd been scared, and he'd made them forget those fears.

"Ready!" Emma and Noah shouted.

"Let me grab something!" Travis scrounged in the utensil drawer and grabbed a cheese grater and a butter knife. He sawed the flat end of the blade against the jagged holes. "All set."

Heath sang Creedence Clearwater Revival's song "Have You Ever Seen the Rain" as they marched around the long, dark pine kitchen table dominating the cozy space. Macaroni rattled inside the boxes Noah and Daryl shook while

Emma banged her pan and Travis sawed on his grate. Sierra added a meow here and there. All in all, not half bad for a family band. One side of Heath's mouth kicked up.

"Hey, what's this?" asked Pa as he entered the front door.

"We're making it rain!" shouted Noah, blasting across the open living space to throw his arms around his grandpa's legs.

"And thunder." Emma clanged her spoon against the pan for emphasis.

Pa hung his hat. "Well now. We sure could use it."

A wire tightened across Heath's chest, constricting his breath. Time to tell Pa about his Nashville tryout before he bailed like Clint predicted. "There's something important I need to talk to you about, Pa."

Pa nodded. "Let me just get a cup of joe first." His normally broad shoulders drooped, and the grooves of his weathered face appeared deeper, his skin slightly gray.

"What's wrong, Pa?" Sierra set down Ginger and hurried to their father. "You don't look good."

Pa ran a hand over his brush of silver hair, then jerked a thumb at the screen door. "Cole's the one who's not doing good."

Travis ducked outside.

"What happened?" Heath measured out coffee grounds and dumped them in the coffee maker. Since his brother Cole's ex, Katlynn Brennan, left after taping a segment for her cable show about the Loveland-Cade family feud, he'd been even more withdrawn than usual.

"Hurt his arm." Pa opened the door and ushered in a hunched Cole, his left arm in a sling, followed by Joy and Travis.

Air whooshed out of Heath's lungs as if someone had just drop-kicked him in the chest. If Cole was laid up, their make-or-break herding season went from daunting to near impossible.

"Are you okay, Uncle Cole?" Emma tugged on his plaid shirt.

Pain edged Cole's smile, and dark unease filled Heath. "I've had better days, but your pretty smile sure makes things better. That and some Percocet."

The unease turned into balls of dread, settling heavily in Heath's stomach. Cole never took pain medication. His arm must be seriously injured. Water overflowed the coffeepot Heath held beneath the faucet before he switched it off.

Emma giggled. "You always say that, Uncle Cole."

He lightly tapped the tip of Emma's nose. "That's because it's always true."

"Can I draw on your cast?" Noah tugged Cole's sling. The dread exploded in Heath's gut like buckshot, and his gaze dropped to the white plaster encasing Cole's left arm. He'd broken it. "Josh has one and he let everyone sign it but me."

"He's mean," Emma griped. "Who wants to sign stupidhead's stupid old cast anyway?"

"Be nice," Sierra chided, her raised hand hiding her smile.

As Heath stared at Cole, his heart cracked open. What did this mean to his Nashville tryout? He poured the measured water into the back of the coffee maker and flicked on the machine.

It was a selfish thought. Shameful…considering his brother was hurt. Heath breathed in the brewing coffee's rich roasted aroma and strove to settle his racing pulse. He opened the fridge and paused before pulling out the milk, letting the cool air wash over his flushed face.

"What happened?" Sierra retrieved mugs. When the gurgling coffee maker quieted, she filled them and added milk.

Cole's stance appeared casual, but he was coiled tight,

hiding the pain. "Wasn't paying close enough attention while fixing the bull pen fence. I got pinned when Diesel charged."

Heath winced. Few survived the force of a two-ton raging bull. With a grateful nod, Pa curled his fingers around the warm mug Heath passed him.

Daryl whistled. "Could have been a heck of a lot worse."

Cole accepted Sierra's coffee and dropped into a seat. "Pa pulled me out."

"Why were you in there, anyway?" Travis clasped his hands behind his back and frowned.

"Thought Diesel was secured in his pen. Must not have latched the gate last night." Cole dropped his head in his hand.

"I'm just so thankful you're both okay." Joy reached across the table and managed to pat both Cole and their pa. Despite the late hour, their new stepmother looked stylish—and matching—as always in a blue polka-dot blouse tucked into a blue skirt that complemented her silver bob and hazel eyes.

"How long do you have to wear the cast?" Heath's temples were starting to ache. The scalding coffee burned his tongue, but he kept sipping anyway.

"Six weeks." Pa's expression was pale and strained. "Which is why Joy and I are canceling our honeymoon."

Heath's jaw hit the floor. Coffee splashed over the rim of his mug when he set it down. They needed every hand, but Pa couldn't cancel his special trip with the woman he'd waited for all his life. They had to figure out a way to make this work. "Daryl and I can handle things, Pa."

Pa shook his head, lacing his fingers with Joy's. "We need at least three full-timers. Maverick's on his bull-riding tour. Travis used up his vacation last week for the wedding, Sierra's running her practice, and we can't afford to hire another hand."

A weight landed on Heath's shoulders as he rubbed his fingers along his temples. He couldn't leave his family ranch when they needed him. Couldn't try for the record deal after all. The feeling that his dreams were slipping through his fingers cut deep into him, making misery of his bone and tissue.

Heath clenched his jaw and dragged in a deep breath. The contract was a long shot anyway. No sense pining for it. Instead, he'd work around the clock to ensure things ran smoothly during their cattle drive while his father honey-mooned. Staving off foreclosure mattered most. Heath's life had never belonged to him anyway; it'd been stupid to think otherwise, even for one night.

Cole lifted his head slowly. "Sorry, Pa."

"Stop me if I'm overstepping, but..." Joy's mouth pursed. "Maybe one of my kids could lend a hand? We have plenty of help with my nephews visiting this sum-mer. We could spare someone experienced."

Everyone sat perfectly still. No one spoke or even ap-peared to breathe. A Cade working Loveland ranch? Un-thinkable...yet they had to consider it.

"Forget it." Joy pulled off her frameless glasses and cleared the fogged lens with a napkin. "I shouldn't have interfered."

"You're part of the family, darlin'." Pa smiled tenderly. "It says Joy Loveland on our marriage certificate, don't it?"

"Yeah." Sierra threw an arm around Joy. "You're one of us. I'm proud you're my stepmother."

"Me, too," Heath, Daryl, Travis and Cole chorused.

"And our grandma!" shouted Emma and Noah, whose simultaneous attempts to climb on Joy's lap went from shoving to a WWE match before Daryl banished them to opposite sides of the table.

"Sorry, Joy." Daryl stared down his kids until they apol-ogized, as well.

"After raising six kids, five of them boys, I don't break easy." Joy's hands shook as she wiped beneath her eyes. "I couldn't be prouder to call you my stepchildren and grandchildren. Hopefully, once the trial's over, we'll all become a real family, too. I want that more than anything."

Heath spied his doubt in his siblings' eyes. They'd never get along with the Cades, not with so many years of bad blood between them, no matter how the feud started, especially with their face-off in court next month. Joy was the exception.

In the week since she'd moved in, Heath had noticed subtle improvements. Family dinners happened every night. Baskets of freshly laundered clothes appeared on their beds daily. And the moment anyone mentioned a food preference, the item materialized in the fridge the following day.

Is this what having a mother is like? Heath had caught himself wondering since the wedding. He'd devoted his childhood to pleasing his real mother, to smoothing things over and making others happy. Having someone else take care of him and his family left him unsettled…and feeling almost unneeded, if that made any good sense.

"Let's not talk about the trial for now," Pa said, gruff. "Joy, who should we ask to help?"

She tapped her chin. "Jack's working across the state as a sheriff's deputy. James is ranch manager, so we can't spare him. My nephews are learning the ropes and don't have enough experience. Jared's touring with Amberley so that leaves either Justin or Jewel." No mention of Jesse, of course, the son she'd lost to violence related to his opioid addiction.

"Justin?" Cole exclaimed. "Heck no, not unless you want the place burned down. Remember the Fourth of July when he decided to light fireworks from the church steeple and set the roof ablaze?"

Joy smiled widely at that, and Heath's stomach plummeted. If not Justin, then the rancher assisting him would have to be…

"Who would you pick, Pa?" Daryl wiped fudge from Noah's chin.

"I'll let our range boss decide. He's in charge of ranch operations while I'm away." All eyes turned Heath's way.

Heath's stomach twisted something awful, and he opened his mouth, but he didn't know what to say. Jewel's dogged determination to free the spare, her no-nonsense efficiency in mounting the new tire and her dry, quick wit had impressed him.

Her challenging, irritating and obnoxious personality, not so much. She was a tough, experienced, capable cowgirl, whose mouth would be a constant source of aggravation. Kelsey had given him until summer's end to agree to a wedding date, and he needed time, space and peace on the open range to stop bucking his future…something he'd never get riding alongside the brash redhead.

Worse, the connection he'd felt with Jewel last night, the way his thoughts kept straying to her today, warned him of trouble ahead if they spent too much time together.

"Heath?" Pa prompted.

Time to pry his tongue off the roof of his mouth. There was nothing for it. "Jewel." Heath scraped back his chair. "If you'll excuse me?"

He trudged to the porch and leaned over the railing, soaking up the fresh air. Twilight was still at the stage where it was more lavender than onyx, with the fireflies just beginning to turn on and off in the yard. Standing there with the birds chirping in the trees, the crosscut-sawing of the crickets and a cattle dog snoring at the top of the stairs, was usually restful.

Heath shoved his hands in his pockets, yanked them out again, then laced them tightly behind his back, unable to settle his mind. Spirit. Heart. All around him, broad-shouldered mountains rose, penning him in, pinning him down.

Goodbye, Nashville.

He squeezed his eyes shut as a burning knot of emotion formed in the back of his throat. Without other prospects, he'd have to accept Kelsey's father's offer to become a partner in the supply business.

He'd have to set a wedding date.

Give up gigging.

Music.

He sucked in a sharp, stinging breath, then blew it out. He heard a fluttering overhead and then the hoot of an owl, which for some reason struck him as menacing.

At least his new, lucrative job meant he could help keep Loveland Hills on secure financial footing. It wasn't the life he'd dreamed of, but it was the one he'd been dealt.

Best he accepted it.

Besides, he loved Kelsey…didn't he? They'd been together for so long he wasn't always sure. Their relationship was comfortable, like a pair of worn slippers…and just as boring. But that was typical of people who'd been together as long as he and Kelsey had, he'd heard.

The door banged open behind him, and Pa clapped him on the back. "Jewel will be a whole lot easier on the eye than Justin."

Heath shifted from foot to foot and swatted away something feathery, a moth. Looks weren't everything. He'd watched Jewel at local rodeos through the years; she was a talented roper and rode as well as any man. The question was: Would she listen to him and take orders? Between her and Justin, he'd wager her daredevil brother would be easier to handle, despite what Cole said. This year's herding had to go off without a hitch. The stakes were too high for mistakes.

"You sure you'll be okay handling the cattle drive while I'm away?" Pa asked. "Joy's fine canceling the trip."

Heath jerked his lips into a smile big enough to ease his father's concerns. Pa deserved to be happy. "You bet, Pa."

His father's tense expression softened. "Never thought I'd have this second chance with Joy. I appreciate it, son."

"No thanks needed. It's what family does. We're always here for each other."

Pa nodded. "So, what was the important thing you wanted to tell me?"

Gnats whined in Heath's ears and tree frogs piped. He stared at the distant moon and shook his head. "It wasn't that important."

Which was true.

Nothing was as important as keeping his family happy and at peace. Now he just needed to make peace with it himself…

And manage antagonistic Jewel Cade while driving cattle through one of the worst droughts in his state's history.

His fingers clenched around the rail once his father strode back inside. What had he just signed up for?

CHAPTER THREE

JEWEL INHALED THE COMFORTING vanilla scent of Ma's neck as she hugged her tight in the Lovelands' circular drive. The morning clouds were a deep, ominous gray. They churned like muddy waters stirred up from the bottom of a lake, mirroring her mood.

She dropped her head on her mother's shoulder and closed stinging eyes. How had her plan to become Cade Ranch's range boss crashed and burned in less than twenty-four hours? She'd be working Loveland Hills for the next month, her chance to prove herself to James gone. Despite a sleepless night, she still hadn't completely processed it all.

"I'm going to miss you, honey." Ma's hazel eyes searched Jewel's when she stepped back.

Above her earnest face, the stately poplars surrounding the Lovelands' homey ranch house swayed. It reminded Jewel of a Hallmark Christmas ornament, with its white-spindled, wraparound porch, a honey-colored porch swing and wide front steps. Lacy, leaded-glass transoms were open above every ground-floor entrance to let the breezes flow through. Yet none of its tranquility made her feel welcome…or at home.

"Are you sure you're all right with this?" Ma probed.

The collective gazes of the Cade and Loveland siblings, gathered to see their parents off on their honeymoon, pressed Jewel like invisible hands. Judging, weighing, testing… She shoved back her shoulders and snapped up her chin. "Of course. Heath could use a lesson on what real ranching looks like."

Her brothers' guffaws rang out. Beside a clump of large-leafed hostas, Heath and his siblings shifted in their boots, stone-faced and tight-lipped. Typical, obstinate Lovelands.

They didn't even flinch at her jab. How was she supposed to spend a month with them? Concrete had more personality.

At least the children got along. Javi darted around flowering bushes with Daryl's son and daughter, screeching, "Tag, you're it!" Everything was in bloom on the expansive property. Daisies, trumpet lilies and purple coneflowers mingled in raised beds while brightly colored petunias lined a flagstone walkway.

Her eyes clicked with Heath's, and her heart added an extra beat. In a black cowboy hat pulled low over his lean, handsome face, his brilliant blue eyes piercing beneath the brim, he was rugged, gorgeous and—she gave herself a shake—off-limits.

When Ma begged her to help the Lovelands last night, Jewel reluctantly agreed. Her mother always sacrificed for her family. She deserved the honeymoon of her dreams. Would Jewel lose her range boss spot to Justin if he impressed James in her absence?

Boyd stood behind Ma and spanned her waist with his hands. His features settled into stern lines as he scrutinized the group. "All y'all are gonna get along while we're gone, right? No dustups."

Sierra stepped forward and kissed her father and Ma. "Of course." She shot them a wide smile, turned and narrowed her eyes on her siblings until they grinned, too, the entire group joining so they resembled a bunch of crazed clowns, no doubt. "We're family now."

Boyd and Joy exchanged a worried glance.

"Sierra's right." Heath ambled over to Jewel. His unhurried, loose-limbed grace turned his Wranglers, black boots and fitted white T-shirt into something like poetry…the easy-to-memorize kind that branded itself inside you. He set his palm on her back in a gesture halfway between a clap and a hug. Her body tensed in awareness. The subtle scent of his clean skin, salty and slightly smoky, made her breathe deep. "We're family. Right, sis?"

"Right, little brother." Her cheeks ached with the nonstop grinning. Technically, she was only a day older than Heath, but she'd exploit the age difference for all it was worth.

"Little, huh?" He arched an eyebrow and stared down from his great height. Like all Lovelands, he was mountain-sized and tree-tall, even bigger than her brothers. She squirmed slightly in his hold. If she couldn't impress James this month, she'd sure as heck prove herself equal to any Loveland and hopefully, in the process, find a way to still be named Cade Ranch's range boss.

"It's not the size of the dog in the fight…" she murmured beneath her breath.

"It's the size of the fight in the dog," Heath finished, a twinkle in his luminous eyes. "Is this our first fight?"

"One of many to come." Overhead, birds sang in the poplars and small white butterflies flitted in a small patch of sage. Jewel's stiff cheeks eased, her grin becoming genuine until she caught herself. What was she doing smiling, for real, at a Loveland?

"Hey!" Justin catcalled. "Whatever you two have going on over there, can you save it for after Ma and Boyd leave?"

Jewel jerked away from Heath, and his hand dropped. Red stole up over the collar of his T-shirt, the same type of heat bleeding into her cheeks. "Knock it off, Justin." Her fist shot out and Justin danced back, rubbing his shoulder.

"Truth hurts, don't it?" His white teeth flashed inside his dark beard.

"I'll show you what hurts." Jewel advanced, scowling, fist cocked.

"Jewel!" Her mother's horrified gasp stopped her dead. Her arm fell. Heath's disapproving expression made something inside her wither and curl into a tight ball. Fine. She wasn't a lady. Didn't measure up to his standards of womanhood, just like her father believed. Well…she didn't care. She lived by her own standards and was doing fine.

Just fine.

"Use your words, Aunt Jewel," piped up Daryl's little girl.

Okay…maybe she wasn't doing fine when an eight-year-old lectured her about behavior.

"Time for us to go or we'll miss our flight." Boyd held open the pickup's passenger door. "If we have to come home early on account of any mischief, you'll wish we hadn't."

Jewel rolled her eyes and Heath's mouth twitched as they exchanged a swift, secretly amused look that meant nothing.

Absolutely nothing.

"No mischief, Pa, promise. Like Sierra said, we're family." Heath caught everyone's eye until they nodded along, heads bobbing like a clutch of chickens.

"I have faith." Ma's mouth curved into a smile. "You'll do just fine without us. Love you!" And with that, she gripped Boyd's hand and stepped up into the truck's cab.

Boyd angled his head toward the pickup. "What she said." He hopped in behind the wheel and slammed the door shut.

"Goodbye!" everyone hollered as they drove away, returning Joy's wave through the rear window.

As soon as the pickup disappeared, their smiles whisked off their faces. Justin's mouth twisted into a snarl. Cole drummed thick fingers on his cast arm.

James sauntered over to Heath. "Nice act, but we're not your family."

"Your ma says so," Heath countered. A cattle dog joined the children. It raced around the perimeter—barking madly—but Heath whistled, and it came bounding up to him. "Down, girl." He tousled her mane affectionately, and she gave a resigned whimper and curled herself at his feet.

"Let's keep a couple of things straight." James planted his boots wide. The remaining Cades and Lovelands crowded close. A flashback to their softball game pileup last month had Jewel bracing. "One. Jewel is here only because of Ma, not out of any sense of kinship with you. Right, Jewel?"

She struggled to nod under Heath's keen stare. James was right. She'd never volunteer for any other reason…the way Heath's T-shirt stretched across a well-defined chest and a toned stomach—the kind of stomach that put six-packs to shame, notwithstanding.

Lordy, he was one beautiful, brawny cowboy.

"We already figured that out, genius," Cole uttered with infuriating calm.

Heat rolled off Justin in waves. "Yeah? Why's that?"

"Because whenever anyone needs help, Cades usually just throw money at it." Scorn darkened Cole's accusation.

Jewel opened her mouth to argue, then snapped it shut. Her family gave generously to local charities, whereas the Lovelands gave their time, always the first to arrive when someone needed aid. Then again, time and a pair of hands was all they had to offer since, as her grandmother would have said, they didn't have two nickels to rub together.

"At least we've got money to send," Jared insisted.

"Money you've made for a hundred years while denying our easement to the Crystal River." Fury dripped from Darryl's words.

A vein started to protrude from Jared's forehead. "The one taken away after *your* cattle trampled *our* property and bred with our longhorns?"

The shouts of the playing children filled the sudden, tense silence. Daryl's daughter was spinning under a dogwood tree, her head tipped back and her arms flung out. The boys raced each other to a fence post and back.

If only life could be that uncomplicated again…

"Lie," Daryl charged. "Your ancestor's brother judged the case instead of recusing himself. He stole it from us."

James shrugged. "Then why didn't your family appeal?"

"Our family wouldn't have had enough money to pay for a lawyer." Heath pulled off his hat and damp strands of dark hair clung to his temples. "Driving cattle farther to reach the Crystal River means herd depletion. Loss of revenue."

Jared made a sweeping motion with his hand. "How do you have enough money to hire a lawyer now?"

"None of your business." White appeared around Cole's clamped lips.

Sierra gave an exasperated huff. "Our attorney's taking twenty percent."

"Of the five million you're suing us for in damages?" Jewel demanded, dragging in air too fast.

"That's right," Heath said evenly.

"You'll never win." Justin's boots crunched on the driveway's gravel as he paced.

Cole stepped in front of Justin, blocking his way, and leaned down so the tips of their noses nearly touched. "Guess we'll see next month."

Another silence fell, this one heavy and muffling, like a blanket. Heath shot Jewel an inscrutable look, then waved his hands. "Let's leave this to the lawyers. For now, we'll honor our promise to our parents."

"I didn't promise nothing," spat Justin, eyeball to eyeball with Cole.

"Me neither." Daryl puffed his broad chest.

"Daddy, how come you're so mad?" Daryl's little boy, Ned… Nick…no… Noah looked up at his father with a worried frown.

Daryl's tense expression softened when he glanced down at his child. "I'm not mad."

"You look mad," asserted his daughter, whose name started with an E… Emma. "And the Cades are nice. Javi and I are BFFs." She looped her arm through Javi's.

"I don't like girls," Javi added, the innocent comment diffusing the tension as smiles and muffled snorts circled the group. "But she's my cousin—her and Noah, right, Pa? More family is always good, isn't it?"

James studied his son and shook his head. "Guess kids can teach the adults now and again. Let's go."

One by one, Jewel watched her family leave, exchanging waves or hugs. Cole, Sierra and Daryl strode away next. Only then did it hit her. She'd be living in enemy territory, around the clock, as the extra ranch hand they needed for an outfit of this size. Sure, her ranch was only five miles away, but it might as well be light years in distance from the family, the only home, she'd ever known.

"Where's your gear?" Heath asked.

Jewel nodded at her stallion, Bear. His black tail slapped at flies beneath the poplar she'd tied him to. "In the saddlebag."

Heath cocked his head. "What about the rest?"

"Rest of what?"

"Clothes? Toiletries? Girl stuff…makeup?"

Her face scrunched. "I brought a comb, a toothbrush and toothpaste. Deodorant. Underclothes. I'm assuming you have soap and laundry if my jeans need a scrub."

"Won't you want to spiff up every night? Change outfits?"

She scowled at him. "Cowgirls don't 'spiff up,' we dust off. And do I look like I care about outfits? Makeup?"

The intensity of his close stare nearly rocked her back on her boot heels. "Guess I thought, like most women…"

"I'm not most women."

"I can see that."

She jammed down the rising sense of not measuring up, untied Bear and led him around. "Where can I stable him?"

"This way."

She followed Heath to the rear of a well-kept barn. The smell of fresh manure drifted through an open window. Inside the lofted space, they traveled across creaky, straw-littered floorboards. While its finishes were outdated, the water system hand-pumped, the horses appeared well cared for in roomy stalls.

After settling Bear and feeding him his favorite treat—apple-flavored licorice—she threw her arms around his neck. "Don't be scared, Bear," she whispered. "This is just temporary."

He nickered, and she released him to join Heath at the other end of the barn. He waved her into a small room where he'd spread Loveland Hills' survey map on a desk.

"Here's where we're driving cattle today." He pointed out a spot.

"The calves have all been vaccinated?" At Cade Ranch, they didn't go to pasture without protection.

"Yesterday." Heath leaned over to smooth a folded map corner, and his arm brushed hers. The brief touch, in this intimate space, did something funny to her knees, softened them somehow so they dipped slightly.

She propped a hip against the desk to keep her feet under her…to battle the irresponsible urge to lean closer to him. "Us, too. Are they weaned?"

Heath shook his head. "Shots are stressful enough. We don't separate them."

"We don't, either."

"Huh."

"Huh." Their eyes clung for a moment, and she noticed a thin band of black surrounding his brilliant blue irises.

When Heath cleared his throat, she remembered to breathe. "Anyways. I'll need you ready to go in an hour."

Jewel peered at their destination, noting the coordinates, the elevation. "We can't go there."

Heath frowned. "Why not?"

"It's your southernmost point…the most exposed to the drought. I bet forage sorghum grows there, right?"

"Some sorghum, but mostly ryegrass."

"But sorghum is hardier in extreme weather," she countered. "There'll be more of it."

The beginnings of a crease developed between Heath's eyebrows. "What if there is?"

"We've never had a drought this bad. Extreme dry weather causes prussic acid to build up in sorghum grass, which will weaken the cattle. It slows their ability to take in oxygen, might even kill some."

Heath rubbed the back of his neck. "And you know all this because…"

Outside the office, the horses nickered and shifted in their stalls. "I read. Go to conferences."

Shock splashed across Heath's face. "*You* read about cows."

One shoulder rose. "Yeah—so?"

"Took you for more of an outdoorsy type than a bookworm."

"Who says you can't be both?" Her shoulders shot up, nearly reaching her ears. Why did everyone want to put her in a box? If life was a road, then shouldn't you be allowed to change lanes? Take detours?

He stared at her for a long moment and nodded. With his vibrant eyes and near-heavenly features, he looked like she imagined an angel would. He had cheekbones and a jaw you could cut glass with, a face any artist would die to sketch—or touch. And those full, expressive lips were parted. "Look, the Lovelands have been driving cattle in this pattern for over a hundred years. We always start here. It's how my father wants it done."

"He's not here. *You* are."

A muscle feathered in Heath's jaw. "And I'm doing it Pa's way."

"Don't you ever just do what you want?"

He stilled, his expression as shuttered as any Loveland's. Yet something in the corners of his eyes, a darkening, a creasing, betrayed his discontent. Was he dissatisfied with his life? Impossible. Soon he'd be married to the daughter of a wealthy family, about to have it all, respect, money, prestige.

Whereas she…she'd continue being just another hand on her family ranch if she didn't get the range boss job.

She must have made a noise because Heath's gaze lasered into her. Sparks of electricity crackled from his deep blue eyes. "Let's get something straight. I call the shots."

Their breaths came a little faster, harder, as they stared each other down. "Still doesn't make you right about the pasture," she snapped. "I'd make a better range boss."

"Then why aren't you Cade Ranch's range boss?"

Her heart throbbed like a giant open wound. She willed away the sting of his words and pressed on. "James promised to give me the job if I proved myself this summer. Since I'm stuck here, I'll prove it on Loveland Hills instead."

"What's that mean?"

"I challenge you."

Heath's frown deepened. "To what?"

"To prove who's the better rancher." She gestured between them. "Cade versus Loveland."

"We're on the brink of foreclosure," he responded in clipped tones. "I'm not playing games or keeping score."

Jewel picked up a pen and clicked the tip in and out. "I'm not playing, either, but I *will* be keeping score." She dropped the pen and peered up at Heath. "And I intend to win."

Heath made a quick, sharp, shaking-away motion with his head. "Play whatever games you want but know this... I'm in charge of everything on this ranch, including you."

Her fingers curled in, nails biting into her palms as anger flushed through her system, hot and bitter. Oh, the terrible, crushing, breath-stealing burden of people who thought you didn't measure up. "You'll never be in charge of me."

"We're doing it this way, end of story. Be ready to head out in an hour." He turned on his heel, strode away, then paused in the doorway. "I'm the range boss. Not you."

He tossed those last two words at her like he was throwing down a gauntlet—the one she'd been battling her whole life.

Challenge accepted.

She stomped to Bear and flung her arms around his neck. "Miserable, stubborn, know-it-all Loveland," she whispered into his thick mane inhaling his comforting, musky scent. "I can't stand him," she insisted, wondering who she was trying to convince.

James didn't take her seriously, and now Heath?

Her skin tingled like a thousand fire ants were marching all over it. Heath had a lot of lessons to learn, one of them being to never underestimate a woman.

Especially her.

From here on out, it was war. Cade versus Loveland, and may the best rancher win.

HEATH LIGHTLY TAPPED his spurs into his mare's sides and cantered along the line of trudging Brahmans. With his index finger and pinkie in his mouth, he whistled three sharp blasts. Blue wheeled around from the front. The cattle dog raced toward a pair of heifers who'd paused to graze. A few jaw-snapping lunges got the hungry animals moving forward again.

With a yank, Heath freed his kerchief from his back pocket and mopped his dripping face. It was drier and hotter than the center of a haystack, despite the lack of sun. The Loveland rain dance had conjured only clouds…and a different kind of storm. His gaze swerved to the petite redheaded rough rider who effortlessly drove the cattle ahead of him, her body in perfect sync with her enormous black stallion. In the distance, their destination, a southern valley with abundant greenery and a natural spring, beckoned.

Was Jewel right about the sorghum grass?

She hadn't spoken since they set out a couple of hours ago, her silence bugging him for no good reason. His family rarely talked when working. Besides, he wanted this time on the range to make peace with his future as a married businessman, yet his thoughts kept returning to his and Jewel's earlier argument.

She'd acted as though *she'd* save the day by steering them from this pasture and prove herself a better range boss. It'd blasted away his usual patience. He'd had to remind her who was in charge.

His stomach twisted, and his back tensed.

What'd gotten into him?

You're under my control...

His words echoed in his ears. Who spoke like that? Shirtless guys on the covers of Sierra's romance novels, that's who. Not him. Not before Jewel blasted into his life, intent on shaking it—and him—up.

With a slight tug, he slowed his Appaloosa, Destiny, and plodded alongside the bawling cattle. Their heads bobbed as they lumbered on dry, rocky ground. Choking dust rose. Up ahead, Jewel expertly headed off a small breakaway trio and nipped them back into the group. In the rear, Travis patrolled the end of the herd, keeping an eye out for stragglers or predators.

Why had Heath acted like a demanding jerk before? Jewel triggered something inside him, a part that wanted to assert itself even when he knew the disastrous consequences of putting his wants ahead of others. A disturbing image of his mother on the night of Cole's sixteenth birthday momentarily blinded him. Just in time, he spotted a depression and guided Destiny around it. Her hooves clattered over bedrock.

Jewel wasn't to blame for his actions. He was chafing inside his own life. A mustang resisting the bit. Sometimes he felt as though his life was like a railroad car that had been shunted onto a side track—all the wasted, carefree years of his youth spent worrying about his mother's moods, her well-being, her effect on the family. And now here he was, still lagging behind, still not on the main track, worrying he'd look back on his adult years and wonder what he'd accomplished beyond making others happy.

And shouldn't that be enough for any man?

To please is a disease.

He frowned and touched his spurs to Destiny again. Instantly, she transitioned into a trot, then a gallop before he pulled her up alongside Jewel. "Nice work."

Her pert nose lifted, the only indication she'd heard him. Beneath her white Stetson, her face was pink; she suddenly looked pretty. And dainty. Thick leather reins disappeared inside one small hand. The other rested on her jean-clad thigh. It was shapely for it being so short, he observed before tearing his eyes away to gaze at the nearing pasture. "You've ridden with your brothers all your life?"

"What else would I have been doing?" she asked from the side of her mouth, eyes locked straight ahead. "Playing dolls? Dress-up? Baking? This is the twenty-first century. We have things like electricity now...and women have the vote..."

He flushed. "I get that. My sister Sierra was more interested in caring for the animals, and Kelsey, she—"

Jewel's loud, noisy yawn cut him off. When she finished, she angled her face his way, one eyebrow arched, her expression mock-innocent. "Sorry, what was that again?"

A reluctant smile tugged up the corners of his mouth. Fine. She wasn't interested in hearing about Kelsey and honestly, he wasn't even sure why he'd brought her up. Invoking her name erected an invisible wall between him and Jewel. It was a reminder he was taken...though who, exactly, needed the reminding? With a jolt, he recalled an invitation to dine with her family tonight. His throat tightened. Would they expect some kind of an announcement?

"How long have you had your horse?" he asked, eyeing Jewel's enormous mount. The stallion had to be seventeen hands, yet Jewel rode him effortlessly, clearly in control.

The dimple appearing in her freckled cheek fascinated him. "Eight years. His name's Bear."

"Good name."

"Your Appaloosa's pretty. What's her name?"

"Destiny. I figured wherever she took me was where I was supposed to go."

Jewel's dimple disappeared. "You're the one guiding her. You choose where you go, not Destiny."

Her words struck him momentarily mute. Before he could speak, Jewel gasped. "What's that!"

He followed her finger point into the looming pasture and took in the overgrowth of sorghum, the wilted leaves, the lack of ryegrass, just as Jewel predicted.

"The grass," he began, but she cut him off again.

"*No!* That!" She spurred Bear forward, leaning low over his neck, her red braid lifting behind her.

"Yah!" Destiny responded to his cue and gave chase.

They'd nearly caught up to Jewel when she stopped Bear on the edge of the grazing area and vaulted from the saddle.

"Look."

He followed her nod and spied a buzzing cloud of flies over a dead animal. A large animal. Was it…?

"This one of yours?" Jewel pointed to a motionless cow.

His stomach turned as he eyed the brand on its flank and the ear tag. "She went missing a couple of days ago. We've been looking for her…" He eyed the white foam around the Brahman's mouth and pale gums. A dark suspicion grabbed him by the throat. His gaze swept over the yellowing field of water-deprived sorghum, then to the approaching herd. They were walking to their deaths if they got any closer.

"Prussic acid poisoning."

Jewel glanced up at him sharply when he spoke.

He braced for the "I told you so" that didn't come. Instead, Jewel nodded, leaped into her saddle and grabbed Bear's reins to yank his head up from the deadly plants. "Let's turn them around."

The top of the herd began descending the small slope, just yards from the poisoned forage. "No time to waste."

Together, they sprang into action, hustling the cattle, arcing them left and back. At his whistled commands, the cattle dogs streaked to and fro in a blur of white and black. Jewel was like a scarlet lightning bolt as she thundered along the front line, waving her bright red kerchief, spooking the cattle to change course. She was fearless, as bold as she was skilled. He'd be darned if Cole could do as good a job turning the massive herd back on itself.

"What's going on?" Travis shouted over the panicked bellows of the confused, hungry Brahmans.

"Pasture's no good. Stay here and run any off that get by me or Jewel." He charged forward on Destiny, his heart pounding hard enough to come out of his chest when he spied a drop-off hidden by a copse of spruce. If they didn't control the herd while turning it, they might stampede to their deaths.

Yet hotheaded Jewel was surprisingly cool under pressure. She applied pressure when needed and eased off when it wasn't, her small features set in fierce concentration. She was as tough a cowgirl as he'd ever seen when she faced down one of the larger Brahmans determined to get by her. Without hesitation, she drove Bear forward, hollering, "Yip! Yip! Yip!" until the cow balked at the last minute and turned. Others followed suit and gradually, after hours of painstaking work, they had the cattle back home, watered and hay fed.

He'd expected Jewel to gloat, but she'd been all business, and darned if he didn't miss sparring with her when they'd finally gotten the situation under control.

At last, he mounted the stairs to the house, bone weary and longing for a shower. Jewel's voice stopped him before he reached the top tread.

"You still haven't said it," she drawled.

He turned and flicked the brim of his hat up off his soaked brow. "Said what?"

"That I was right." She climbed past him and stopped on the top step, meeting him eye to eye.

He sighed. "Fine. You were right." She'd saved the herd today—no denying it.

"And…" she prompted.

He stared at her steadily. "Thank you."

"Yes, and…"

He lifted a palm to the rosy orange sky, then dropped it. "What else is there?"

"You'd be a better range boss than me." Her lips curved into a smirk.

The tension was palpable between them, and instinct

told him it ran deeper than the fact that their families were enemies. "I'm not saying that."

Her eyebrows quirked. "But I bet you're thinking it."

"You're a mind reader now?"

"Nah, I'm just clever." The smirk spread, revealing even white teeth against her freckled face, the contrast unconventionally attractive. "And I also think I'm hilarious."

He bit back a laugh and slid by her into the house, shaking his head at her brashness.

"Oh, Heath?" she called, and he stuck his head around the doorframe. One of Jewel's hands lifted a single finger; the other rounded into an O shape. "Cades one, Lovelands zero."

The smile lingered on his face as hot water pounded on Heath's sore muscles while he twisted beneath the showerhead's spray minutes later. Jewel sure had an ego, but she had the talent to back it up, too. He snapped off the water, wrapped a towel around his waist and sauntered from the steam-filled bathroom.

"Oof!" He collided with someone—someone much too petite to be one of his brothers. Small, calloused hands landed on his bare chest. His muscles clenched as his heart stopped and then sped up.

Jewel Cade's enormous brown eyes trailed up his contracting abdomen to his face. "Travis said I could find an extra deck of cards up here." Air separated her halting words. She yanked her hands down. "We're playing Texas Hold'em. Want to play?"

He shook his head, wordless. No. He did not want to play with the aggravating redhead who nettled him like a burr. Her soft mouth parted, and the tip of her pink tongue appeared on her generous lower lip.

"Come on, Heath, don't you want to live dangerously?"

He pictured icicles dangling from barn eaves, his breath frosting winter air, the sting of sleet hitting his cheeks…

anything to stop the temptation to sample her full lips. “Kelsey wants me over for dinner.”

Jewel’s sparkling brown eyes dulled and darned if he didn’t want to make them shine again. *Get out of here*, he ordered himself, yet his feet had other ideas and stuck him in place.

“But what do you want?”

“Peace.” He ducked back in his room and slammed the door. Her chuckle wove through the thick pine anyway. He paced to his closet and savagely buttoned on the dress shirt and pants Kelsey bought him for his birthday. His rough fingers fumbled to knot the tie. Once, twice…five times. He yanked off the noose. Kelsey’s impending frown flashed in his mind’s eye.

Contrary to Jewel’s opinion, he already knew he wasn’t suited for this ranching life, let alone the one awaiting him once he married. Or maybe it was the other way around and his life didn’t suit him. Either way, he needed to resign himself to it…if she’d just leave him be and stop challenging him.

Was that too much to ask?

When it came to Jewel, his money was on yes.

In the hall, he’d wanted to kiss the everlasting smirk off her face. She tested the limits of his self-control, self-denial and unselfishness.

That, of course, was the problem.

Some part of him apparently liked being unrestrained and taking what he wanted. It’d be his downfall, though, if he didn’t keep his distance from bold, spirited Jewel Cade.

Hopefully, dinner with Kelsey would give him clarity. A loud, raucous laugh erupted from downstairs, Jewel’s shout mingling with his siblings’. He jammed on his hat and clomped outside. He sure wasn’t getting any peace here, not with a certain redhead underfoot and messing with his head.

CHAPTER FOUR

"COME IN. COME IN," boomed a male voice behind Heath.

He jerked his hands from his pockets, dragged his eyes off the waxing moon and whirled to face the Timmonses' open front door. Bright light, spilling down tiered brick steps, silhouetted the outline of a short and stocky man with a head as round as a cannonball.

"You haven't changed your mind about joining us for dinner, have you?" A belly laugh accompanied the question, punctuating the apparent ridiculousness of the notion.

"Only about twenty times." Heath doffed his hat and trudged up the stairs into the grand two-story home.

"Hah!" Sam Timmons clapped Heath on the back. "Changing your mind about joining us on steak night… good one."

Only Heath spoke the truth. During the long drive into town, he'd battled the impulse to turn his pickup around. He glimpsed his clenched jaw in the foyer's gold-framed mirror. Even though he found Jewel irritating, he'd rather play cards with her and his siblings than endure a night of Kelsey's parents' digs about his humble upbringing or their expectations for his and Kelsey's future.

Speaking of whom…

Kelsey glided through an open pocket door, paused before him and leaned close to pat his cheek. He fought back a sneeze at her overly sweet perfume. "We're not letting him escape that easy, are we, Daddy?" Her green eyes sparkled through a thicket of black lashes.

"No indeed, Dew Drop." Sam's barrel chest swelled as he gazed affectionately at his only child. "You've caught yourself a good one."

Heath cleared his constricted throat, his insides wriggling like a worm on a hook. "She hasn't reeled me in yet."

"Famous last words," Sam guffawed.

"Let's say hi to Mama." Kelsey inclined her head, the platinum strands of her upswept blond hair gleaming beneath a chandelier. "She's been anxious to see you all day."

Sam wagged a finger at Heath. "Anxious for you to set a wedding date."

Pressure settled on Heath's shoulders.

"Daddy." Kelsey swatted her father's coat sleeve. "You're terrible. Stop pressuring Heath."

Heath choked back a laugh. Now *that* was amusing, considering her ultimatum to agree on a date by summer's end. "Your daughter's doing a fine enough job on her own."

"What's he talking about, Dew Drop?" Sam's snub nose wrinkled, and his amiable expression faded slightly. "You're not chasing after Heath…making a spectacle of yourself, are you?"

"Of course not, Daddy." Kelsey rested her head on Heath's shoulder and her stiff hair dented slightly. "We've been together forever. Heath's crazy about me."

"Or just plain crazy," Heath muttered beneath his breath as Sam strode across the marble floor and disappeared into the formal living room.

Kelsey gripped Heath's arm. "What's gotten into you?"

Good question. Usually he acted the part of attentive boyfriend, no matter what the Timmonses threw his way, but tonight he hadn't the patience for it. "What do you mean?"

"You're—you're not yourself."

"Maybe this is me and you've never noticed." He'd just lost a chance at his dream, narrowly escaped a livestock disaster and spent a long day sparring with know-it-all Jewel. She'd accused him of never doing what he wanted and yes, he'd admit it, she had a point. Putting others ahead of himself was grating on him lately.

Kelsey's fingers trailed up his dress shirt's buttons. "I know you better than anyone."

Heath's heart turned over heavily as he nodded.

"We're meant to be married," she pressed. "Why else would we have stayed together this long if we weren't perfect for each other?"

Heath's lips flattened. Problem was, lately he'd sensed a change in himself, a restlessness when they were together. Instead of the old excitement he'd felt when he saw her, he had a sense of obligation and even boredom…completely unfounded since Kelsey was as kind and giving as ever.

Had he changed? Or was he just outgrowing his feelings for Kelsey? On the other hand, the pressure of setting a wedding date might be giving him cold feet. He should just pick a date already. He'd probably feel relieved. No more second-guessing whether he was marrying Kelsey because he felt he had to instead of wanted to. He had every reason to love her.

Her hard work and generosity in creating his mother's scholarship also left him beholden to her. After he'd unforgivably failed his ma, Kelsey found a way to honor her and keep her memory alive. It didn't erase his guilt, but it made it possible to live with himself.

"Where's your tie?"

Heath's neck muscles clenched at the slight frown tugging down the corners of Kelsey's mouth. "Didn't want to bother with it since it was getting late."

Kelsey waved her hand. "It's okay. I—I shouldn't have mentioned it. It's just—appearances are so important in my world."

Her world.

The entitled, stuffy life he'd enter when he gave up gigging and ranching to say, "I do."

He counted backward in his head. Years with an erratic mother taught him to speak softly and stay neutral. And—

of course—he *was* a Loveland, and Lovelands locked away their emotions. Problem was, when you denied them long enough, you forgot how you really felt in the first place. "Looks aren't more important than manners."

"Appearances are everything, honey," she said gently, with a kind smile that felt the tiniest bit condescending. "Besides, punctuality is for schoolchildren and trains, not real people."

Heath stared at her false eyelashes, her colored hair and the chin implant she'd gotten three years ago, wondering what passed for "real" these days. A vision of Jewel, covered in dust, her cowlicks standing up every which way, her teeth white against her freckled face, flashed in his mind's eye. She was as real and raw as it got.

"What are you smiling about?" Kelsey bumped his shoulder with her own. "Can I guess?"

He startled. "Nope. Not in a million years." Why did the cocky cowgirl occupy so many of his thoughts?

"You're keeping something from me." Kelsey's brow furrowed.

He bristled, resenting her prying even when she had every right to as his fiancée. "If I am, that's my call."

"Kids?" a woman called before Kelsey could respond. "I've poured the champagne."

"Coming," Kelsey hollered back. Her concerned gaze pinned Heath in place. "Can we talk about this later?" When he nodded, she rose on her tiptoes, so their mouths were almost level. "How about a kiss?"

He half-heartedly obliged, anticipating the familiar sticky-peach taste of her favorite lipstick before easing away.

"What am I, your whiskered great-aunt?" Kelsey threw her arms around his neck. "Kiss me like you mean it, gorgeous man."

"Kelsey!" Her mother appeared in the archway, one

beringed hand resting on a cocked hip. As they broke apart, Darla Timmons smiled tightly, her unlined skin making it hard to gauge her age. She could be thirty-five going on sixty. "If you two lovebirds are done, we're ready for predinner drinks."

"Of course." Kelsey tucked her hand inside the crook of Heath's arm and hustled them into the formal living room.

Tasteful neutral-colored wallpaper covered ten-foot walls ending in white crown moldings. Elaborate sofas and chairs, grouped together before an oversize hearth, were covered with patterned pillows matching long drapes pooling on an inlaid wooden floor. His boots sank into the plush rug as he crossed the room to Kelsey's parents.

"Why, don't you look handsome." Darla handed Heath a champagne flute with a stem so thin he feared he'd snap it just by looking.

He held it gingerly and inhaled the fruity scent fizzing from its surface. "Thank you, ma'am."

"What are we toasting?" Darla asked, raising her glass. Some of the bubbly splashed over the top and down the side of her hand as she lurched slightly on her heels. Heath instinctively steadied her with a firm hand on her elbow.

"Do we have anything to cheer, Heath?" Sam asked.

Three pairs of eyes turned to him. Heath raised his glass and said what was expected. "To Kelsey, the most beautiful gal in Carbondale."

Glasses clinked, and Heath downed the sweet bubbly in a single gulp.

"She's not getting any younger." Sam snagged a shrimp from an ice-filled crystal tray and dipped it in cocktail sauce.

"Daddy!" Kelsey smoothed the tight skin beneath her chin. "I'm not even thirty yet."

"But you will be in a couple of years." Darla tottered down onto the couch, patted the cushion next to her and shot Heath a pointed look. “Tick tock. When am I getting grandbabies?”

“Would you like something to eat, ma’am?” Heath perched beside her and whisked away her glass in hopes she’d forget it, and her nosy question.

“See,” Darla trilled. “This is why you’ll make a wonderful son-in-law. Good manners and such a thoughtful young man.”

“He’s a good boy, all right.” Kelsey patted his cheek.

“And when will the happy day be?” Sam leaned a hip on a grand piano, a Steinway no less, one Kelsey confided had never been played. Heath’s fingers itched to touch its keyboard. The songs he would write on such an incredible instrument… Only once he moved here, he’d be as silent as the Steinway, a decoration without a purpose. Appearances mattered to the Timmonses—not substance.

“We’re setting a wedding date by the end of summer.” Kelsey’s lips curved as she peered at him over her champagne glass rim. “It’ll be a Christmas wedding.”

“That’s not settled yet.” His fingers clenched. Kelsey acted as if their marriage was a foregone conclusion and maybe it was…but his heart hadn’t made peace with it yet. Once he’d successfully moved the herd and handed the ranch back to his father, would he be ready to begin a new life with her? Hopefully, his regret over missed opportunities in music would fade once he had a wife and children to occupy him instead.

“Stop messing around, Heath.” Kelsey playfully swatted him. Her parents’ gazes pinged between them.

An elderly man wearing a bow tie cleared his throat from the archway. “Dinner is ready whenever you are, ma’am.”

Darla inclined her coiffed head. “Thank you, Matthew.” She wobbled to her feet, one hand clutching Heath’s extended arm. “Shall we?”

Once seated, Kelsey cleared her throat and pointedly stared at Heath's cloth napkin, then at his lap. Perversely, he tucked it into his shirt collar like his father instead of draping it on his lap as expected.

Kelsey dropped her fork, then paused by his ear as she reached for it. "Why are you acting like this?"

He shrugged, his back teeth clamped together. She'd called him a good boy before, something he'd labored to be all his life. But what if he didn't want to be so good all the time? Jewel's smug smile, her stupid scorekeeping game, and his urge to even it up tomorrow and prove he was the better range boss added an extra beat to his heart.

"So, how's the ranch treating you these days?" Sam waved over Matthew, who added a dollop of creamy dressing to Sam's salad before setting the silver carafe on the table.

"Good." Heath helped himself to a dinner roll, broke it in half, and slathered it with butter.

"Can't say I'm complaining about the weather. I haven't had to spray-tan in weeks." Darla shook her head at the approaching server and poured herself a generous glass of red wine.

"Mama, the doctor said no more sun after your skin cancer." Kelsey speared a lettuce leaf and lifted it to her mouth. "Why just this morning, while I was volunteering at the free clinic, the doctor diagnosed a malignant melanoma."

Darla waved her off and downed more wine.

Kelsey dropped her fork, grabbed her mother's glass and placed it out of reach. Admiration swelled. Growing up, they'd bonded over their experiences with alcoholic mothers and the toll they took, a battle Kelsey continued to wage. "Besides, you don't want to get ugly freckles, do you, Ma?"

Heath pictured Jewel's red face earlier. With every bit of

her skin colored in, she'd resembled a tomato…or maybe an apple since her face was heart-shaped with a pointed chin she sure liked jerking at him.

Kelsey stopped nibbling on her salad. "Now why are you smiling again, Heath?"

Heat blazed up his neck. It was none of her business. He'd lost his dreams, but he'd keep his own counsel. "No reason."

"People who are getting married shouldn't have secrets from each other." She speared a cucumber slice with her fork and pointed it at him.

"Simmer down, Dew Drop." Sam's blunt features twisted wryly. "All the Lovelands keep to themselves."

"They're tight-lipped—" Darla lifted her napkin to her mouth "—cowboys," she finished with a hiccup.

"Heath isn't like them." Kelsey signaled Matthew to grind more pepper over her salad. "He's more refined."

Heath made a point of flicking crumbs from his navy shirt. Kelsey mouthed "stop" at him, a line forming between her brows.

Sam's fork chased a cherry tomato around his salad plate. "Let's hope he's a better businessman."

Heath stiffened at the insult. "My family's run Loveland Hills for over 130 years," he fired back, his voice hard. Despite the hardship Jewel's family had imposed, the Lovelands intended to run the ranch for 130 more years, with or without their water rights restored.

Sam lifted his white napkin and waved it like a flag. "No offense meant. But ranching is a whole lot different from running a business empire like mine." He dropped the cloth, shoveled a tomato in his mouth and chewed before he continued. "Will you be ready to take over when I retire next year? I'll be giving it to you once you and Kelsey are married."

"What about Kelsey? She's got quite a head for business." Heath caught the brief flash of surprised pleasure in Kelsey's eyes before they dropped to her plate. As long as he'd known her, she'd worked in her father's offices when she wasn't volunteering or in school. She'd started as an assistant, insistent on an entry-level position to learn the business from the ground up, and gradually worked her way to project manager.

Sam flicked his hand sideways, dismissive. "Dew Drop can keep her job, of course. But we need someone in charge who'll be taken seriously. Command authority."

Heath poured more dressing on his salad. "I take your daughter's talent quite seriously."

Kelsey's knee bumped his beneath the table, and he caught her half smile from the corner of his eye.

Her father harrumphed. "This is a man's business. Don't get me wrong, Dew Drop's got a good head on her shoulders, but I need someone with cattle ranching knowledge and know-how. A strong leader the company will follow."

Heath chewed thoughtfully, then swallowed. "I'd never expect Kelsey to follow me."

Sam goggled at him, then turned to his wife. "Did you hear that?"

"It's this generation, Sam." She poured the rest of the wine into her empty water glass and made a face at a frowning Kelsey. "Equal sex or something."

"You won't turn the company over to Kelsey unless she's married?" Heath eased to the side as Matthew whisked away his salad plate.

Sam spat an olive pit into his napkin. "I need to know she's going to be taken care of."

"I can take care of myself, Daddy." Kelsey reached for a bread roll, then buttered it. "Though I'm grateful Heath will be by my side."

"How soon can you start working for me?" Sam continued, as if he hadn't heard Kelsey. "You need to learn the ropes."

"Not until the beef auction and after that...we'll see..." he finished vaguely, earning a glare from Kelsey.

"Now, I'm known to be a straight talker, so don't take offense, Heath." Sam sawed into the thick round cut of filet mignon Matthew placed before him.

Heath braced himself, and Kelsey's hand landed on his knee beneath the table, squeezing.

Darla shook her head at the offered steak, lifted her wineglass and murmured, "Here we go."

After a couple of bites, Sam set his fork and knife on the edge of his plate. "My friend's the president of Colorado Financial. He thought I should know your family's in dire straits before I allowed Kelsey to tie herself to you."

Heath bristled, knowing where this conversation was heading. Due south.

"We wouldn't want anyone to think you're after her money," Sam concluded.

"Daddy!" Kelsey rose from her chair. "Take that back! We've been together so long Heath's practically a son to you. You know him better than that. He'd only marry me for the right reasons."

Was a sense of obligation a "right reason"?

Heath's clamped, back teeth shot a flare of pain into his temples. Sam had no right to use his connections to get financial information about his family. "Money isn't a consideration for me."

At least, it wasn't a deciding one. He had thought about using his salary to help the ranch, but it'd be money he earned, not took...

Sam choked slightly and swallowed hard, downing a long gulp of wine. "Son. Money should always be a consideration."

"Heath loves me." The utensils jumped when Kelsey slapped her palm on the table.

Did he? Lord, he hoped so. "Good folks care about their independence and integrity most…and privacy. You had no right to investigate my family."

"When it comes to ensuring my daughter's happiness, everything's my business." Sam tapped the side of his wineglass with a buffed fingernail. "And you'll never convince me people don't care about money the most."

"Well—you're wrong." Kelsey subsided back in her chair and cast an apologetic look Heath's way.

Heath opened his mouth to argue with Sam further, but finding no good possibility of convincing his audience, he inserted a bite of steak instead. The rich, beefy flavor melted on his tongue as he chewed, thinking hard. Money didn't buy happiness. Would he be happy with Kelsey and she with him? He'd be doing what was expected of him and maybe that'd be enough. "The chance to supplement my family's bank account with my earnings would be appreciated."

"Now we're getting somewhere." A puff of steam escaped Sam's baked potato as he slit open its center. "No harm in helping out your ranch since it'll belong to my grandkids."

Now it was Heath's turn to swallow funny. He coughed to clear a bit of meat from his throat and took a deep pull of water. "I'm sorry, sir, but you're wrong. Loveland Hills belongs to all of my siblings. My children will get their fair share, no more, no less."

Sam frowned, wineglass clenched so hard in one hand, Heath thought the man might shatter it. "If we're putting up money to keep it afloat…"

"Daddy, enough with the business talk. You're boring Mama to death." Kelsey nodded to her mother, whose lowered eyes and tilted posture suggested drink had more to do with her condition than conversation. Like him, Kelsey avoided words like "drunk" or "passed out." There was too much shame attached to them.

"Another time then," Sam said firmly, his tone brooking no compromise.

Heath's entire body clenched like a fist. No doubt they'd circle back to this conversation next time they met up, and the one after that and the one after that… They'd never leave him in peace until he and Kelsey set a date and booked a venue. Would he be at peace then, too?

A couple hours later, Heath and Kelsey lingered on her front steps. Overhead, the moon had crested, splashing silvery light on the perfectly manicured lawn. Automatic sprinklers arced streams of water over grass so thick it'd feed twenty, maybe thirty head. He ached at the waste of it, his mind turning to tomorrow's cattle drive destination. Would the natural spring they sought still be flowing given the unrelenting heat? The herd couldn't handle another setback like today.

"Are you sure you have to leave so early?" Kelsey threw her arms around his waist and snuggled her head against his chest.

He breathed in the scent of her hair spray and gently disentangled himself. "I've got an early start. In fact, I'll be sleeping on the range some nights, and won't see you much for the next few weeks."

Which was exactly what he needed to figure out his mixed-up feelings…

Kelsey sighed. "Won't you be glad when those days are behind you?"

When he remained silent, she pressed a kiss to his cheek. "That's why I adore you. You're so loyal. You never speak bad about anyone, especially your family."

It was too dry of a summer for mosquitoes, but a warm

wind rustled the leaves on nearby trees. "Are you going to set your parents straight about us?"

Emotions shifted like sea currents beneath her made-up face. "About what?"

His eyebrows met over the bridge of his nose. He might be a people pleaser, but that didn't mean leading someone on. Kelsey knew where they stood, no matter how she kept insisting to the contrary. "That we haven't set a date and that we aren't necessarily getting married at Christmas."

"You're right." She blew out a breath. "And I appreciate what you said to Daddy…about me being able to run the company."

"I meant it. You don't need me."

Kelsey seemed to be looking somewhere far beyond him; it took a visible effort for her to drag her gaze back from that distant place. "Daddy thinks I do."

There was a moment of silence that lengthened into awkwardness as they faced each other warily, unsure how to proceed. "I had a chance to go to Nashville for a try-out," he blurted.

Her long lashes beat the air, and her mouth formed an *O* before she recovered herself. "Had? As in you turned it down?"

He nodded.

"And you said no for me?"

A deep breath lifted his chest. "I said no because Cole broke his arm and Pa left on his honeymoon. I couldn't leave the ranch shorthanded."

Kelsey's shoulders rose. "Is that all you care about?"

"Right now, it's all hands on deck."

Her lips pressed into a seam. "You know how I feel about your music. You can't keep gigging forever. It's time to grow up. Settle down. I want you to become a respectable business- and family man."

"Music's respectable," he insisted, the words hot on his tongue. Music was his life. Or had been.

"It's a pipe dream. Like chasing after the end of the rainbow."

"You don't think I can make it?"

"You're talented, Heath. But it's no guarantee of success, and this life is." She made a sweeping gesture with her hand to encompass her expansive home. "You'll never have to struggle or worry about your family, because we'll help take care of them."

When he remained silent, she slid her hands into his. "You *are* going to set a date with me, aren't you? It'd be so romantic to arrive at the church in a sleigh..."

He squeezed her petal-soft fingertips, then withdrew. "I've got a lot going on. I can't focus on us when I need to keep the herd intact through a drought."

Her features sharpened. "I've given you ten years, Heath. Don't keep stringing me along."

"I won't."

She sighed. "Problem is I only want you."

He donned his hat and adjusted it on his head, thinking what to say. Then again, maybe he should just run. "Are you sure I'm all you want? Neither one of us has ever been with anyone else or considered another kind of future. What if we're just together because it's comfortable? Expected?"

Her eyes fled his and she seemed not to breathe for a moment. The sprinkler system trickled in the quiet. Then she gave herself a shake and her lips wobbled into a smile. "Of course I want you. What a crazy thing to say."

He cocked his head, sure he hadn't imagined her pleasure when he'd suggested she could run the company alone. "I'd better get going. Daryl, Jewel and I are starting at five a.m."

Kelsey's nose scrunched. "Jewel? Jewel Cade?"

He stopped at the base of the stairs and a stream of water smacked against his boots. "Yes."

"I didn't know you were working with her."

He stared up at Kelsey's uncertain face. "She's filling in this month. Is that a problem?"

"Will she be sleeping on the range with you?"

That brought him up short. A strange emotion pitched his stomach, like the moment a bull-riding chute gate sprang open. "I suppose. Daryl's got some family issues going on, so it'll probably be mostly me and Jewel."

"You can't. It's inappropriate."

Heath stared her dead in the eye. "It's not negotiable."

"You shouldn't be spending nights alone with another woman when you're engaged," Kelsey exclaimed. "Think how that'll look to other people!"

"I don't care what anybody thinks. She's good at what she does." Heath curled his fingers into his sweating palms and shoved them deep inside his trousers. "And she's my sister now."

"*Step*sister," Kelsey insisted.

"Same difference." Heath studied his boot tops, uneasy. He never lied...yet somehow it felt like he'd just told a whopper.

"Is that how you see her?"

Heath shrugged. "She's just a temporary ranch hand... and an annoying one at that. I'm only interested in how fast she can rope and ride."

Jewel was no threat to Kelsey.

What a crazy thought...yet it stuck with him. He couldn't deny his eagerness to even up the score tomorrow and prove who was the best range boss. Guilt swamped him. It'd been a long time since he'd felt as excited to see his loyal and patient fiancée.

"She can't give you this." Kelsey leaned down, placed

her hands on his shoulders, and smashed her mouth to his. Their teeth banged together.

He recoiled, rubbing his throbbing canine to see if she'd cracked it. "You don't have to worry about Jewel Cade."

"You've known her for ten seconds and we've been together for over ten years. Who's worried?" Then, without a word, Kelsey dashed back in the house and slammed the door.

Heath jogged down the brick path, yanked open his pickup's door and started up the engine, reversing out of the driveway at breakneck speed.

Was his haste to escape Kelsey's accusations or to hurry back to his sparring match with Jewel?

He couldn't deny he looked forward to working with his annoying new ranch hand much more than he should.

CHAPTER FIVE

THE SHRILL RINGING OF the Lovelands' old rotary phone assaulted Jewel's eardrum and snapped up her drooping eyelids. Since she was the only one awake to answer it, she set her coffee on the kitchen table and snatched up the handset. "Loveland residence."

"Honey, I was hoping I'd catch you before you set off."

Jewel's heart swelled at the familiar sound of her mother's voice. She dragged the receiver and its long cord to the table, dropped into a chair and cradled it between her ear and shoulder. "What time is it over there?"

"Midday, which means noon in London. So many funny words here. Did you know *chips* means French fries and *crisps* means chips?"

"Sounds confusing." Jewel focused blearily on the wall-mounted clock. Five a.m. Any minute now, Heath would appear to start the second day of their cattle drive. Her heart thumped in her ears and her palms grew clammy. She'd gotten up extra early to beat him here, to set the tone…to prove she was the best range boss, not him.

"And the trunk of a car is called the boot," Ma continued. "When the taxi driver asked Boyd if we'd like him to put our luggage in his boot, Boyd said, 'Mine might fit, but the wife's brought more than a toothbrush.'" Joy's giggle drew a chuckle from Jewel despite her jumping stomach.

She spooned sugar into her coffee and chased it with a long pour of milk. The brew's scent stung her nose and expanded her lungs. "Sounds like you two are having fun already."

"We had a lovely meal after we settled into our hotel last night and today we're going to see Buckingham Palace."

Jewel stirred her coffee, dropped the spoon onto a napkin and lifted her steaming mug. "Make sure to match your hat to your outfit so everyone thinks you're the queen."

Ma tutted. "Now why didn't I think of that?"

Hot coffee scalded Jewel's tongue as she took a cautious sip. "Bigger question is why did I?"

"There's a softer side to you, Jewel, no matter how many quills you cover yourself in."

Jewel straightened her slouch when Heath sauntered into the kitchen, his brown hair wet and clinging to his high cheekbones, his blue eyes hazy until they landed on her. "I'm not prickly."

Heath lifted a skeptical brow and strode to the coffee maker. The play of his muscles beneath his fitted gray shirt snared her attention and stole her breath.

"I've got a way for you to prove it."

"How?" Jewel sneaked a glance at Heath's broad back as he poured himself a cup, her eyes trailing over the worn Wranglers that hugged his long legs. Why did the most irritating man also have to be the most handsome one she'd ever seen?

"I need you to fill my spot on the Flower Gala planning board," Ma said in a rush. "It helps raise thousands of dollars each year for animal and wildlife conservation."

At Jewel's coughing fit, Heath's head whipped around. His deep blue eyes searched her flushed face until she subsided back in her chair. "I thought Sofia was taking your place."

"We'd planned on it, but James called. Seems she's having some troubles with her first trimester."

Jewel's heart clenched for her sister-in-law. "Is she okay?"

"Oh yes. The doctor just wants her to take it easy and spend as much time off her feet as possible. Jewel, I hate to ask you, but..."

Jewel sighed. Family. Equal parts love and suffering. "Of course, Ma. What do I need to do?"

A chair scraped against the tiled floor as Heath dragged

it back and dropped into it. He hung his head over his coffee. With his eyes closed, he inhaled the curling steam rising off the surface before drinking the brew.

"Attend the weekly meetings, share your thoughts and offer to help make calls, organize, set up, tear down… there's no end to the work that needs doing."

"That's work?" Jewel scoffed. She and Heath reached for bananas from the basket set in the center of the table. When their fingers touched, it was as if an electric spark shot up her wrist. Neither of them moved for a long moment and Jewel couldn't feel her heart. She jerked her hand back as if she'd touched a live wire.

Her ma's chuckle flowed through the phone. "Just wait and see."

Jewel's fingers stopped mid-peel as suspicion crackled inside her. "Am I going to have to wear a dress to this Flower Gala thing?"

"Sofia can lend you one. And your grandmother was petite like you. I have some of her gowns hanging in my old closet."

Jewel savagely bit off one end of the banana and chewed. "But Grandma liked ruffles. Lace." She swallowed hard. "Pink."

"That's a wonderful color for you. You'll look pretty."

"*Pretty* and *me* are two words that don't go together."

Heath leveled her with a speculative stare that curled her toes inside her boots.

"You have your own kind of beauty if you'd stop scowling once in a while."

Jewel relaxed her pursed mouth and smoothed her pinched brow. "When do I scowl?"

When Heath guffawed, Jewel mouthed "shut it" at him, then continued, "Plus, you're my mother. You have to say that."

"It is part of the job description," Ma said blithely. "But in your case, it also happens to be true."

A tabby cat butted her ankle, then trotted to Heath, who scooped it up and stroked its arching back. "What if I'm on the range overnight and can't get into town?"

Heath's eyes clicked with hers and something dark in their sapphire depths stalled her breath.

"Boyd's going to talk to Heath so he and Daryl can arrange to cover for you those nights. In fact, is Heath there?"

Jewel gulped down the last of her banana. "Yeah. Heath's here." And way too present for her liking. "Want me to put him on?"

Heath extended a hand.

"In a moment. Are you getting along okay with the Lovelands?"

Jewel shook her head at Heath, and he dropped his hand to his mug handle. "I kept the herd from getting poisoned yesterday." She launched into the tale, relishing the way it made Heath's mouth flatten and a muscle jump in his jaw. Why she enjoyed getting under his skin as much as she did was a mystery, but it was entertaining to see one of the tight-lipped Lovelands lose their precious self-control. She concluded her tale with, "A Cade saved the day."

Heath pulled the kind of face that told her simultaneously that she was a show-off, and that this was no surprise to him whatsoever.

Joy laughed softly. "I'm sure they appreciate it."

"Heath said just yesterday I was the better range boss." Jewel tapped her chin and moved the phone away from her mouth. "Right, Heath?"

He glowered at her.

"Tell Boyd 'hi' for me," Jewel added.

"I will," Ma promised. "Love you, honey."

Jewel reluctantly said goodbye, handed the phone to Heath and paced to the open window. Her eyes stung as she stared out at the pink-gray dawn and the brightening world of green hills rolling up Mount Sopris. This was the first time she'd ever been apart from her family. She'd never thought of herself as sentimental, had only ever cried once, at her brother Jesse's funeral…yet the idea of her only parent being half a world away left her feeling as empty as a picnic basket after a church supper.

As Heath's deep voice rose and fell behind her, she leaned her forehead against the warm window frame edged in gold light. All this upheaval was to blame. Last night, she'd lain awake in her attic room, thinking over the day's events, replaying her tense exchanges with Heath on a continuous loop. Thoughts of him dining with Kelsey and her family earned her pillow a hard punch or two as she'd tossed and turned. It was none of her business who Heath spent his time with, but for some stupid reason she couldn't fall asleep until his headlights swept up the drive and his boots thudded up the stairs.

A moment later, she sensed Heath behind her as he returned the receiver to its cradle. The warmth of his body seemed to steal into hers before he cleared his throat. His breath stirred the small hairs on the back of her neck that'd escaped her braid. "Looks like another hot one out there."

Peering over her shoulder, she caught his eyes on her face and flushed. Up close, he smelled like Ivory soap and line-dried laundry. Just a couple of inches separated their mouths. If she stepped on his toes and rose on hers, then…

"We'd better get hustling if we're going to make it to the spring before noon," she blurted, her rapid-fire sentence full of air.

One side of Heath's full mouth kicked up. "And it sounds like you've got to be back in time to give your expert opinion on flowers and galas."

Jewel bristled. "What's so funny about that?"

His eyes swept down the length of her faded shirt, rumpled jeans and worn boots. "Is that what you're wearing?"

"So now you're my stylist?"

His nose held a telltale ridge, and his eyes crinkled in a way that suggested there was almost no human behavior he had not seen and, perhaps, been slightly amused by—especially from her. "I'm just saying, you might want to do a little more than 'dust off.'"

"I am who I am. I don't care who likes it."

"Suit yourself," he said calmly, as infuriatingly unfazed as ever. Heath half turned, then stopped, the movement quick and efficient. Although he was tall and broad like his brothers, he moved with a kind of gentle economy, as if he had absorbed the effort of not damaging things just from his size. "Go saddle up the horses while I wake Daryl." Without another word, he strode away.

She made a face at his retreating back. Fine. She would suit herself. What did it matter what anyone thought, least of all a Loveland?

Yet she wondered if she cared, just a tiny bit, about one particular Loveland's feelings toward her more than she should.

Six grueling hours later, Jewel plodded alongside the herd through a narrow chasm. The heat was in full bloom, her entire body sticky with sweat. Dust rose from the hard-packed ground. All around her the sounds of the herd spelled out the urgent quest for life-saving water, hooves striking bedrock, cattle bleating and the musky smells of sweat, livestock and dung. She scanned the vista for signs of the natural spring they sought.

As she brought Bear behind Heath's Appaloosa, his rich, deep bass reached her ears. He sang something lilting and haunting, a tune about distant shores and long hard miles, all in search of true love. Despite the soaring temperature transforming her shirt into wet rag, goose bumps rose on her slick skin.

Every note Heath sang came from another place, another time. It moved through her powerfully, like the blast of wind before a storm, stirring her flagging spirit. Her fatigue fell away. Even the cattle seemed to pick up the pace. Their ears pricked forward, and their hooves lifted higher.

When he finished, she sneaked a glance at his profile. Like his brothers, he was otherworldly handsome, but his nose was a bit shorter and straighter, his smile more boyish.

"Did you like it?" he asked without taking his eyes off the herd. His back swayed, his athletic body one with Destiny.

"Like what?"

"The song."

She pushed a strand of hair back from her face "Oh—I—uh…wasn't paying it much mind."

He slid her a quick "gotcha" side-eye, his gorgeous mouth twitching, and all her thoughts evaporated. In the silence her heart drummed in her chest, and stifling air curled, damp and sticky, beneath her shirt collar. It took her a moment to find her voice. "What kind of song was it?"

"Thought you weren't listening."

"Forget it." She was about to urge Bear forward, but Heath held up a hand.

"It's an Irish folk song. My mother taught it to me." His voice broke on the word *mother* and his jaw grew taut.

The words settled in the air between them, heavy as the oppressive heat.

"Cows like Irish ballads?" she teased, hoping to dispel the strange sense of intimacy building between them.

"They soothe the savage beast." He yanked his hat low against the slanting rays.

Was he talking about the Brahmans or his ma? Jewel knew the tragic story about his mother's suicide and the whispers of her alcoholism and mental illness. The Cades had their share of tragedy, but the Lovelands had suffered, too.

A different image of Heath Loveland, country musician/cowboy heartthrob, appeared in her mind—a boy who'd grown up singing to quiet his troubled parent's heart. His music was a gift, not just a talent. It'd helped Jewel escape her pain, too, when she'd sought out his gigs following Jesse's death.

A breathless quiet descended as they rode until a flash of blue water caught her eye. Her chest expanded with relief. "There it is!" she called.

Heath's head snapped her way, and he met her wide smile. The light in his eyes turned them a brilliant cerulean blue. It sent her heart tumbling straight down into her belly. "You never should have doubted it."

"I—I—"

"Was wrong?" Heath's smug expression, his slightly sardonic smile and his direct gaze left her, briefly, winded.

"Was being realistic." She lifted her braid off the back of her steaming neck. "Between the temperatures and lack of rain, I would have sworn it'd be dried up…but…"

"You were wrong."

The Brahmans streamed around them in their haste to get to the water. Daryl rode up from the back to keep the front edge moving straight.

She glared at Heath, her hand tight around the reins. "Fine."

"Say it."

"Say what?"

A mischievous tilt to his upper lip appeared. "Say you were wrong."

"Don't be childish."

He pulled his sweat-soaked T-shirt away from his chest. "You made the rules of the game, darlin', not me."

"I thought you weren't playing."

Heath's slow grin sent fire across her cheeks as he cast a long glance in her direction. "Let's just say it's grown more appealing of late."

"Now that you've scored a point?" Jewel waved a sarcastic hand, then swiped at the perspiration dripping in her eyes.

"So, you admit this round goes to the Lovelands?"

Before she nodded, a squeal erupted from the back of the herd. She and Heath wheeled their mounts around and spied a pair of wolves leaping at a straggling calf. A chill blew through her.

Heath swore a blue streak and tore off, riding fast and low over Destiny's neck. Jewel squeezed Bear's sides and flicked open the clasp holding her long rifle in place. As her horse thundered beneath her, she dropped the reins, hauled out her firearm, chambered the bullet and sighted the attacking predators down her scope. Before she could squeeze off a shot, Heath vaulted from his saddle into the melee. She lowered her gun.

Was he crazy?

Three cattle dogs appeared beside him. They flew at the wolves, snarling and biting as Heath scooped up the injured calf, laid it across his saddle and leaped up beside it.

"Don't shoot!" he called to Jewel when he spied her gun. "Blue and the gang will handle them."

Heath's faith in his cattle dogs quickly proved true. Within minutes they'd chased off the predators, then loped back, thankfully uninjured.

"How's the calf?" she called to Heath.

"I'm taking it to the stream to see how bad its leg is."

A moment later she joined him by the water. Pink tinged the crystal flow streaming from the natural spring as he carefully washed the calf's leg. Its mother bellowed nearby. In the distance, she spied Daryl weaving in and out of the herd, now drinking and grazing, his eyes scanning the tree line for more predators.

"This little guy got lucky," Jewel observed, absently petting a hovering black-and-white cattle dog as her eyes traveled over the scrapes on the calf's rear leg.

Heath dried the appendage, applied antibiotic cream, then swatted its rump. In a flash, it scampered to its mother and nudged beneath her stomach to nurse. "He's going to be okay."

She rolled her eyes up to the sky and blinked fast, relieved.

"You're not getting soft on me, cowgirl, are you?"

She was conscious of the sudden lump in her throat. No one saw that side of her—or bothered to notice. “Nah. Just got something in my eye.”

His eyebrows raised as if to say *really?*

“Does that happen a lot up here?” She tried to swipe the dirt clinging to her neck with fingers that were still stiff from gripping the reins all day.

“What?”

“Predator attacks. We don’t see them often on Cade land.”

“That’s because you don’t have to drive them this far into the mountains to find water.” He shot her a significant look.

She bristled at the accusation in his voice. “That’s how the maps are drawn.”

“You could change that.”

“I’m no surveyor.”

“No, but you could convince your brothers not to fight our case and reinstate the easement.”

“I’d have a better chance of talking that sun into not setting.” She nodded to the yellow blaze of light beaming from the cloudless sky. “Besides, where would we get the five million to pay the settlement?”

“What about Cora’s Tear?” he asked, referring to the fifty-carat sapphire brooch and family heirloom that’d started the feud between the families over 130 years ago.

“That’s part of my trousseau,” she said automatically, waving off a nagging fly.

“Your what?” Heath crouched down to the stream and splashed his face with water.

“It’s a thing for brides—in case I get married.” Not that it’d ever happen, but Cora’s Tear always went to the oldest girl in the family, so right now, the jewel was hers until she passed it on.

Water beaded on the ends of Heath’s long lashes as his eyes crinkled in amusement. “You?” he snickered. “Getting married?”

She jerked back, his words echoing—no, actually taunting her. Anger rose in her swiftly. "Why's that so funny?"

Shaking his head, Heath straightened slowly. "Just can't imagine it..."

"I don't see you getting hitched any time soon," she accused. "Shouldn't you have a wedding date by now?"

His mouth opened and closed and the flash of vulnerability in his eyes pricked her ballooning anger...and left her wondering. Didn't he want to marry Kelsey Timmons, the prettiest, richest gal in Carbondale?

"Not that it's any of my business." She crushed her hat between her hands.

"It's not," he said curtly.

"Good."

"Fine."

She slammed her hat over her head, his irritation feeding hers. "All right then."

"Since when does Jewel Cade ask for permission anyway?" Heath drawled.

His words stopped her from the glorious stomp-off she'd planned. "What do you mean?"

"Can't imagine you doing anything just because it's what others want, like getting married or risking the cattle. You proved that yesterday. You don't see these animals as just a dollar sign." He slid calloused fingers through her cowlicks. "See. Even your hair won't bend."

A pulse of pleasure bubbled in her veins. No one had ever noticed how hard she worked to reduce the cattle's stress or took her attempts seriously. Not her father or even her brothers. Yet Heath gave her much-appreciated respect. It made her feel warm and liquid-filled, as though all her tension with him had been a solid thing and now was not.

"This spring isn't enough to hold the herd for more than a day or two." Heath dropped his hand and continued when she didn't speak. "Defy your brothers and let's drive them to the Crystal River when your family's longhorns aren't around for our Brahmans to bother. No harm, no foul."

Her head snapped back, and she gaped at Heath. James's warning returned to her.

You know how those Lovelands are. They know how to sweet-talk a lady.

"You must think I'm a fool," she murmured, shaking her head.

"I think a lot of things about you," he said slowly, his voice gravelly, his eyes intent. "But fool ain't one of 'em."

She inhaled sharply but the air stuck in her throat. "You're trying to sweet-talk me."

"If I was, would it work?" His brows flew up.

"Not a chance." Her boots splashed in the stream as she stomped across it. Whatever she thought she'd read into Heath's expression earlier, she was dead wrong.

He was trying to soften her up, lull her, so he could take advantage of her—and darned if he didn't have a shot if she wasn't more careful.

"Oh, Jewel," he called, stopping her. When she turned, he held up each of his index fingers. "Lovelands-Cades tied up."

"Don't count on scoring again." She slid her boot into Bear's stirrup, slung her leg over the saddle and trotted him away, fast. She needed to keep her distance from Heath Loveland or she'd lose more than just points.

She valued her independence too much to ever get romantically involved with anyone. Heath, however, might be the one guy able to penetrate her shell if she wasn't careful.

CHAPTER SIX

THE SUN HAD started to slide across the mountaintops, its orange glow diffused by the purple-gray air of evening, the scorching temperatures dropping with it. Heath studied the sun's gentle fall and the lengthening shadows creeping toward him, thoughts of the formidable Rocky Mountain skyline and the fact that nobody was truly free filling his mind. Perhaps all freedom—physical, emotional, personal—really only came at the cost of somebody or something else.

Out on the range today with Daryl and Jewel, he'd felt free. Yet each sunset brought him closer to setting a wedding date with Kelsey, a decision that'd change his life forever. Whenever his mind turned it over, his thoughts became dark and clouded, full of dead ends and treacherous paths leading him right back to where he'd started.

Jewel rode up beside him. Astride her enormous stallion, her large brown eyes were nearly level with his. "Are we going to check the injured calf again?"

He nodded. "I'll have the dogs separate it from its mother."

"Why call them back?" She angled her face and tracked the black-and-white canines circling the grazing herd. "A real rider could separate them in five minutes flat."

"Five?" he scoffed, though the number was nothing to sneeze at…for Cade standards. But Jewel rode with Lovelands now and the sooner she understood the difference, the quicker she'd lose the giant chip on her shoulder.

"Why?" She squinted at him from beneath her black Stetson. "How fast could you do it?"

"Three."

Her brows shot up and disappeared beneath her brim. "Liar."

"I've got nothing to prove." As Heath watched, the sun

vanished, and the orange sky began to turn periwinkle blue. "Standards are higher on Loveland Hills."

She recoiled. "You're saying Cades have lower standards?"

He shrugged and bit back a grin at the strangled noise escaping her.

"Then I'll do it two minutes." She urged Bear forward.

"Wait!" he hollered, but Jewel ignored him and plunged into the milling cattle. Uneasy Brahmans scattered at her approach. He swore under his breath. If one of the large animals spooked the wrong way, she'd be thrown or worse. Adrenaline surged through him, making his muscles twitch.

Nothing for it.

He and Destiny gave chase. Ahead, Jewel circled a rope over her head as she systematically pressured the calf's mother until the pair broke from the herd, the calf following its parent as expected. Then, with well-practiced ease, she released the loop to fall neatly over the Brahman's head. Admiration replaced Heath's irritation as Jewel expertly backed up Bear, tightening the restraint until the panicked cow settled.

"Time?" she called once Heath lassoed the calf, secured the rope to his saddle and hurriedly checked its leg.

"It wasn't five minutes," he admitted. The abrasions looked clean as he washed them and applied antibiotic ointment.

"It wasn't three, either, I'd wager." Jewel retrieved her rope, coiled it and secured it to her saddle.

"Might have been under," he muttered from the side of his mouth. "You still disobeyed an order."

"Range bosses don't take orders." She shot him a cocky grin over her shoulder before trotting ahead on Bear. "I'll get some wood. You start the fire."

He opened his mouth to remind her *he* was range boss,

but she was already out of earshot. As she trotted away, she held up three fingers, two on one hand and one on the other.

Cades two. Lovelands one.

Irritating, aggravating, infuriating cowgirl.

He rode to a clump of bedrock, tied up Destiny, grabbed a lighter and started a blaze with scrub.

"How'd the wound look?" Jewel approached minutes later with an armload of wood. She dumped it beside the crackling fire he'd coaxed to life inside a stone circle. Nearby, the Brahmans had mostly settled for the night, standing motionless in the field surrounding the spring, their tails flicking at nagging flies. Daryl circled the herd astride his mount. His indistinct calls to the cattle dogs carried on the still, balmy air.

A whiff of woodsmoke curled beneath Heath's nose. "Dixon's going to be okay."

Jewel, crouched beside the fire, leveled him with a wide-eyed look. "Do you name your calves?"

Heath ducked his head. Why had he let that name slip? Something about Jewel's mix of prickly temper and surprising sensitivity left him rattled and unsteady. Her brash talk and mischievous smile distracted him, made him laugh and kept him off-balance. "They each deserve one, don't they?" A defensive note entered his voice. "Even if it's for only a short while."

A shower of orange-red sparks floated skyward as she dropped a log on the fire, brushed off her pants and rose to join him on the large rock. Beneath the odor of horses and sweat, the faint scent of her soap, fresh and natural as the spring burbling nearby, teased his nose. "I name them, too."

Heath gaped at Jewel. Rough, tough, take-no-prisoners Jewel named her calves? It didn't surprise him, somehow. Her hard shell hid a softness he grew more curious to know by the minute.

"Don't tell my brothers," she added, fierce. Despite the gathering darkness, he glimpsed red deepening her freckled face.

"I won't if you promise not to tell mine."

Her small, calloused hand slipped into his and pumped it up and down. "Deal."

Heat flared in his gut. Her skin was rough, yet the strong length of her fingers, the shape of her hand, fit perfectly in his, and a fierce longing to hold on to the strange sense of completeness seized him.

"Let go, Neanderthal." Jewel yanked back, blushing.

Shocked, he opened his hand, and the sudden release sent her sprawling backward into the dirt. He rushed over and gripped her shoulders. "Jewel! Are you all right? Jewel!"

Without warning, she grabbed his shirt collar and twined her leg in his, flinging him away as she rolled. He landed on his back. Hard.

The thick air, now hazy with smoke, muffled her laughter. She bounded to her knees and pressed her palms to his shoulders. "Pinned you!" An enormous grin broke out over her face, and she whooped like a cowboy.

"Wrong!" He wrapped an arm around her shoulders, maneuvered her beneath him and braced his weight on his palms. The brush of her compact, muscular body against his set his heart afire and turned his sinews to stone.

Their breaths quickened, mingling in the small space separating their mouths. The cockiness faded from Jewel's eyes. In its place, the yearning he'd glimpsed the night of his last gig returned. No one ever looked at him the way Jewel did. Her gaze took in everything about him, inside and out, good and bad; she saw all that, and her rosy lips parted in a slow smile. Heat reddened his ears, colored his throat.

"Are you two eight or twenty-eight?" drawled a voice above them. One side of Daryl's mouth curled as he peered at them from atop his dapple-gray stallion, Remington.

They scrambled to their feet, careful not to look at each other. "That was nothing." Heath brushed the grass from his shirt. His breathing had almost returned to normal, though his heart was pumping overtime.

Had he almost kissed Jewel?

"Looked like something." Daryl patted Remington's neck when he tossed his head and sidestepped a leaping bullfrog. "Emma acts more mature, and she *is* eight."

Heath rubbed his bristled jaw. Daryl had a point. He shouldn't let Jewel goad him so easily. "Don't insult Emma, now. Isn't she turning nine next week?"

"Got a birthday party for her, too." Daryl's gaze swerved to Jewel. "You're invited, of course."

Her white teeth flashed. "Thank you."

Heath cast a wary glance at the thickening twilight. "You'd best start back if you're going to catch a ride into town with Sierra."

Jewel heaved out a long-suffering sigh. "I'd rather sleep on the range than go to some flower party meeting."

Daryl held out a flask. "Maybe this'll take the edge off."

Jewel downed a swig of whatever Daryl carried. Must be something hard, Heath guessed, given Jewel's watering eyes and wheezing as she struggled to catch her breath.

"Easy, girl." Heath clapped Jewel on the back.

"What's in there?" She wiped her mouth with the back of her hand. "Lighter fluid?"

Daryl tucked the flask back in his saddle bag. "Moonshine. One hundred percent Rocky Mountain gold. It'll put hair on your chest." Daryl cracked a rare smile. Heath eyed him with concern. Ever since he and LeAnne started having troubles, his outgoing brother had grown more somber and withdrawn, the only company he kept his kids. Regardless of his marital issues, he remained a devoted father, though.

"Did you make this?" Jewel gasped.

"Guilty." Daryl's deep dimples flashed.

"That should be illegal." She tore off the kerchief tucked into her T-shirt's V-neck and fanned herself. The glimpse of damp, creamy skin momentarily mesmerized Heath. She wasn't freckled everywhere…

"Now that you mention it, I believe it is." Daryl held Bear's halter as Jewel hoisted herself in the saddle.

"Does Travis know about 'Rocky Mountain gold'?" she asked, referring to their brother, the county sheriff. He was the latest in a long line of Loveland lawmen who'd served Carbondale for over a hundred years running.

"I plead the fifth."

Jewel cracked up laughing at Daryl's quip. Then, with a wave, she rode off. A pang of longing filled Heath as she grew smaller and smaller before disappearing over a ridge. Did he want Jewel to stay? He should be glad he and Daryl were watching the cattle tonight, yet a sense of loss dogged him.

"You like her." Daryl ripped the top off a bag of trail mix, shook some into his hand and passed it to Heath.

Heath's fingers clenched around the plastic. "You're losing it, dude."

"Question is," Daryl continued, pinning Heath with a discerning look, "what are you going to do about it?"

"I'm already spoken for."

"Are you?"

Pressure built in Heath's chest. It felt like he was slowly suffocating. Air seeped out of his body, and he couldn't coax it back in. "About to be."

"Then how come you can't quit staring at Jewel?"

A picture of the wisecracking cowgirl, her eyes brewing with mischief whenever they landed on him, her full mouth stretched in a taunting smile, rose in his mind's eye. "I don't like her."

Daryl shook out a bedroll, dropped down on it and laced his fingers behind his head. "Keep telling yourself that, bro. Maybe you'll even convince yourself."

"So now *you're* giving relationship advice?" Heath laid out his sleeping bag, then leaned back on it, his palms denting the slippery material as he stared up at the emerging stars. Fireflies blinked on and off in the brush.

Daryl laughed, a harsh scraping sound. "Guess I'm the last person you should listen to."

The naked pain in his brother's voice filled Heath with regret. "Is everything all right with you and LeAnne?" Daryl was silent so long, Heath slid him a sidelong glance to see if he'd fallen asleep. "You don't have to tell me."

"No," Daryl said gruffly. "It's a fair question. Haven't answered it yet myself. Lovelands don't have the best track record with relationships. Cole went toe up with Katlynn, Pa and Ma…well…you saw how that went. Heck, even Wyatt Loveland lost his Cheyenne wife when she died after childbirth, right after he bought Loveland Hills. Maybe Pa's broken the Loveland curse with Joy, and you'll be the next lucky one…if you figure out which gal to give your heart to." Daryl closed his eyes, and the faint lines around his mouth deepened. "Trust me when I say, choose carefully."

Heath recalled LeAnne's older sister, the gal Daryl had dated in college. Everyone had assumed they'd marry until Daryl's surprise shotgun wedding to LeAnne. The reason he left one sister for the other remained a mystery, but it wasn't the Loveland way to pry.

"I won't be choosing Jewel." Heath stretched out and

crossed one boot over the other. The buzz of crickets lulled him into a drowsy state.

Even if he weren't engaged to Kelsey, Jewel was every kind of wrong for him. He preferred not to ruffle feathers, while the wild child thrived on stirring things up and doing as she pleased. She challenged his authority on the range, second-guessed his decisions or flat-out refused to follow his orders.

Yet working together made it harder to see her as the enemy. He dropped his hat over his face. Despite her freckles, cowlicks and lack of any effort to put on makeup and dress up, Daryl was right. Heath's eyes strayed her way too often. She was all hard edges and scrawny, not his type at all, but he found himself wanting what he couldn't—shouldn't—want.

His irritating attraction had to stop…along with his rising regard for the scrappy, independent cowgirl. There was a lot to like about Jewel Cade.

Too much for comfort.

Uneasiness twisted inside, the restlessness of waiting to see what he wanted…

And what he would do about it.

"ALL IN FAVOR of tea rose garlands, raise your hands," directed Mrs. Grover-Woodhouse. At her stern, nasal voice, Jewel's knees knocked together beneath the Flower Gala planning committee's conference table. She had a long history with her formidable ex-principal full of after-school detentions where Jewel had learned to write "I will not leave my seat," "I will not talk in class" or, her favorite, "I will not use my compass as a weapon" a hundred times in under ten minutes.

Jewel tucked work-roughened hands beneath her dusty jeans and strove not to squirm amid the dressed-up ladies. A haze of expensive perfume had her battling a sneeze.

Mrs. Grover-Woodhouse peered over a pair of bifocals at the raised hands. "Those opposed?"

All eyes turned to Jewel.

Her heart sped.

"Miss Cade, are you in opposition to tea rose garlands?"

Jewel gazed at the rainbow of manicures surrounding her, shook her head and dug her ragged nails into her chair seat. She'd die before she'd give them something to mock… or shame her mother for. When she'd arrived at the Lovelands' ranch house minutes before nine, she'd barely had time to untack Bear and wash her hands and face before hopping in the truck with Sierra.

"She wouldn't know a tea rose from a teacup," Lara Tomlin, one of Kelsey Timmons's sidekicks, whispered behind a raised hand. Kelsey quickly smothered a laugh.

"I know one of 'em breaks when smashed over your head." Gasps of disapproval greeted Jewel's growl.

Kelsey widened her eyes. "Are you low on sugar, honey? How about some juice? Sweet tea?"

Jewel ground her teeth. Classic Kelsey. In public, she acted like Carbondale's sweetheart and dedicated volunteer, but Jewel knew better. Deep down, she only cared about herself, from the top of her expertly highlighted hair to the designer shoes she bragged about buying while on a recent trip to Italy. Looks and money mattered to Kelsey…which meant Heath cared about them, too. Why else would he be with someone so materialistic? If he liked women like Kelsey, he'd never give a cowgirl like her a second glance.

Not that she wanted him to.

"Miss Cade?" prompted Mrs. Grover-Woodhouse with raised, drawn-in eyebrows.

"I'm fine with the garland," Jewel muttered.

"Thank you." Mrs. Grover-Woodhouse scratched a

check mark next to her list, then raised her head to scan the group. "Let's open the discussion on beverages."

Jewel fought off a yawn as a debate raged about punch with sherbet (tacky according to Kelsey's faction) or a champagne punch (considered sinful by the more stringent churchgoers).

Sierra kicked Jewel under the table, then gave the slightest of eye rolls when Mrs. Berry concluded her "demon liquor" speech by popping a pill—a prescription of course…

Jewel swallowed a laugh. For a Loveland, Sierra wasn't half bad. They'd sung along to old Shania Twain songs on the drive over with the windows down, the radio cranked, neither caring how awful they sounded until a pickup stopped alongside them at a light. The driver had winced and raised his windows, his horrified expression only making them screech louder.

"Jewel Cade." Mrs. Grover-Woodhouse tapped her pencil. "We haven't heard from you on the topic."

"Me?"

Mrs. Grover-Woodhouse's pencil stilled. "You are a member of this committee, are you not?"

"Unfortunately," Lara whispered.

Jewel cleared her throat. "Yes, I am."

"Which type of beverage do you suggest?"

"I'm more of a Mountain Dew kind of gal."

Lara and her crew giggled—including Kelsey.

Mrs. Grover-Woodhouse's withering stare quieted the group. "Soda is not an option."

Warmth flooded Jewel's cheeks. "It should be," she pressed on. "Not everybody likes things so fancy."

"It's a gala, after all," Kelsey chimed in smoothly. "Fancy is the point."

Lara's eyes dragged over Jewel's crumpled T-shirt and jeans. "For civilized folks, anyway."

Jewel's gaze circled the group of nodding heads, all save

Sierra, who shot her a sympathetic look. With a groan, she shoved her chair back. She was a fish out of water and making a spectacle of herself. "If y'all will excuse me."

Out in the hall, Jewel fired off an SOS text to her brother Justin begging for a ride. Sierra's footsteps echoed behind her.

"Wait! Don't leave."

"I'm making a fool of myself." Agreeing with anything Kelsey said stuck in Jewel's craw, but she had a point. Jewel didn't belong in the "civilized" feminine world of tea rose garlands and champagne punches. The ranch, range and saddle were the only places where Jewel belonged; stupid her for even trying.

Sierra placed a warm hand on Jewel's shoulder and squeezed.

"Lara's the one who's acting like a jerk."

"It's no act," Jewel said evenly. "She *is* a jerk."

Sierra cracked up so hard she snorted, which, in turn, got Jewel laughing until they both held their sides, bent at the waist.

"Ain't that the truth." Sierra wiped her streaming eyes. "Don't tell Heath I said so, since she's Kelsey's best friend."

"Do you think he loves her?" Jewel asked, unable to resist the urge to satisfy her curiosity.

Which was all it was.

Just idle curiosity.

Sierra's short nose scrunched. "It's more complicated than that. Heath always puts what he wants and needs aside to take care of everybody else. We used to call Heath the mom whisperer. He was the only one who could soothe her when she got in one of her moods. I think he's so used to making others happy and playing the role of knight in shining armor that he doesn't know how to save himself."

"So, the more Kelsey acts like a princess, the more Heath likes her?" If that was the case, Heath would never care for Jewel since she valued her independence and… Whoa—why was she suddenly worrying about who Heath cared about?

You nearly kissed him on the range earlier…

Sierra shook her head slowly. “The more Heath thinks Kelsey’s depending on him, the more obligated he feels, the harder it is for him to walk away.”

“What could she need him for?” Through the distant doorway, Jewel glimpsed the back of Kelsey’s elaborate upswept hair, pearls dangling from her ears. “She’s got money, looks, one of the most respected names in the county…”

Sierra’s narrow shoulders lifted, then fell. “Some women don’t feel complete without a man on their arm.”

“I’d rather have a horse.”

“I’m rather partial to animals over relationships myself.” Sierra shot Jewel a conspiratorial smile. “Now why weren’t we friends in high school?”

Jewel studied Sierra’s open, friendly face. “Because our families were—are—mortal enemies.”

Sierra half laughed. “Right. Almost forgot about that. Now we’re stepsisters.”

“I’ve never had a sister.” The idea filled her with a strange sense of wonder. She’d only ever had her brothers to compete against and prove herself to…what would it be like to have someone to simply talk to? Confide in? Sing karaoke Shania Twain with?

Sierra squeezed Jewel’s arm. “Same. Just a bunch of annoying brothers.”

They exchanged nods, and a palpable sense of camaraderie swelled the space between them.

“Won’t you come back to the meeting?” Sierra hitched up the slipping strap of her sundress. “I can take you home, but I wish you’d stay. Don’t let Lara and Kelsey’s crew chase you off.”

"They haven't," Jewel automatically denied, despite the unease twisting her gut. She never backed down from two-ton bulls, yet judgmental women had her running for the hills. Why? A motorcycle engine rumbled in the distance, then grew louder. "But I texted Justin to pick me up on his way home from Fresh Start. That's probably him now."

Sierra's face fell. "Shoot. Next time, then."

"Maybe," Jewel mumbled, then impulsively hugged Sierra before racing outside. The air was fresh and cedar-scented. Her lungs gulped it down as she straddled the bike behind her bearded brother and donned the helmet he passed her.

"Everything all right in there?" Justin twisted around in the banana seat and eyed her. "Looks like you've been chewed up, spit out and stepped on."

"That about covers it. Let's blow this pop stand."

"Got it." The motorcycle sped out of the parking lot and Jewel rested her chin on her brother's broad shoulder, her hands linked around his middle as they raced home.

"Hey! It's Aunt Jewel!" Javi pounded down Cade Ranch's porch steps when they pulled up twenty minutes later. His terry cloth Superman cape, a perfect match for his briefs, flapped behind him.

When he flung himself at Jewel, she staggered back a few steps. "You're getting big."

Javi puffed out his skinny chest. "Pa says I've already grown half an inch this summer."

"I bet you have." Jewel pushed back his damp hair. The scent of the honeysuckle bushes crowding the porch filled the darkness with a heady aroma. "Much more and you'll be as tall as me."

Javi's smile fell and he chewed his lip. "It's okay to be little. Don't feel bad, Aunt Jewel."

Jewel pressed her curving lips flat and said, gravely, "I appreciate that, honey. Where are your parents?"

The screen door creaked opened and Sofia's pretty face, backlit by the interior light, peered out anxiously. Her features smoothed when she caught sight of Jewel, Javi and Justin mounting the stairs.

"There you are, Javi." Sofia briskly toweled Javi's hair as she steered him inside. "You know better than to go outside after your bath."

Javi wriggled as Sofia swiped his ears with Q-tips. "I heard Uncle Justin's bike and look—here's Aunt Jewel, too."

"Hey, girl." Jewel took in Sofia's thin frame and pale face. She'd lost weight since Jewel had last seen her. "You feeling okay?"

Sofia dropped onto the sofa once she'd sent Javi upstairs to don his pajamas. "The first trimester's always the hardest."

James appeared on the landing overlooking the two-story living room. Their wailing four-month-old baby, swathed in pink fabric nearly matching her tear-streaked face, flailed in his arms. "Jesse's not following the bedtime schedule."

"Just show her the clock. She's sure to go to sleep then," Justin drawled, his voice dripping with his usual dark sarcasm.

Jewel shot Justin an amused look. James, the second oldest in their family, was a total control freak. He ran his life, and everyone else's, on a tight schedule even Grand Central Terminal would envy.

"Pa?" Javi peeked his head out of his bedroom door. "I dropped my juice, and my blanket's all red."

Sofia began to rise, but Jewel forestalled her. "I'll get Jesse. James, you take care of Javi."

James met Jewel halfway down the stairs, passed over the fussing child and shot her a grateful look. "Good to have you back. You've been missed."

"Yeah, right," she scoffed, hiding her pleasure at the rare brotherly affection. Did he miss her enough to name her range boss yet?

Sofia reached for Jesse, but Jewel plunked down on the floor with the baby instead. "Take a break. This is what aunties are for."

She stripped layer after layer of pink from the squirming child until she wore only her diaper. Jewel confirmed it was dry after a quick check. Once she laid Jesse on a blanket, Jewel blew into the baby's belly while Justin dangled his Harley-Davidson key ring over her head. Jesse's cries subsided into hiccups, then silence, then coos of merriment.

"Thank you!" Sofia dashed away tears. "I don't know why I'm so emotional this pregnancy."

"You just gave birth to this one." Jewel crossed her eyes and stuck out her tongue at Jesse, winning her a gummy smile. "Don't beat yourself up. I wish I were here to help you more."

"You just want to beat me out as range boss, admit it." Justin quit playing with the baby, sauntered to the sofa and sat, stretching out his long legs.

"I am beating you." Jewel covered her face with her hands then opened them, playing peekaboo to Jesse's delight. "I'm working miracles over at Loveland Hills."

"Ma mentioned you saved the herd from sorghum poisoning." Justin shook his head. "You'd think Heath would have more sense than to lead them south during a drought."

"They don't have many options," Jewel said, strangely defensive of Heath. "It's not like they can get to the Crystal River easy."

"And whose fault is that?" Justin demanded. "Not ours."

Jewel shrugged, her stomach knotting. Her brother spoke the truth, but riding with the Lovelands blurred lines a bit.

"You're not taking their side, are you?" James clomped down the stairs with Javi. "I warned you about Heath trying to charm you into feeling sorry for them."

"Simmer down, James," protested Sofia. "There's nothing wrong with seeing both sides."

"I'm going to Emma's birthday party!" Javi, now clad in a superhero-patterned pajama shirt and bottoms, raced into the kitchen. "They're having a princess cake!"

"Remember your loyalties, Jewel." James slipped a pacifier into Jesse's mouth. "And what happened to her nightgown?"

"That wasn't a nightgown, it was a pink straitjacket." She tickled Jesse's rounded tummy. "Look how much happier she is naked."

James slid Jesse's chubby arms into a onesie. "Don't corrupt my daughter."

"Don't turn her into some pampered girlie girl, either." Jewel frowned at her brother, thinking of Kelsey's well-heeled group and how out of place they'd made Jewel feel.

Where would she ever fit in?

Her eyes drifted to the darkness beyond the window panes, picturing the pastures she'd ridden from childhood. As Cade Ranch's range boss, she'd always have a place where she belonged, where she didn't feel less than others.

"This is Emma's birthday invitation!" Javi dropped a purple card onto Jewel's lap. "Will you be there?"

"Your mother and I haven't decided if you're going yet, Javi." James slid his fingers into Jesse's waving fist.

Javi's left-sided dimple vanished. "Emma's my friend."

Justin picked up the TV remote and turned on a Rockies game. "Our families are having a dispute."

"What's a dispute?" Javi asked.

Sofia patted the empty cushion beside her. "An argument."

Javi flung himself into it. "Then use your words so you stop fighting."

"It's not that—" the crack of a bat and the roar of the crowd at the baseball field interrupted James "—easy."

Javi leaped up, scooted in front of the TV and blocked the view. "Yes, it is! Emma's my cousin now and Grandma Joy said family always sticks together."

"*Cades* always stick together." Justin craned his neck to glimpse the action accompanying another cheer.

"Grandma Joy's a Loveland," Javi pointed out with powerful child's logic. "Will you still stick by her?"

An appalled silence descended, muffling all but the baseball announcer's babble. Sofia rose slowly to her feet and slipped her hand in Javi's. "We'll talk more about it tomorrow. Say good-night to your family."

Javi scampered up the stairs, stopped on the landing and cupped his hands around his mouth. "Night, Lovelands!" he shouted at the windows then dashed into his room.

"I'll be darned." Justin dropped his elbows to his knees and craned his head to peer up at the empty banister. "Javi's one strong-headed Cade."

"He's made up his mind, all right." James slipped the pacifier from his now-dozing baby's mouth.

"You should let him go." Jewel ruffled the floor rug's fringe with the tip of her boot.

"It'll only encourage his crazy idea about us being close with the Lovelands." James brushed a finger over Jesse's rounded cheek. "They're the ones suing us for millions we can't afford."

"We could sell Cora's Tear."

James gaped at her. "Who gave you that stupid idea?"

"I can guess," Justin muttered through clenched teeth.

Jewel met her brothers' hard stares dead-on. "Heath mentioned it."

At James's bitter laugh, Jesse's eyes flew open. He lifted her to his shoulder and patted her back. "Of course he did."

"It's not like that," Jewel insisted, cringing inside at how naive she sounded. "Whether you accept it or not, we're a family—the most dysfunctional, messed-up one in the county, maybe even the state, but we are family now."

James's brows lowered. Just then, the porch door opened and two of their cousins, Hayden and Graham, sauntered inside, doffing their hats. They were tall, lean young cowboys with red cheeks and cropped brown hair. "We've got the cattle settled for the night, James. What'd you like us to do next?"

"Best ask your range boss." James nodded at Justin.

Jewel bristled as Justin conferred with the boys about tomorrow's drive. "He's not officially the range boss."

James laid Jesse back on the blanket and swaddled her. "Not yet. Best remember your loyalties, or I'll make it permanent."

Her heart momentarily stopped, then resumed a frenetic beat. "Is that a threat?"

James's dark eyes rose and lasered into hers. "Let's just say, for now, it's a friendly reminder."

And one she'd needed to remember, Jewel thought, as she drove back to the Loveland ranch in a borrowed pickup, or she'd lose everything she'd worked her whole life to achieve.

If she failed to become range boss, who was she?

Not her own person. Not someone people looked up to.

She'd be no one important.

Just like her father raised her to believe.

From now on, no more letting Heath get under her skin or sweet-talk her. She'd focus solely on the job: keeping the Loveland herd intact.

As for her heart, she needed to guard it, too, lest a sensitive singing cowboy turn her from the path she'd chosen.

CHAPTER SEVEN

SWEAT DRIPPED IN Heath's eyes as he rode Destiny alongside the plodding, bellowing herd. Overhead, the intense sun bore down and cracked the earth. Everything was still, breathless, insects and animals alike sheltering beneath rocks or trees. He stared at the hazy sky, watching two vultures with their white-tipped wings circle slowly, deliberately, waiting for something somewhere to die.

The weather report predicted another record-breaking day of dry heat. Had he gambled correctly in driving the cattle from the natural spring to the next pasture? They'd lingered for nearly a week, nipping the forage down to its roots, but water alone couldn't sustain the cattle. Worry twisted his gut. What if the next grazing area's water hole had dried up?

"Some of 'em are getting gut fill." Beside him, Jewel stared straight over Bear's black head. He tore his eyes from her dainty profile and followed her gaze to the lumbering Brahmans. Concern burned in his chest as he noted their bouncing abdomens. Ribs and hip bones jutted slightly beneath thick gray hides. They weren't starving, not yet, but they were losing weight. If the next pasture didn't have enough water, some of the more fragile members of the herd would be at risk.

"Noted." Heath clucked to a lagging Destiny, and she picked up the pace to tramp up a steep incline.

"We should have moved the herd a couple of days ago."

Jewel's know-it-all tone set his teeth on edge. "The spring's one of our most reliable water sources. I wasn't in a hurry to leave it."

"If we hadn't overgrazed it, we could have returned in a couple weeks." Jewel screwed off the top of her canteen and drank a long gulp before passing it over.

He nodded his thanks and guzzled the tepid, slightly metallic-tasting water. “What do you mean?”

Jewel’s calloused fingers brushed his when he returned the canteen. His breath quickened at the sandpaper feel of them. Her skin was as rough as her manner, yet it electrified him somehow. “Pastures should be grazed for only a day and then returned to after a two-week break. It allows for regrowth. The idea is to raise the pasture with the livestock.”

He turned Jewel’s words over in his mind. “Makes sense.”

“Of course it does,” Jewel blustered. From the corner of his eye, he caught her pleased grin. An answering pulse of happiness loosened his joints and lowered his shoulders. He liked making Jewel smile. Too much.

“Is that part of the herd health report you gave your brother?”

“Not that he’s going to read it,” Jewel grumbled.

“I would.” The cattle dogs’ barking and Daryl’s “yip yip yip” filled the sudden silence. Heath sneaked a sidelong glance at Jewel. Her features seemed frozen in place, and her knuckles shone white against the tan leather reins. “If you’ll let me.”

“Why would you do that?” When she turned her head, he met her wary brown eyes straight on. “I’m a Cade, aren’t I?”

“I won’t hold that against you.” He mopped the back of his steaming neck with his kerchief. “Much.”

Her low belly laugh gave his heart legs; it leaped like a spring hare in his chest. “You’re admitting Cades know more than Lovelands,” she chortled.

“One does anyway.”

Jewel’s rose-colored mouth dropped open before she snapped it shut and lifted her chin. “Darn straight,” she vowed. “I’ll email you a copy.”

“All right then.”

"All right."

A companionable silence descended as they rode. The steady clop of their horses' hooves striking hard-packed soil, the lowing of the cattle and the panting, galloping dogs, tongues lolling, filled the quiet. Destiny picked her way across the rugged terrain. Loose rocks threatened to slide out from under her shoes if Heath didn't keep a close eye on her footing. Some of the ravines were so steep, they never saw sunlight.

"Sierra said you left the Flower Gala meeting early the other night."

Jewel guided Bear around a depression. "Couldn't stand another minute of that hen party."

"That bad?"

"They debated about rose versus blush-colored napkins for almost an hour."

"Aren't they both pink?"

Jewel let loose a long-suffering sigh. "Exactly. At least I got to see my family afterward."

He didn't respond immediately. Instead, his gaze drifted over her melancholy face and then down to her clenched hands. "You miss them."

"Yes."

"Sorry you're stuck here." He cleared his throat. "With me."

"It's—uh—not so bad," she replied, her voice tight.

"How's your family?"

"James said not to let you sweet-talk me."

His nostrils flared with a heavy exhale. "What's he worried about?"

"That you'll persuade me to drive the Brahmans through our land."

His shoulders stiffened. "I'm hoping you'll come to that conclusion on your own. The herd's growing frailer."

Jewel's teeth appeared on her bottom lip. "They'll make it."

"All of 'em?"

"All of them."

"What if the next watering hole isn't big enough? Or the one after that?" He tore off his hat and thrust his fingers through his damp hair. "How much longer can they go on? We've got weeks ahead of us without a drop of rain forecast."

Jewel swiped her face with her kerchief. "Weathermen get it wrong."

"Satellites don't. Look. We could create a fenced area leading across Cade land for us to drive our cattle straight to the Crystal River. They won't mingle with yours or cause any property damage."

Jewel turned her head away, her jaw set. "It'd restrict our cattle's movement."

"Not much or at all, if we time it right." In the distance, Heath watched Blue square off against a runaway Brahman. The cattle dog crouched, refusing to back down, until the large animal balked and rejoined the herd. Heath could relate. Going head-to-head with Jewel was a test of wills… one he was determined to win. "We could use temporary fencing and break it down as we leave."

"No."

"Why?" Frustration brewed deep inside. Jewel still clung to their old feud and the divisions he wished no longer divided them, especially when the cattle needed to reach the river soon.

"I can't go against my family."

His skin tingled, and the back of his throat burned. Whatever control he had snapped like a rubber band. "Because they've been so loyal to you?"

Jewel jerked back as if she'd been slapped, kicked Bear into a gallop and streaked off in a cloud of dust.

"Dang it!" He urged Destiny after her. "Jewel!" he shouted to be heard over the stomping, mooing cattle. "Hold up!"

"Leave me be!" she hollered over her shoulder.

He pulled Destiny up alongside her. "Listen to me!"

She averted her head and dashed away tears—tears he was furious at himself for putting there. "Why?"

"Because I'm sorry."

Her eyes were shiny black as they locked onto his again. "What for exactly?"

"I shouldn't have brought your family into it."

She studied him, stone-faced. "And?"

"Plagued you about the Crystal River access." He pulled his sticking shirt from his chest. "I won't bring it up again."

One eyebrow rose. "And?"

"And?"

Exasperating woman. What was she after now? Her fingers drummed on the rope she'd used to lasso calves earlier when she'd spied pink eye. His muscles clenched. Fine. He'd say it if only to make her smile again. "You'd make a good range boss."

"Better than you."

He choked on a laugh. "Don't push it."

"I'm not sure your fragile male ego could handle it."

His shoulder lifted in a lopsided shrug. "If that lets you sleep at night."

"Oh, it does, it does." The mischief in her eyes twisted his lips into a wry smile.

Jewel was as entertaining as she was infuriating. And for all her bragging, she could put her money where her fast-talking mouth was, he thought as she cantered away to nip a breakaway pair back into the herd. He was starting to find more common ground with the unruly cowgirl than his perfect fiancée, which left him equal parts uncomfortable, guilty and exhilarated. She was his resourceful work partner, but that was as far as it could go.

Her continued attempts to outdo him were both annoying and humorous. Maybe she held her own with the Cade boys, but she was riding with a Loveland now. Big difference he'd say out loud if he didn't think it'd be bragging.

Nah. He let his actions speak for themselves and had found himself flaunting his skills, too. She brought out this unfamiliar tendency as well as the urge to bend her over his arm and kiss her.

What was it about the boastful cowgirl that set his thoughts in directions they had no right to go?

Once they reached the pasture, he paused to let his senses drink in the fresh mountain air, the sweet smell of wildflowers, the bellowing cattle. He wanted to imprint the moment in the folds of his memory, preserve it like one of his mother's flowers between pages of her books. To remember: this is how it felt to be happy.

Free.

"Oh, give me a home, where the buffalo roam," he sang once he dismounted and tied up Destiny, the words springing from him without conscious thought. "Where the deer and the antelope play..."

He heard Jewel approach on Bear and felt her eyes on him. As he launched into the chorus, a slightly flat alto joined him.

"Home, home on the range!" Jewel belted, singing with more enthusiasm than finesse, an amusing assault to his ear. She tethered Bear and then retrieved the camping gear stowed in her saddlebag.

Their voices mingled as they set up a makeshift camp, growing louder and twangier as he added extra country flourishes that got her giggling between words. When they finished with a rip roaring "Yee-haw!" they dissolved into laughter.

"Where've you been hiding all that talent?" he teased when they quieted again.

"Under a rock where it belongs." Jewel handed him a pot for him to fill from the nearby creek and scratched her peeling nose. "Wish I had your gift."

"It's not doing me any good." Her sharp glance made him wish back those telling words. He hurried to the thankfully flowing stream and dipped the kettle into it. The water level was the lowest he'd ever seen it for this time of year, he noted with a sinking heart. They wouldn't have much time here. Maybe a week. Tops.

"But you still like gigging, right?" Jewel asked when he returned.

"Yes." *While he could...* He hooked the kettle onto a rod stretched across an old firepit and lit a pile of leftover logs from last season. "Got a show Friday night if you want to come," he shouted as Jewel filled a coffeepot in the stream. "Daryl and Cole can take the night watch."

Jewel returned, dumped pungent grounds into the pot, then hooked it beside the dangling kettle. "What about Cole's arm?"

"As long as he's just watching the cattle, he should be fine." Heath dropped slices of bacon into a four-legged cast-iron skillet he planted on the edge of the fledgling fire. "He can drive up to the pasture on the ATV."

"Okay," she said after hauling out a bag of potatoes and placing it between them. Her paring knife neatly peeled off the skin. "I'll go."

A wave of pleasure rushed through him. He wanted Jewel at the show just as much as he wanted her riding beside him. No logic applied to any of it, yet it didn't change those indisputable and darn inconvenient facts. He flipped open his utility knife and grabbed a potato.

"What about Kelsey? Is she going?"

Heath schooled his features into blankness and pinned his eyes on the potato he circled with his blade. "Nah. She never comes."

"Never?" Jewel's voice rose in disbelief. Water splashed when she dropped her potato into the kettle.

"She's not a fan of the honky-tonk scene." Heath's knife slipped. He winced and brought his stinging thumb to his mouth.

Jewel's hands flew over another potato, neatly divesting it of its skin in one, circular cut. "Has there ever been anyone else besides Kelsey?"

"Dating, you mean?" Heath flipped the sizzling bacon with the side of his knife and his stomach grumbled at the salty hickory-cured scent. When Jewel nodded, he said, "No."

Jewel added three more potatoes to the now-steaming pot of water. "Ever been tempted to date anyone else?"

Heath cracked his tense neck side to side. "Nope."

Jewel's thick eyelashes fell to her cheeks, all her attention on the potato she peeled. "You must really love her, huh?"

A heavy, breathless feeling flooded Heath's chest. "How about you?" he countered, sidestepping the question he still needed to answer. Understanding grew cloudier every minute he spent with Jewel. "Ever been in love?"

Jewel snorted as she passed over the last tuber. "Only with my four-legged partners."

Heath stared into her gorgeous eyes. "But someday…"

"I'm never getting married." As if to underscore the point, water from the boiling kettle struck the fire with a loud hiss.

One side of his mouth curled as he watched Jewel remove the kettle, raise the metal rod another notch and reattach the pan. Jewel might not consider herself domestic, but she sure knew her way around a campfire cookout. "Famous last words."

"I mean it." Jewel retrieved mugs from their packs, hollered to Daryl to join them, and poured out the fragrant coffee. "I won't give up my independence for a man."

"What if you met a man who didn't want you to change?" His mind turned to Kelsey and all the changes she demanded: stop gigging, quit ranching, work in her family business. He hadn't asked her to give up anything. Not one thing.

The unfairness of it struck him, followed by equal parts resentment and guilt as he sipped the tongue-scorching brew

Jewel passed him. Did he have a right to those feelings? Kelsey had always been generous with him and his family.

"You're talking about a rainbow-colored unicorn right there." Jewel tipped up the brim of her hat and perspiration glistened on her freckled brow. "He doesn't exist."

He swallowed the urge to declare himself that unicorn and gulped more coffee instead. Growing up with a mother who'd blamed her family for tying her down and crushing her dreams convinced him to never stand in the way of others' choices.

"Besides," Jewel continued, her eyes darting to watch an approaching Daryl, "even if he did exist, it wouldn't make a difference. Like my Pa said, I'm not the girlie-wife type."

"Not all men care about that." Outrage—for Jewel—stung him, sharp as a wasp. He set down his coffee and stirred the browning bacon. The melting fat crackled and splatted. "And why let your father's opinion define you?"

"It doesn't." Despite Jewel's bluster, it was clear that she, like him, had been affected by a negative parent. Another line of connection tethered itself between them. "All I care about is being free." She poked the tip of her knife into the boiling potatoes to test their softness.

"But you've gone on dates…you're not against that, are you?" Strange how the thought of other men, teasing Jewel, holding her hand, kissing her, made his teeth clamp tight.

"I've never gone on a date or had a boyfriend," Jewel blurted, red-faced.

"Have you ever been kissed?" He whisked the skillet from the fire's edge to let it cool while they waited to slice the potatoes into it for frying. Surely Jewel wasn't completely inexperienced…

He caught a glimpse of her tortured expression before she leaped to her feet and stalked off, hands balled at her sides.

"What set her off?" Daryl hopped off Smoke, grabbed up his coffee and closed his eyes with a blissful smile as he sipped.

"Ah, you know, women..." Heath responded vaguely. Craning his neck, he stared at Jewel's retreating back, mentally berating himself. He knew better than to pry.

Why did he want to know the answer so badly?

He didn't intend on being Jewel's first kiss, though he'd come close the other day. Still, the thought stayed with him as he began slicing the cooked potatoes, his mind returning to Jewel's expressive, beautiful mouth as she laughed, sneered, teased. Did he want to be her first kiss...and her last? The idea brought him up short. This was uncharted territory, one he was in no position to explore with his future predetermined once he girded himself to accept it.

He dumped the potatoes into the skillet, added a chopped onion and returned it to the fire. Even if he was interested in Jewel—crazy as that'd be—she wanted to be independent, free. It wasn't like she'd ever want to be tied to him...

Kelsey's concerns about him spending time with Jewel returned to him. This forced proximity was messing with his head and confusing his already-cloudy heart. From now on, he needed to prioritize Kelsey and fight his unwelcome feelings for Jewel if he stood any chance of making up his mind by summer's end.

"I LIKE YOUR hair down."

At Sierra's compliment, Jewel fingered the slightly damp waves skimming the off-the-shoulder blouse Sierra had lent her for Heath's performance tonight. Not that Jewel had fussed with her appearance...much. She breathed in the fresh coconut-and-vanilla scent of her body wash (also borrowed) and eyed her pressed jeans and polished boots.

So much for just dusting off. This cowgirl had spiffed up for reasons she didn't want to think about, since she suspected Heath was smack-dab in the middle of them.

"I—uh—didn't have time to braid it." Jewel winced

slightly at the fib. It was partly true. She'd spent so long agonizing over what to wear, she'd barely had time to scoot out the door to claim her spot on the edge of Silver Spurs's already-crowded dance floor. Her heart drummed, and her skin tingled with anticipation as she stared at the stage's instruments, microphones and amplifiers awaiting Outlaw Cowboys.

When would Heath and the group begin playing? The familiar excitement to lose herself in their music thrummed inside her, harder than ever. She'd discovered more sides to Heath than just heartthrob singer. Sometimes he acted like one of her annoying older brothers, poking and needling her, showing off in the saddle and even prying into her love life. Why had he been so interested in her dating history or whom she'd kissed? Or more accurately…hadn't.

On the other hand, he had a caring, protective side. He took pains to safeguard even the littlest members of the herd, like the injured calf. What's more, he wanted to read her herd health report, which meant he didn't dismiss her like her brothers. He respected her, which was all she ever wanted. Yet deep down she craved more than the sensitive cowboy's respect.

When he'd asked her whether she'd change her mind about relationships if she met a man who valued her independence, she'd scoffed, then wondered. Could Heath be the unicorn she'd joked about?

An almost-married unicorn...

"You should leave your hair loose more often." Jewel tuned back in to Sierra. "It frames your pretty face except…" A line appeared between Sierra's delicate blond brows. "If these two strands were pulled back with a clip it'd really show off your eyes. Mind if I…?"

"Do I have a choice?" Jewel grumbled with more good nature than bite.

"No," Sierra said through a smile.

Jewel sighed and subjected herself to Sierra's fussing,

enjoying it more than she'd imagined. Even her ma learned early on to hand Jewel a comb and back away fast. Sierra, on the other hand, seemed undaunted by recalcitrant subjects. Her unflappability must come from years working with the local wildlife population. If rattlers and raptors failed to fluster you, a curmudgeon of a cowgirl didn't pose much of a challenge.

With quick, practiced moves, Sierra whisked back some of Jewel's hair, secured the locks behind her ears and stepped back, lips pursed. "Perfect. You look like Karen Gillan."

"Who?"

"She played Amy Pond in *Doctor Who*." Sierra lifted her voice to be heard over a cheering group crowding a pool table while a Little Big Town song blared from wall-mounted speakers.

Jewel shrugged. "I don't watch many movies."

"It's a TV show." Sierra twined one of Jewel's waves around her finger, then pulled it forward to dangle over Jewel's collarbone. "Time-traveling Brits in space."

"So, I look like an alien?"

Sierra's deep blue eyes twinkled. "No. Amy Pond's a human—and pretty, like you."

Jewel fanned her face as more customers shoved through the door. The stench of body odor, spilled beer and crushed peanuts wove in the humid air. "Quit saying that or I'll start believing it." When they'd gotten ready, Sierra had showered Jewel with so many compliments she'd worried her swollen head might send her airborne. Sierra had even conned Jewel into a facial mask guaranteed to turn her skin to porcelain.

If porcelain had freckles…

Just her luck Heath had walked in before they'd washed off the green goo. When he'd drawled he preferred her freckles, he'd rendered her speechless and blushing like a schoolgirl. Her teeth gnashed at the downright embarrassing effect he had on her. Luckily, Sierra had mistaken her speechlessness for hurt and rushed to assure Jewel Heath was just acting like a typical, irritating big brother and not to mind him…only Jewel couldn't stop "minding" him. He was getting under her skin, burrowing into her thoughts and coming dangerously close to her heart. Not a brother-sister type of feeling at all.

"You *should* feel pretty. Look." Sierra nodded to the bar. "That cowboy has his eye on you."

Jewel glanced at a leering bearded man wearing an enormous cowboy hat and a leather trench coat over fringed chaps. He waggled overgrown eyebrows at her and raised his beer mug. When he guzzled the brew, foam striped the furry animal masquerading as a mustache on his upper lip. "I think he's either an alien or Sasquatch."

Sierra's cheeks bulged as she fought to swallow a mouthful of pop. "Don't make me laugh when I'm drinking!" she sputtered after she set the glass down on the table behind them.

"Then don't set me up with a Klingon."

Sierra wagged a finger. "And you said you didn't watch TV. Nice *Star Trek* reference, by the way."

"I watched *The Wrath of Khan* in a drive-in once."

Over Sierra's shoulder, an old-time popcorn maker exploded to life when a server flipped the switch, the salted, buttered kernels popping harder than a Fourth of July finale. "Wish the Sunset Drive-in hadn't shut down."

"Heard some new owners are reopening it soon."

Sierra clapped her hands. "We should go."

Jewel nodded to the man at the bar. "I've got my date…"

Sierra snorted. "You might need to bring a cattle prod."

"Or a phaser." Jewel gave an approaching group of staggering men the stink-eye until they swerved away to play darts.

"If things get weird you could always say, 'Beam me

up, Scotty' and—" Sierra stopped and made a face. "That was too far, right?"

Jewel chuckled. "We crossed the line way further back than that."

"Look. Heath!" Sierra started to drag Jewel to the hall by the restrooms, then stopped short. "Now what's *she* doing here?"

Jewel flickered Heath a quick glance, then frowned at the sight of Kelsey, clad in a white one-shouldered mini-dress and gold jewelry more fitting for a cotillion than a honky-tonk. Her loyal henchman, Lara, sipped a glass of white wine beside her. "Heath said she never comes to his gigs," Jewel said, trying and failing to keep the disappointment from her voice.

"This must be her first time...and she looks uncomfortable." As they watched, Kelsey seemed to fold into herself, her shoulders curving forward, her gold bracelets sliding as she clasped her hands in front of her. Lara's disapproving expression suggested she smelled something bad.

"He didn't mention it when he invited me." A sinkhole opened in Jewel's chest, carrying her heart down with it. She stopped fussing with the strings closing the front of her pretty shirt. Stupid her for reading too much into Heath's invitation. Even dumber was letting down her guard around him. *Again.*

"He invited you?"

Jewel fidgeted under Sierra's assessing stare. "It didn't mean anything."

"Of course not," Sierra said slowly, sounding unconvinced and the tiniest bit amused. The Little Big Town tune ended, and the babbling voices and clinking glasses grew louder.

"There's nothing going on between Heath and me," Jewel insisted, then felt twice as dumb for sounding defensive. And guilty. Okay. Fine. Maybe something was going on...but clearly only on her side, more fool her.

"You're dating Khan anyway, right?" Sierra teased, and Jewel grinned back, thankful she'd let the topic drop.

One nice thing about the Lovelands, they never pried, except for Heath. Jewel frowned. She was discovering a lot of good about her family's old archrivals—the Lovelands were devoted to one another and cared about their land and its animals as much as her own. They'd been talking nonstop about Emma's upcoming birthday party as if it were the event of the year. They treated one another, and especially the children, with the kind of devotion she'd give her own offspring.

She lost herself in the pleasant thought, then tamped it down. Mothering was not in this prickly cowgirl's future.

A drumroll announced the start of the set, and Heath pulled loose of Kelsey's grip to jog onstage. Outlaw Cowboys' bass player, Clint, pounded a twangy beat and Heath grabbed the mic. Feminine howls of appreciation rose. In a fitted collared shirt, rolled up to his elbows to reveal strong forearms, and Wranglers hugging his long, muscular legs, Heath Loveland snatched the air from her lungs. Her chest burned as his full lips parted to sing the group's opening song.

Every other noise receded save his bass voice. While his fingers flew over his electric guitar, he infused every note with emotion and meaning. He was gorgeous. Magnetic. A star. In that moment, he stopped being her nuisance of a cattle drive partner, her family's arch rival and became the man she'd been dreaming of and thinking about nonstop.

It took her until the chorus to realize he sang a Prince song he'd rearranged into a driving country tune. The gravel of his voice added another dimension to it, an alluring one dancing along her spine and making her shiver.

His sapphire eyes locked on Jewel's and he sang about wanting a kiss.

Her lungs quit right along with her heart. Was he singing to her? Singing about kissing her? Ever since he'd cornered her about whether she'd ever done it—she hadn't—her overactive imagination conjured Heath as her first lip-lock, no matter how wrong the thought.

"Hey, Kelsey!" Sierra's shout dragged Jewel from her trance.

"Hey." Kelsey inclined her head. "May I?" At Sierra's nod, Kelsey wedged herself between them, followed by Lara, who forced Jewel to step back. The artful pile of Kelsey's blond hair now partially obstructed her view. Great. Awesome. Just what she'd come to see.

Then again, what had she seen? Surely Heath wasn't singing to her about a kiss. He must have been looking at Kelsey when she'd come up behind Jewel and Sierra.

Had to be.

To think otherwise was dangerous.

Kelsey's appearance at Silver Spurs proved she cared about Heath. Stupid Jewel for thinking the couple might not be suited, that Heath would do better with someone else like…

Like who?

Her?

Crazy. But somehow, somewhere the thought had taken root recently. She needed to stop it before she made a fool of herself and lost focus on becoming Cade Ranch's range boss. If she kept the Loveland herd intact, despite dangerous weather and challenging terrain, she'd leave little doubt she was better than Justin. He had plenty of help and Crystal River access.

"How's everyone doing tonight?" Heath shouted when Outlaw Cowboys ended their first set. Jewel hooted along with the appreciative audience in response.

"You don't have to scream like heathens," Lara griped.

"Woo-hoo!" hollered Sierra directly in Lara's ear. "Heath!"

Kelsey summoned a weak smile. "I think I need earplugs."

"Not the best way to hear a band," Jewel sighed, exasperated at Kelsey and Lara's complaining. Why come at all?

"I'm here to check in on Timmy Logan's fund drive." Kelsey nodded her chin to a manned table selling Solo cups for unlimited beer to fund a local boy's bone marrow transplant. "And for Heath, not his music."

"Same difference," Jewel insisted. How could Kelsey separate the two?

Heath *was* music…it seemed as much a part of him as the blood in his veins and the oxygen in his lungs.

When Outlaw Cowboys swung into an original song about the home that could have broken a child, but built the adult instead, Jewel lost herself in Heath's music again. He was undeniably talented. His good looks aside, some intangible quality connected him to others, especially Jewel. He sang with the same emotion crowding her heart, his lyrics telling the story of her life, as if he understood her—or some mysterious part she sensed more than she knew.

Her throat ached as he sang about the troubled childhoods that made you, not broke you, the hard lessons you learned, the mistakes you'd never repeat. Jewel's father had dismissed her. Would she be as strong now if not for his rejection? She'd come through the fire transformed into forged steel as Heath's lyrics promised. Nothing would bend her again, she vowed, singing along hoarsely. The powerful song deserved a spot on the radio—the Country Music Awards even. She believed in Heath's music. Why didn't he—or Kelsey?

"So? What'd you think of our boy?" asked Clint a couple hours later when he and the group joined Jewel, Kelsey, Lara and Sierra at the mostly cleared out bar.

"He's very talented," Jewel said, speaking directly to Heath. His eyes widened and bored into hers.

Kelsey pecked Heath's cheek, then recoiled. "You're so sweaty. Can we leave now? The fund drive's finished."

"Where's the fire?" Remmy, the group's drummer, signaled for some drinks, passed the bartender their Solo cups, then leaned a shoulder against one of its wooden pillars. "This is the first time you've seen the show."

"You liked it?" Heath ducked his head, and his eyes flitted to Jewel.

"Of course." Kelsey stepped in front of Jewel. "I'm glad I came out to support you."

"You came for the fund-raiser." An edge entered his voice. "I didn't see you smile once."

"The show rocked." Jewel angled around Kelsey, not about to be sidelined by her. "You should have a recording contract."

"That's what we've been telling him." Clint passed out the beer and sipped foam spilling over his Solo cup's brim. "He should be taking advantage of his opportunity in—" He cut off when Heath shot him a hard look and shook his head.

Jewel's gaze swung between Heath and Clint. Was Heath passing up an opportunity to pursue his music career? It'd be criminal if he did.

"You guys gonna help pick up the place?" called Silver Spurs's owner.

Clint grumbled. "Are we the talent or the cleanup crew?"

"As long as we're getting paid, who cares?" Remmy grabbed a bucket of suds and Clint and Heath followed behind him to bus the tables along with the waitstaff.

"What'd Clint mean about an opportunity?" Jewel collected the empty Solo cups littering the bar top.

Sierra sprayed a citrus-scented cleaning fluid over the surface. "He hasn't mentioned anything. My family operates on a need-to-know basis."

"Has he mentioned it to you?" Jewel eyed Kelsey. How much did Heath confide in her?

"That's between me and my soon-to-be husband." Kelsey toyed with her engagement ring.

"If you're getting married, when's the date?" Jewel challenged, hiding her disappointment at Kelsey's pronouncement. She'd known Heath would marry his long-time fiancée, but to hear it in concrete terms hit her with blunt force.

Was she jealous?

"We're getting closer to setting one." A defensive note entered Kelsey's voice. "Not that I'm worried. I know how Heath feels about me. If I sensed I wasn't wanted, I'd leave."

"Like how you came to your senses and excused yourself at the Flower Gala committee meeting," interjected Lara. "We all have our lane. Yours is the off-road kind."

Kelsey nodded sympathetically. "Not everyone's cut out for society."

Jewel stepped forward so fast Lara and Kelsey scrambled backward and clutched the seats behind them to keep from tumbling on their designer butts.

"Get this straight," Jewel growled. "My opinion matters, as you'll find out at the next Flower Gala meeting."

And with that, she stalked from the bar. Sierra hurried after her, calling, "Stop." Only Jewel wasn't going to stop.

Or let others intimidate her again.

Maybe she viewed the Cade Ranch range boss position the wrong way. It'd give her power and shield her… but she'd be tougher still if she tapped into that strength on her own, wherever she went, in any situation. Even a Flower Gala meeting.

Wasn't it about time she tried?

CHAPTER EIGHT

JEWEL COUGHED, EYES WATERING, as she groped for baking pans in the smoke-filled oven, glared down at the blackened cake tops, then stomped to the garbage. Another disastrous attempt. She'd never baked so much as a batch of Rice Krispies treats—were they baked?— let alone a princess fairy cake…no pressure. With a muttered oath, she dumped the ruined contents in the trash. What if she let Emma down? With Daryl out searching for Emma's MIA mother and party guests arriving in just three hours, Jewel had offered to put on the party rather than let a dejected Daryl cancel it.

And she'd been regretting the impulsive gesture ever since. If her pride hadn't gotten in the way, she would have—should have—begged the local bakery to fit it in their schedule today.

Fast strides carried her to the sink, where she tossed in the pans, ripped off her oven mitts and flicked on the faucet. Her elbows jerked as she scrubbed with warm sudsy water, then dropped them with a clattering bang on the countertop to dry.

"What'd those pans ever do to you?" Heath sauntered into the kitchen and sat on a stool. With his cheek resting in his palm, his elbow planted on the counter, he looked half-asleep, his dark hair rumpled, his marine-blue eyes hazy and warm and doing all kinds of strange things to her sudden, staccato-beating heart.

"I think they're trying to kill me." She grabbed a dish towel and swirled it over the cake pans. "Or at least send me to a burn unit."

Heath chuckled softly, linked his fingers overhead and stretched. Jewel's breath caught at the glimpse of flat, toned stomach revealed by his rising shirt. "And why are you here, baking, on your day off? I thought you'd be home."

"LeAnne went out last night with the girls and didn't come home. Daryl's out looking for her." The shouts of the children, playing on the tire swing outside, filtered through the window screens.

"She's been doing that a lot lately." Heath frowned. "Did Daryl say anything more?"

"He planned on canceling Emma's birthday party." Jewel greased the pans, added a pinch of flour like her mother did, and tapped the sides of the pan, shaking the powder over the butter layer. "I offered to help so he could keep searching."

"By burning down the house?" Heath ambled over to the coffee maker and poured himself a cup. The warm appreciation in his eyes belied his teasing tone.

"I probably would have woken you in time to get out." Jewel grabbed some eggs and cracked them on the side of a mixing bowl.

Heath's lips twisted in a wry smile. *"Probably?"*

"Can't lose my sparring partner." Jewel beat the eggs until they turned yellow and foamy, then added a teaspoon of vanilla.

"You'd miss me?" Heath set down his coffee, eyed the cookbook cake recipe and measured flour into another bowl.

Jewel unwrapped a couple of butter sticks. "Let's not get ahead of ourselves, Sir Please-a-Lot."

Heath's dark hair swished across his forehead as he angled his head to eye her. "Sir Please-A-Lot?"

"It's catchy, right?" Jewel grinned, full-out, as she dumped the butter in a plastic container and set it in the microwave to melt.

If getting under Heath's skin was wrong, then she didn't want to be right. The legendary tight-lipped Loveland self-control wasn't easy to crack, but she loved a challenge and the glimpses of intense emotion Heath occasionally revealed. The timer dinged, and she grabbed the melted butter.

"*Something*, anyway," Heath grumbled, using a fork to stir baking soda and salt into the flour mixture. White puffs rose.

"You don't have to help." Jewel poured the butter into the mixing bowl and added sugar. "It's your day off, too." She raised her voice over the whirring blades as she swirled them through the mixture, combining ingredients.

"How much do you know about throwing fairy princess–themed birthday parties?" Heath pointed to the glittering pink decorations covering the kitchen table.

Jewel slowed the mixer and reached for the beaten eggs. "I didn't know much about girlie stuff, even when I *was* a little girl. I always just wanted to be one of the boys."

"Not all girls are the same." Heath's shoulder brushed hers as he added flour to the batter in between pours of egg.

"I'm not the feminine type." Her voice grew husky, her skin tingling in awareness at the feel of Heath's muscular biceps against her bare arms. "Not like Kelsey."

Heath tapped the last of the flour mixture into the batter bowl. "That's not a bad thing."

Jewel's eyes lifted to his. "No?"

"No." The sincerity in his voice, the heat spiraling in his eyes as he gazed down at her, softened her joints. Her lungs heaved to drag in more air. What was Heath saying? Did he think she was as good as Kelsey?

It shouldn't matter. In fact, she needed to not care at all...yet a humming vibration began in her chest and spread to her toes.

"It's hotter than Hades out there." The back door opened, and Maverick Loveland, home in between bull-riding gigs, ducked to avoid the top of the old-time door header as he strode inside. "Travis is with the herd." He tipped his hat at Jewel, then hung it on a peg. "Where are you planning on driving the cattle next so I can scout it out?"

"Saw Grass Overpass."

"Dewey Fields."

Jewel and Heath spoke simultaneously, then glowered at each other. Last night, they'd debated the two pastures past midnight. Jewel argued that Dewey Fields, while being more exposed to sunlight, was superior because of its irrigation-supplied watering hole. Heath, however, wanted to hit the overpass first because of its shade and the likelihood of good forage for the hungry herd.

Maverick raised his dark eyebrows. "Which one of you is range boss?"

"I am," they insisted, in stereo, followed by a synchronized, "No, you're not."

Maverick shook his head, picked up the bowl and dumped an even amount of batter into each pan. "I hear you two clucking, but I can't find the nest."

"He's the crazy one." Jewel took the pans from Maverick and carefully placed them in the oven with a murmured prayer.

Blessed be the fruits of a domestic interloper.

"You're the one broiling cakes." Heath cranked down the temperature knob as Jewel peered around his broad back.

"Broil?" She lifted her toe and scratched the back of her opposite calf.

"Are you trying to barbecue this cake or bake it?" Maverick's deep chuckle diffused the tension.

Jewel dropped onto a stool and buried her head in her hands. "Why did I volunteer for this? I've never cooked a thing in my life besides water."

"You cook water?"

At Heath's scoffing words, she lifted her head and glared. "For tea."

"Well. That's something," Maverick said stoutly. "Where's Cole and Sierra?"

"Sierra's out on call. Something about an orphaned fawn." Jewel watched Emma and Noah as they took turns leaping from the tire swing. "I'm not sure about Cole."

"He went up to the cabin again last night," Heath said heavily.

"He's been worse than ever since Katlynn left." Maverick shoved his hands in his worn jeans.

Heath nodded. "He knows when the party starts, though."

"If he doesn't show up, I'll haul his sorry butt down here." Maverick's boots clomped on the wooden floor as he crossed to the door and settled his hat back on his head. "In the meantime, I'll check Dewey Fields *and* the overpass."

"Will you have enough time?" Jewel asked.

Maverick shot her a grin. "Just save me a piece of that cake. It's been a while since I've had good barbecue."

The door clicked shut behind him, and Jewel rubbed her aching temples. "I tried to charbroil a birthday cake."

Heath poured her a glass of sweet tea and passed it over. "We'll get through this."

She sipped the lemony drink. "We?"

"We're partners, aren't we?"

She hurriedly raised her glass to hide her involuntary smile. Partners. She liked the sound of that. Pushing to her feet, she set the oven timer, then turned to examine the pink decorations. "How much of these are we supposed to use?"

Heath held up a packaged princess castle centerpiece. "All of it. Daryl's been buying supplies for weeks now."

"He dotes on Emma." Jewel tore open a bag of pink balloons.

"Spoils her rotten." Heath's cheeks bulged as he inflated a balloon. With a deft flick of his wrist, he tied off the bottom. "He's a good dad. All fathers love their little girls."

"Not all do." Jewel blew hard into a balloon, expanding it in one, furious breath. With a snap, she tied it off.

"Jewel?"

"I'm just sayin', some are more like Darth Vader than Andy Griffith." The taste of rubber lingered as she placed another balloon between her lips.

"Who are you really talking about?" Heath prodded.

Jewel lifted one shoulder in a lopsided shrug as she blew up another balloon, then another and another.

Heath's large hand, warm and rough, closed over her free one. "Your dad?"

She yanked her hand away and knotted the balloon. "I don't want to talk about it."

Heath cocked his head and studied her for a long minute. "I'm a good listener."

"Not much of a talker, though." Jewel gathered up the balloons a few minutes later and began tying some to the backs of chairs.

"What's that mean?" Heath cut lengths of pink-colored ribbon and passed them to her.

"Clint mentioned something about a music opportunity…"

Heath shoved back his chair and strode to the oven. "Better check on the cake."

"What was he talking about?" Jewel looped a ribbon around one of the balloons, securing it, then used the side of the scissor to curl the bottom.

"Nothing." He slid a toothpick into the center of the puffed white cakes, then closed the oven door again.

Jewel's mouth watered at the delicious buttery vanilla scent. Would this attempt succeed? If so, it'd be the first domestic thing she'd ever succeeded at except changing Jesse's diapers. According to her brothers, she had the maternal instincts of a copperhead snake, which, incidentally, eat their own young. So, yeah, not a vote of confidence.

"Nothing you want to talk about, you mean." With another scissor slide, the ribbon bounced in a long curl.

"Fathers and music…" Heath returned to the table, his expression shuttered, his shoulders tense. "Two subjects we're better off avoiding."

"Right," she agreed, yet a part of her yearned to open up to Heath. Maybe it was his music, or his sincere face, but she felt safe around him. Not judged. Challenged, too, but in an empowering way. Her father had never listened to her. Her brothers indulged her in debates up to a point, their wishes already a foregone conclusion. Heath, however, argued with her like an equal. Around him she was solid, visible, heard.

How odd that on Loveland territory, she no longer felt lacking. She eyed the heap of pink decorations and gritted her teeth. No matter how much sparkle she inhaled, she'd repay this accepting family by giving Emma the most girlie, fairy-princess party of all time.

Which made her a fairy godmother, if fairy godmothers wore Wranglers and Tony Lama boots. She peered at the clock and curled another ribbon.

Bibbidi-bobbidi-boo…

"Where'd you buy this cake?" James mumbled around a mouthful of frosting a couple hours later. "Amazin' Glazin'?" Over his shoulder, a blindfolded Javi thwacked a unicorn piñata hanging from the living room's exposed-beam ceiling. A group of cheering kids bounced on the balls of their feet and prepared to pounce on the imminent candy shower.

"I made it."

James stopped chewing and goggled at Jewel. "You?"

"With some help from Heath."

Heath passed the stick to Emma, tied the bandanna around her eyes and spun her three times before releasing her to swing at the unicorn. His white teeth flashed in a broad grin. What a smile. Like all Lovelands, he was a natural with kids. Affectionate, warm and firm without being harsh. He'd make a good father someday. *If* a gal was looking for that kind of thing—which she was *not*.

"I see." James drew out the two words.

"You don't see anything." Jewel cut another piece of cake, plopped it on a paper plate and passed it over with a fork and napkin to a waiting child. When he smiled his thanks, his teeth were the same bright pink as the frosting covering the tiara-wearing doll. She and Heath had stuck her in the center of the cake layers decorated to resemble a ball gown.

"You two sure looked cozy helping Emma unwrap her gifts. You're baking together, riding together…what's next? Picking out china patterns?"

"Heath's already engaged," Jewel huffed. A cheer rose from the children when Emma pierced the piñata. They descended on the falling candy, scrambling for pieces, trading favorites on the spot with each other. When a couple of boys began a shoving match, Cole and Maverick stepped in to break it up.

"Not officially." James stopped to give Javi a thumbs-up when he waved a handful of Tootsie Rolls at them. "And why isn't Kelsey here, then? Emma will be her niece."

As if on cue, Emma raced over and flung her arms around Jewel's knees so hard she staggered. "Thank you, Jewel! I love my party. It's so pretty and pink."

James nodded approvingly, rocking his four-month-old, clad in a ruffled pink gingham dress and matching bonnet. "I like the fairy-princess theme."

Emma peered up at him. "I'm not supposed to talk to Cades except Javi, Jewel and Grandma Joy."

"Why's that?" James tucked his dozing daughter's head into the crook of his arm.

"Just because!" Emma raced away to join the kids now

pinning a diamond-ring cutout on a princess poster. Sierra passed out cardboard pieces to each child in line, hollering "Step right up!" like a carnival barker.

"That's about as good an excuse as I've heard yet." Jewel spoke from the corner of her mouth, her eyes on Heath as he laughingly stopped one child from pinning the ring on another child's forehead.

"You know what the issues are," James insisted.

Jewel moved around the table collecting abandoned cake plates. "I thought I did."

"What's your opinion now?"

"The Lovelands aren't much different from us," she said over her shoulder as she headed for the garbage. "They're family-oriented, supportive of their neighbors and community, hardworking, moral people."

"Stubborn, tight-lipped and grudge-holding, too." James switched little Jesse to his opposite shoulder and rubbed her back. She belched softly.

"I'd hold a grudge, too, if my neighbors stole my water access rights." Jewel poked toothpicks in the cake and stretched plastic wrap across it.

"You're calling your own family thieves?" James's jaw clenched. "You've sure gone over to the other side. Will you sit with them or us when we go to trial in two weeks?"

"What's wrong with seeing both sides?"

"If Loveland Brahmans traipsed across our land, they'd damage our property, overgraze, and mix and breed with our longhorns. That'd make your job as range boss harder."

Jewel hefted the cake platter and carried it from the table to the counter. "I'm not looking for easy. I want what's fair."

"Fair for the Lovelands, you mean. You're not winning yourself any points with me right now."

Jewel whisked off the plastic pink table covering, balled it up and tossed it out to make room for the tiara-decorating craft supplies. "Stop holding that over me. Judge me on my merits, not by how much I agree with you."

"I'm the final say."

Jewel lined up glue bottles, plastic tiaras and multicolored "stones." "Maybe I don't need your approval anymore."

Before James could respond, the children crowded around the table, grabbing the supplies. Sierra crouched between the kids, helping, while Cole and Maverick circled. Heath picked up the piñata and princess poster mess.

"Can boys be princesses, Pa?" Javi twisted the silver headpiece in his hands, naked longing on his face.

"They can be anything they want to be."

James frowned at Jewel for hijacking whatever his intended answer would have been.

"Is that true?"

Heath squeezed Javi's shoulder, joining them, his eyes locked on Jewel. "Your aunt's right. No one can tell us who we are. We decide for ourselves."

Javi's gap-toothed smiled flashed. "Then I'm Princess Superman!" He tore off, grabbed a red triangular stone, and squished on a chair beside Emma, who seemed to have amassed every pink stone on the table.

"Princess Superman, huh?" James shook his head slowly. "What's that even mean?"

"It means he's not letting others define him."

At her words, Heath raised his eyebrows, and her admission about not being a girlie-girl, the wifey-type as her father once told her, returned to her.

James wandered away to help Javi, leaving Jewel and Heath alone. In silence, they watched the babbling children. Save for a couple of squabbles, all ran smoothly.

"We did a good job," Heath said without taking his eyes off the kids.

She nodded, then cleared her throat. "Any word from Daryl?"

"He found LeAnne playing pool at Silver Spurs."

"Is he driving her to the party?"

"She's been drinking, so he's taking her to their cabin, then coming on his own. He's cut up over missing so much of it already."

"Poor Daryl. Did he say why LeAnne stayed out all night?"

"Lovelands don't pry. He'll tell me what he thinks I need to know."

Jewel bit her lip, irritated at the stoic family. You had to talk about your problems. Otherwise they festered inside. Denial never worked. Then again, she had no right to ride that high horse. She'd never told her brothers, or mother, how she really felt about her childhood. They knew she wanted the range boss job, but she'd never explained why, or how Pa's dismissal had hurt her.

Maybe keeping things in had a way of holding you back. Would admitting her pain, her insecurities, free her of them?

After another beat of silence, Heath leaned forward to grab an unclaimed tiara. "What color jewels would you like, *Jewel*?"

Her hand rose to finger the loose waves Sierra had conned her into styling when she'd returned from her orphaned fawn emergency. "The only thing this head wears is a cowboy hat."

"Why's that?" Heath glued purple stones in a heart-shaped pattern to the tiara.

"I—I'm not the princess type."

"Who says?"

She opened her mouth to say her father, then snapped it shut. How much of her identity was her own? What kinds of things, experiences, people had she rejected simply because she thought she wasn't suited for them?

"Here." Heath slid the tiara on her head, his hands lingering on the side of her face. They trembled against her skin slightly, and her heart jumped to the base of her throat.

"You look like a princess to me," he whispered, hoarse.

"Which one?" she murmured, keeping her voice low in case it cracked and revealed the emotion flooding her.

"Sleeping Beauty."

"Why?" She was freckled, redheaded, skinny…if anything she should be one of Cinderella's stepsisters.

"Because a handsome prince hasn't kissed you yet."

"What if I don't need one?"

"Maybe—" he drew closer "—you want one."

"Uncle Heath, can we do the birthday parade now?" Emma called.

They broke apart, and Jewel's cheeks stung with heat under James's and Sierra's speculative stares. Whatever they thought was dead wrong. Nothing was going on between her and Heath.

Nothing.

So why had her lips been puckering, her skin perspiring, her pulse racing just then? Heath was right. She needed—wanted—a kiss from him, even if it was stupid and wrong.

Heath squeezed her hand, then strode to the piano. With a flourish, he pounded out a couple of dramatic chords as the tiara-wearing kids lined up. Sierra, Cole and Maverick passed out wands, plastic frogs and glitter-covered blowers.

Heath sang the Beatles classic "Birthday" as the kids marched around the living room, tooting horns, waving wands and shouting "ribbit."

"He's so talented," Sierra said, joining Jewel. "It's such a waste."

"What do you mean?"

"He's as passionate about music as I am about animals. If I didn't get to work with them…" Her voice trailed off and Jewel followed her gaze back to Heath.

Sierra strolled away as Heath launched into another

birthday tune, a personal ode to Emma. Being a princess wasn't about how others saw you, but about how you saw yourself, he sang. Jewel fingered her tiara. What a beautiful message. Heath created lyrics that pierced your heart and made you think. It was a God-given talent.

"Where's Emma going?" The young girl dashed from the group and up the back stairs. When Sierra didn't answer, Jewel craned her neck and spotted her washing platters beneath a forcefully spraying faucet. An oblivious Cole and Maverick marched with the kids while Heath continued to play.

Jewel jogged up the stairs, then followed the sound of muffled sobs to a second-floor linen closet. She knocked on the door. "Princess Emma? It's Jewel."

"P-please go away," Emma snuffled.

"I can't. Party rules." Jewel knelt on the hardwood floor and leaned her forehead against the wood paneling.

"Lovelands don't talk about our feelings."

"But I'm a Cade. The Loveland rules don't apply."

"Oh."

"Why are you crying?"

"I miss Mama."

"I'm sure she'd be here if she could." Jewel crossed her fingers, wishing it were true. How could LeAnne miss her daughter's birthday to play pool?

"She never plays with me," Emma cried. Jewel flattened her hand against the door, wishing she could hug the confused and lonely little girl. "She's never around and always has headaches and spends all her time on the computer."

"She loves you, honey."

"No, she doesn't!"

"My father never noticed me much growing up." Jewel's hands clenched at the admission.

The closet door cracked open and Emma peered out. "How come?"

"I think it's because I wasn't a boy."

"But that wasn't your fault!" Indignation crossed Emma's tearstained face as she emerged to crowd closer to Jewel.

Jewel nodded. Emma was right. Being born a girl wasn't something to apologize for…so why had she spent her entire life blaming herself for it? Her brothers might be bigger and stronger, but she had just as much grit and determination. Even if her father didn't value those qualities in her didn't mean she shouldn't value them in herself. Just like Heath sang: it wasn't about how other people saw her, it was about how she saw herself.

"No, it wasn't my fault." Jewel stroked Emma's soft hair. "That's why it's important not to let other people control how you feel about yourself." She brushed away the tear rolling down Emma's cheek, feeling like a complete fraud. She'd never followed that logic before.

Before now, she amended. The next mirror she passed, she wouldn't ask if she was the toughest of them all, she'd ask herself. Her opinion mattered most.

"So I decide if I'm good?"

Jewel held out her arms and Emma laid her head on Jewel's chest. "Yes. And that you're smart, and capable, and pretty."

Emma lifted her head. "Pa says pretty doesn't matter. Character does."

Jewel nodded, liking Daryl even more for being such a good father. "He's right."

"I think you're pretty." Emma skimmed a finger over Jewel's cheeks. "All your freckles…it's like you're coated in fairy dust."

A throat cleared behind them, and Jewel glanced over her shoulder to meet Heath's eyes. His intense expression turned them a deep, unfathomable blue. "Javi and some of your other guests are leaving."

The girl bounded to her feet. "I've got to hug my cousin!" With a whoop, she practically catapulted down the stairs.

"That was a nice speech." Heath moved closer, near enough to smell the homespun scent of his bar soap and the fresh pine scent of his clothesline-dried shirt.

Her toes curled in her boots. "I hope it helped."

"It did."

They exchanged smiles, then Jewel dropped her eyes, flustered.

"I heard what you said about your father."

"Oh." She shuffled her feet, feeling disloyal. "I was just trying to help Emma."

"I could never please my mother either."

She studied the dark fan of his lashes on his cheeks, the twist of his hands before he stuffed them in his pockets. "Your sister called you the mom whisperer."

Heath hung his head. "She'd always wanted to be a musician, and she blamed us for trapping her here in Carbondale. When I played songs with her, I could help her forget…"

"Forget what?"

"How much she resented us."

"I'm sure she loved you."

"If she did—" Heath voice cracked. He cleared his throat and began again. "If she did, she never would have killed herself to escape us."

"Don't say that…"

"I haven't. Not before."

"Why say it now?"

He shoved his hair from his eyes and peered down at her. "I don't know. Maybe it's like you said. The Loveland rules don't apply with you. Maybe none of them do." He cupped her face and her breath stalled. Was she finally about to have her first kiss? "You're different, Jewel. Not like anyone I've ever met before and if I was free…"

"Yes?" she prompted when he stopped, her heart beating out of her chest.

He released a breath and his hands dropped to his sides. "Forget it. We'd better get back to the party for Emma."

She nodded and watched his broad shoulders disappear down the stairwell, knowing she'd forget none of this shattering moment of connection between them.

With a hand slapped over her face, she paced, a strangled noise gargling in the back of her throat. She would have kissed Heath…even though he wasn't free.

She'd been raised better than that.

Just because she was starting to have feelings for Heath—and yes, she'd cowgirl up and admit it—he was taken.

Off-limits.

She peeked over the rail and watched as Heath handed out the party favor bags to the departing children. He'd be a good parent one day.

Would she? She'd never imagined herself in a motherly role before interacting with the children today. Helping Emma had filled Jewel with warm satisfaction. Maybe she had a maternal side after all. Was she wrong to discount marriage and a family as her future?

Sure, she'd lose some of her independence, but what she'd gain, she sensed, might be far more fulfilling.

Especially with a man who didn't want to change her.

Someone like Heath. A man promised to another woman…

CHAPTER NINE

HEATH STUDIED THE Scrabble tiles nearly filling the board and plunked down an *O* and a *P* with a shrug. It was his best option. Or so he guessed. With the fetching redhead beside him, ready to pounce on his every move, who could focus? Despite the soothing, honeysuckle-scented air filtering through the window screens, and the bullfrogs serenading the balmy night, his body felt like an overwound clock. Awareness stiffened his joints and raised the small hairs on his arms.

"Op?" Jewel's petite nose wrinkled. Wearing a light blue tank top revealing toned arms and a trim waist, her burnished hair flowing around her freckled shoulders, she'd never looked prettier. Or maybe he was coming around to her kind of pretty?

He fought the urge to run his fingers through her waves, teasing them apart. "*Op* is short for operation."

"Hey, I'm not trying to talk you out of it." Then she chuckled and placed *S* and *T* before his *OP*.

"Fine. You got me." Heath's gaze dropped to her beautiful mouth, as rosy as her freckles, then lifted to her sparkling brown eyes. The relentless desire to be her first kiss had already cost him countless hours of sleep. What would she taste like? Spicy and sweet, like a Fireball candy…one of his favorites? "But I'm still ahead."

"And I'm not finished." With a flourish, she added a *B*, *A*, *N* and *K*, using all but one of her remaining tiles. Then she sat back on the couch, her expression triumphant, arms folded across her chest.

"Stopbank?" He summed up the points. Eighty-one—which put her in the lead. Whoever lost tonight had to ride in the rear of the herd tomorrow, a long, lonely day. "That's not a word."

Her eyebrows rose. “Are you challenging me?”

“Heck, yeah.”

She passed him the dictionary. “You'll lose your turn when you find out I'm right.”

“You'll lose those points when I prove you're wrong.” With quick flicks of his fingers, he turned to the *S* section, scanned down the page then stopped.

Stopbank.

A levee.

Exactly what he needed to stop his building feelings for Jewel. With time running out this summer, a wedding date decision waiting at its end, along with a looming courtroom family showdown, he had to rein in his emotions. They threatened everyone and everything in their path.

“What's it say?” Jewel crowded close, and his fingers curled around the book binding at her fresh, clean scent. It was like breathing in sunshine after a spring rain.

“Says you're wrong.”

“Liar!” She lunged for the book. When he held it aloft, her momentum carried her forward, tumbling them down to the couch.

The book dropped from his nerveless fingers. Neither seemed to notice as they stared into each other's eyes, their mouths a whisper apart.

“Jewel,” he groaned, cupping the back of her head. Her soft hair tickled his cheeks as it fell around them like a velvet curtain.

Her dark eyes glazed. “Heath—”

“Yoo-hoo!”

Jewel scrambled backward at Kelsey's call. Heath bolted to his feet so fast he upended the board.

“What are you up to?” Kelsey's heels clicked on the wooden floor once she strode inside. “I've been calling your landline, but you haven't—” At the sight of Jewel, smoothing down her hair with a shaking hand, Kelsey jerked to a stop.

Heath rose and glanced at the empty phone cradle. "One of the kids at the party must have knocked it over." He pressed a perfunctory kiss to Kelsey's raised cheek, searched the floor for the phone and replaced it.

"And you didn't notice?" Kelsey lifted a fingernail to her mouth, as if to gnaw on it, then shoved both hands in her pockets.

"I was beating him at Scrabble." Jewel crouched to pick up the pieces. "You know men. They're only focused on winning."

"I had you until that last move," Heath protested, joining her in retrieving the tiles.

"Dream on." Jewel grinned, and he laughed, unable to help himself. She always made him laugh…when he didn't want to hold her tight and kiss her until they both lost their minds.

"Heath. I'd like to talk to you." Kelsey's voice emerged tight. High. The sound of a steaming tea kettle about to blow.

Jewel dropped the last piece in the box, jammed on the cover, then fell back onto the couch. She jutted her chin. "Don't mind me."

"Alone." Kelsey's lips wobbled slightly before she clamped them tight.

"Let's sit on the porch swing." Heath tugged her outside, wishing, oddly, to reassure Jewel. Her tough expression had shattered when he'd reached for Kelsey's hand, the color leaching from her face. Even her freckles faded to beige.

Something panged inside him. What would he reassure her of? That he cared for *her*, not Kelsey?

Insane.

Yet he might have kissed her if not for Kelsey's interruption. It made him the worst kind of man. Disloyal. Dishonest. A cheater…

The floorboards creaked as they crossed to the wicker swing. When they sat, it swung backward with a tinny rattle of its metal chains. The silence between them was as hard and brittle as glass.

"Aren't you going to say something?" Kelsey crossed a knee over the other, and her heel swung. "Like, 'I'm glad to see you' and 'My, don't you look pretty.'"

He shifted, his stomach churning. "You surprised me. I didn't know you were coming over."

Weak, Loveland. Weak.

Kelsey pursed her bright pink mouth. He didn't have to use his imagination to know it'd taste of chalky makeup. "I need an invitation to see you?"

"When you didn't come to Emma's party, I assumed…"

She plopped her purse in her lap, pulled it open, and yanked out a small, brightly wrapped gift box. "The engravers didn't have it ready in time, and I didn't want to show up empty-handed. Plus, the food bank ran short on diapers, so I had to run to the store and buy a trunk load." She shoved the present at him. "Tell Emma it's one of a kind."

"I'm sure she'll appreciate it." Kelsey…always so generous. Although presents didn't matter as much as being there for loved ones…like a soon-to-be-niece once—if?—they married. The fundamental difference in their values, his for family and hers for money and appearances, yawned wider than ever.

"And…" Kelsey prompted, smoothing a hand over her sleek hair. The complicated half up, half down style practically screamed "don't touch."

"You do look pretty."

He heard a strangled exclamation from inside the house and glimpsed Jewel stalking across the living room to disappear upstairs. A tearing sensation ripped through his chest. He wanted to chase after Jewel… and he wanted to reassure Kelsey he wouldn't disappoint her.

What do you *want?*

He ignored the internal question and tore his gaze from the house to peer at Kelsey.

The corners of her mouth pulled downward. "Aren't you happy to see me?"

"I didn't expect you," he said again, avoiding the question. "And you never come here because of the drive."

"How else am I going to see you? You're spending too much time at the ranch."

When she reached for his hand, he grabbed a lighter instead, flicked it on and touched its flame to a citronella candle. "I'm working."

"Didn't look like work in there." Kelsey's brows lowered. "Maybe you'd rather play board games with that prickly cowgirl."

"There's more to Jewel than meets the eye," he insisted, thinking of how kind she'd been to Emma at the party, how open and vulnerable.

"You're defending her over me?" Kelsey sucked in a raspy breath.

"Of course not," he denied, more to keep the peace than anything else. Strange how Kelsey's feminine softness hid an inner hardness whereas Jewel's tough-as-nails exterior shielded a tender side. It aroused his protective instincts. "Look. You just surprised me."

"I didn't plan on coming until the other night."

His eyes stung at the acrid smoke rising from the candle beside him. "The other night?"

"At Silver Spurs."

Heath planted his toe on the porch planks and set the swing in motion, like he and his siblings had done when they were kids. Pa had always warned them they'd go flying off the porch, but that'd just made them swing harder to see if he was right. What he'd give to sail straight over Mount Sopris, clean up to the moon, above the gravity of his life. Free. "What's that got to do with you stopping over?"

"I thought Jewel might need reminding you're taken."

He tipped his head to the side. "Jewel?"

"She's got it bad for you. She has for a long, long time."

His heart stopped, along with the rest of the world it seemed, as he absorbed her words. "No, she doesn't."

"You're blind. She used to moon over you when you were in 4-H together. And I saw the way she looked at you on stage."

"*She* likes my music." The swing whooshed faster now so their feet rose, weightless, before plunging to earth again.

"What's that supposed to mean?"

He swallowed back the accusations hurling themselves against his gritted teeth. "Just what I said."

"Are you saying I don't like your music?"

"You want me to quit."

"I want you to grow up," Kelsey countered. "And please stop rocking the swing. You're making me motion sick."

When Heath obliged, Kelsey continued. "Do you want to be one of those pathetic middle-aged men singing in honky-tonks, pretending they're young?"

"I *am* young."

"Almost thirty isn't young." She patted his leg.

He pulled away, brushing at her hand like a persistent fly. "Dreams have a life span?"

"Aren't I your dream?" Kelsey cried. "Having a family, a life with me?"

He opened his mouth, but only silent confusion emerged. He did want a family, a wife, but did he want them with Kelsey? They'd gotten engaged so young. He'd planned to grow old with her, but instead it seemed as though they were growing apart.

"If you're not careful, you're going to lose everything." Her eyes swept over his house, then down to the barns and fenced-in pastures. "And I mean *everything*."

"Is that a threat?" Anger cracked through him, like the first tentative step on a newly frozen pond.

"No." Kelsey's head drooped for a moment before she stood and strode away. When she reached the stairs, she paused and gripped the balustrade. "It's an observation. Loveland Hills is going under unless you find the cash to catch up on your mortgage payments."

The swing rocked as he propelled himself from it. "You want the ranch to go under to free me up to be with you."

"How can you accuse me of that?" Kelsey stormed. "Don't you know me anymore?"

When he didn't answer, she flung herself down the steps and into her sports car. It purred to life, low and heavy, like the growl of a predatory cat in the dark.

"Kelsey!" He strode after her, then stopped when she reversed into a one-hundred-and-eighty-degree turn. The car yanked to a halt beside him, and the window slid down.

"Do you still love me?" Her tortured eyes met his.

"Yes," he insisted. But was he *in* love with her?

She closed her eyes and nodded. "I don't know what I would have done if you'd answered differently," she whispered. The glass rose, and she peeled off down the road.

Heath's clenched jaw ached as he watched her vehicle disappear into the night. Even if he wanted out of his engagement, how could he end it without hurting her? They'd meant so much to each other once. She didn't deserve to be jilted after waiting ten years for him.

But would he make her happy if he wasn't happy himself?

Lately, he'd only felt at peace riding the range, working alongside Jewel. She was tart-tongued and prickly, not sweet-smelling and soft like Kelsey. In fact, most times she was downright dusty and smelly…but from hard work. Honest work. Work he admired. Despite being no friend to his family, Jewel gave everything she had to the cattle drive, all except going against her brothers' wishes to cross the old easement.

Maybe her kind of help didn't have the potential to save the ranch the way Kelsey's cash influx could, but he valued it more. Did she labor on Loveland Hills because it was her nature, a promise to her mother, their bet—or…did Jewel have a crush on him like Kelsey suggested?

A strong hand clapped him, hard, on the shoulder. "Women."

Heath turned to study Daryl. The silvery moonlight seemed to deepen the lines around his mouth, dragging down the corners. "LeAnne okay?"

"Nothing a good night's sleep won't cure," Daryl said gruffly as they mounted the stairs. "And some Tylenol."

Heath hid his wince, knowing Daryl wouldn't want his pity.

"How about you and Kelsey?" Daryl asked once they were inside. He grabbed a knife, unwrapped Emma's birthday cake and cut a couple of generous slices. "She left in a hurry."

Heath poured them some milk and touched the cold glass to his burning forehead. "She's got a bee in her bonnet that there's something going on between me and Jewel." He tried to laugh, but the sound emerged like a gasping croak.

Daryl passed Heath a fork. "Is there?"

"No!"

"That was quick." Daryl pulled out a chair and dropped into it, as if he'd been standing all day by sheer willpower alone.

Heath speared a bite and lifted it to his mouth. "I don't have to think about the answer."

One of Daryl's shoulders lifted and fell as he chewed. "Maybe you should."

When Heath opened his mouth to insist the opposite, Daryl lifted a hand to silence him. "Can't thank you and Jewel enough for making Emma's birthday special. You make a good team. And I've seen the way you two look at each other. There's something there."

Under Daryl's piercing stare, Heath's bluster faded. "If there is, I can't do anything about it."

"Why's that?" Daryl slid the side of his fork into the cake and scooped up another bite. "Jewel's good people."

"It'd kill Kelsey."

"What about you?"

"What about me?"

"Do you love Kelsey?"

Heath gulped his milk, probing his heart. "We've been together so long, I must."

"That doesn't mean you're *in* love with each other." Daryl turned his face to stare out the window at the distant lights of his cabin.

Was he thinking of LeAnne?

"You've always tried to please women who can't be pleased, like Ma."

Heath gaped at Daryl. "I was the only one who could, except the night of Cole's party." His voice cracked.

Daryl reached across the table and wrapped his large hand around Heath's wrist, squeezing it. "It wasn't your responsibility. You were a kid who deserved a happy childhood, and she took it from you. From all of us." Daryl released him and scooped up a pink frosting rose with his fork. "Don't waste your future, too. Maybe the person you need to choose is you."

Heath pressed his fork into the cake crumbs, mashing them. Was Daryl right…could he put himself, and his wants, ahead of everyone else?

"I haven't talked much about what happened between me, LeAnne and Cassidy," Daryl said, naming the sisters who'd been estranged after he'd dated one, then married the other.

"You don't have to," Heath rushed to say.

"If it'll help you avoid the same mistakes I made, then I'd be wrong to stay silent."

"What do you mean?"

Daryl spoke without lifting his eyes from his plate. "I married LeAnne because I had to."

"But you loved her…"

With a heavy sigh, Daryl said, "She's my wife now, and she has my loyalty. But I've never been able to make her happy, no matter how hard I've tried, and for that, I'll never forgive myself."

"Because you don't love her?"

Daryl pinched the bridge of his nose. "Because I loved someone else more."

Heath thought of Cassidy, how happy she and Daryl had been when they'd visited the ranch on college breaks. If he'd loved Cassidy, why had he turned to LeAnne?

Daryl shoved back his chair and stood, his shoulders tense, as he strode across the kitchen. At the archway, he turned. The raw pain in his eyes darkened them to black. "Two things about Lovelands. When we love, we love forever. And when we commit, it's forever, too. There are no takebacks for us. Go after what *you* want and get it right the first time. It's the most unselfish thing you could do."

Heath collected the dishes, cranked on the faucet and scrubbed them, his gaze drifting to the brilliant moon.

Was it unselfish to please himself? And if he could choose any path he wanted to, where would it lead? Kelsey insisted Jewel had feelings for him, and he suspected he returned them. Seeing her with the children, he'd glimpsed a softer side that called to his heart. Plus, he couldn't stop thinking about her never being kissed. But if he opened himself up to Jewel, he'd let everyone down and his family might lose the ranch without his financial help. He wouldn't accept Kelsey's generous offer to pay down their mortgage with her trust fund, but he wouldn't have a problem funneling his salary from her father's company to keep them afloat until the drought ended, or the easement was returned.

Still, Daryl had a point. Lovelands were loyal. Whatever road he chose, he'd travel forever. Was two weeks enough time to decide on the rest of your life?

CHAPTER TEN

JEWEL CANTERED BEAR down an old, dried-up riverbed a few days later, her skin sticky with sweat, her breath a harsh rasp in her throat. As she rode, she kept a wary eye on the herd, the other on the sky. Without warning, storm clouds had rolled in, and it was no longer the guileless blue it had been when she and Heath set out. It matched her dark mood.

Kelsey's surprise visit the other night had Jewel's tail up. Fancy Pants had practically planted a flag in Heath's heart to claim him. Worse, he hadn't seemed to mind. He'd even told Kelsey she was pretty. Jewel groaned. She'd never received such a compliment from a man—probably never would. Who'd be attracted to a freckled, cowlicked cowgirl like her? She'd never given her appearance much thought before. Now she spent more time at the mirror than her pretty-boy brother Jared. And for no good reason. Heath wouldn't pay her any notice if not for her ability to help his failing ranch.

Why moon over him?

She glowered at Heath's broad back as he wheeled Destiny around in an effortless pivot to chase after a runaway.

Making a fool of herself, that's what.

Heath's off-limits status should make Jewel glad. She needed to focus on her job and impress James enough to be named range boss. Yet seeing Heath with Kelsey left Jewel hopeless. It was a darned unfamiliar feeling for a gal who'd always believed hard work would earn her what she wanted in life.

And what she wanted was Heath.

She heaved out an aggravated sigh.

No denying it; she was falling for him.

Wind blasted from the west, whirling dust. The tips of

trees were getting pushed and pulled in all directions, and in the distance, thunder rumbled. How much closer was the storm? She studied the racing purple-bellied clouds and a jittery feeling settled in her bones.

"Yaw!" Jewel squeezed Bear's sides, galloping full out as she raced alongside the cantering herd, guiding them as fast as she dared to a sheltered pasture on the mountainside opposite the approaching storm. With rain threatening, thunder growling, they needed to get the cattle to higher ground and out of flash-flood danger. The hard-packed, dry ground wouldn't absorb a sudden rainfall. It'd create a torrent strong enough to sweep a hundred head to their deaths if she and Heath didn't hustle them to safety.

"Yip! Yip! Yip!" called Heath, signaling the cattle dogs. They streaked in a black-and-white blur to keep the frightened animals together. His expression was hard, his body rising in the saddle as he craned his neck to check for stragglers. With Daryl back home tending to a sick LeAnne today, it was just them against the elements.

Rain was coming, Jewel could practically smell it now, but the air was still stifling and oppressive. She twisted around and peered behind her. The riverbed was the quickest route to the sheltered spot. If they didn't make it in time, though, they'd be swept right off the mountain.

Thunder belched through the sky once more. This time, it wasn't nearly as polite and distant as it had been before. The hair on the back of her neck stood on end. A branch snapped. A bird called, a high-pitched sound, like a yelp, and another answered.

"It's moving fast," shouted Heath, pulling alongside her. His shirt clung to his muscular frame. Beads of sweat ran down his handsome, angular face.

"Weather report said only a twenty percent chance of rain," she hollered back. Her eyes swept over the bellowing, tramping herd. Leaves gusted around her like green confetti as the wind began to build, and masses of foliage shuddered and bent as it whipped through a tree line.

"We've got to drive them quicker." He pulled Destiny around and charged to the back of the herd.

Jewel galloped after him. "If we leave the riverbed, we can take a shortcut through that underpass." She pointed to a jagged arch of rocks in the distance.

Heath leaned low over Destiny's lathered neck as they pressured the cattle from behind. "Footing isn't sound there."

"It's less likely to get hit with a flash flood. Better to lose one or two than a hundred."

Lightning cracked and Destiny broke stride, briefly, before Heath gathered her again. "I don't want to lose any!" he hollered.

"Then we won't." She met Heath's eyes briefly and he nodded.

"Bend them left."

Satisfaction flooded Jewel at Heath's faith as she and Bear tore off down the right flank. They began pressuring the cattle to turn. A raindrop fell on her nose, then her cheek. Her heart raced. No! They had to escape the riverbed before the real weather hit. Hustling the cattle up a rocky slope was risky, too, but staying in a flash flood zone was suicide. The Brahmans bellowed, the whites of their eyes showing, as they picked up their hooves and trotted faster still, sensing the imminent danger.

Getting them out of the riverbed, however, meant driving them up and over its steep bank. As they neared the spot, the lead cattle slowed and balked. A sickening feeling in Jewel's gut pinched harder as each second passed.

"Go! Go! Go!" Heath whistled to the dogs. Dodging the Brahmans' kicking legs while lunging at their heels, they pressured them to keep moving, avoiding a pileup at the last possible moment.

Relief surged as the livestock followed their leaders, scrambling up the pebbled soil. Their hooves sought purchase to heave themselves up and over the sides. They began crossing beneath the underpass.

The wind picked up and tore Jewel's Stetson from her head. Her braids whipped around her cheeks. With a solid *crack*, the swollen skies suddenly split above them. Rain peppered the hard-packed soil and rivulets of water rolled down the riverbed. Within minutes they were wet through.

By now only half the herd had clambered up the bank, the rest splashing in water rapidly rising over their hooves.

"Heeeee-yaaaaa!" She yelled so loudly that it felt as if the humid air was scorching her throat when she drew breath. Waving her red kerchief at a pair of hesitating Brahmans, she spooked them in the right direction.

She squinted at Heath through the now-pelting rain. He rode like the devil himself, flashing back and forth as fast as the lightning, urging the cattle forward and left without making them panic. Like her, he knew one breakaway animal could lead an entire group to their doom.

Bear splashed through the rising water. She couldn't judge the terrain beneath them, couldn't predict where a treacherous depression might turn his fetlock or worse. *Compartmentalize. Focus on herding the animals from the imminent threat at hand.*

Swiping the dripping water in front of her eyes, she zipped alongside the cattle, blocking their way when they tried to outrun the rushing water. It now swelled around their knees. The cattle dogs paddled beside them, fighting the current. Thunder rumbled, low and deep, and a lightning bolt hit a nearby tree and sent a limb crashing down.

As each second passed and the weather pressed in around them, her fear built into a hot, urgent creature. It threatened to explode inside her. By now, most of the cattle had made it up the embankment. The remaining Brahmans reared back at the smoking tree limb. Heath, grim-faced and bold, drove straight at them, and they scrambled over the branch to safety.

"Come on!" Heath made a sweeping gesture with his hand from the top of the riverbank.

Jewel eyed the raging water. Just before she urged Bear onto drier land, she spotted a floundering calf, caught in the current. Fear melted her insides. It bawled before its little head disappeared under the raging water. From the corner of her eye, she caught a flash of color just before Heath dived in after it.

Her lungs quit working. With the water moving that fast, Heath might die right along with the helpless animal. She squeezed Bear's sides and sent him sprinting up the embankment. They thundered alongside the now-raging river. Without taking her eyes off Heath or the calf, she uncoiled her rope and began twirling it overhead. Meanwhile, Heath kicked his legs and swung his arms like mad, battling to reach the calf without getting pulled under and pinned beneath the current.

Keep a cool head.

Jewel eyed a piece of deadwood jutting out of the water downstream.

"Grab the log!" she screamed, galloping along the river's edge. If Heath missed it, he'd be lost in the water, drowned.

Fighting back tears, she continued to lasso the rope through the pounding rain.

Please. Please. Please.

Spare them.

Just as the calf's head disappeared once more, Heath grasped it, pulling the animal above the surface and clutching it to his chest.

"Grab the wood!" she screeched, pointing with her free hand at the downed tree several yards ahead of Heath.

He glanced up and briefly met her eyes. The determination she glimpsed heartened her. He wasn't giving up, and neither was she. Just as the water tore him toward its deadly center, Heath managed to hook an arm around the end of the limb, the other anchoring the calf to his chest.

"Hold on!" she hollered.

Heath's feet appeared, dragged off the bottom. The only thing holding him in place was his strong one-handed grip. How long could he withstand the flash flood's punishing pressure?

Jewel gritted her teeth and eyed the distance between her and Heath. She wasn't going to wait around to find out. Timing the moment, she released the lasso and the rope dropped in the water, inches from Heath.

He stared at it, then back up at her, the tendons in his neck taut. To grab it, he'd have to let go of the calf. Jewel hauled back the rope. She knew his choice. She'd make it herself.

Another toss and the rope hit his shoulder. Heath lost his grip reaching for it, and she screamed when he went under. A second later, he popped back up with the calf on the other side of the log, barely holding on. The rain was relentless still, heavy and driving.

Beneath her, Bear shifted back and forth when another bolt of lightning lit up the sky. It illuminated Heath's white face, his blue lips. She had to get him out of there. Now.

Swinging hard, her eyes never leaving Heath's, she circled the rope once, twice, three times, then tossed it, watching as it slithered through the water-logged air to drop over Heath's shoulders. Relief swept through her with tidal force as he shifted his body to ease it down over his torso. She stepped Bear backward to tighten the line. On the other end, the relentless pull of the gushing water worked in opposition.

"Hold on!" she yelled.

He nodded and, to her amazement, began to edge his way along the log toward the shore his arms still wrapped around the calf with only the lasso around him to keep him upright. What incredible strength and balance, she marveled, watching him, as she held the line steady. If he stumbled, he might pull her, and Bear, into the water, too, but she believed in him too much to fear the possibility.

At last, he stumbled up the embankment and set down the calf. It wobbled forward a few steps, caught sight of its mother, and scampered her way to join the rest of the herd now milling in the sheltered area beyond the underpass. Jewel flung herself from her saddle, rushed to Heath and threw her arms around him.

"I thought you were going to drown."

"Not a chance." Despite his brave words, his teeth chattered. Another lightning bolt smacked against the mountainside. "Let's take shelter."

They secured their horses beneath a rocky outcropping then, hand in hand, they struggled across the drenched field toward an old shack sitting inside a copse of trees. The lock was broken, and the shack abandoned, though an old leather harness and empty feed bags remained among the dust and cobwebs.

Clothes clung to limbs, hair to burnished cheeks, and they tumbled, panting, into the shack. The damp walls and earthy darkness made the space feel more like a dungeon than a respite from the storm.

Heath grabbed a burlap cloth and wrapped it around her shoulders, pulling her close. A sneeze ripped from her. His gaze roamed from the top of her soaked head to her squelching boots. "You're soaked."

"So are you."

He shrugged. "I'm waterproof."

"You shouldn't have jumped in after that calf."

"Why? Because you were going to?" When she nodded, he chuckled. "Guess that makes us a pair."

"Does it?"

The smile faded from his face and warmth spiraled in his eyes. His rough hand cupped her cheek. "Thanks for getting me out of there."

She held up four fingers on her left hand and three on her right. "Cades ahead by one."

He caught her hand and brought it to his mouth, pressing a kiss to the center of her palm.

"Heath," she groaned, turning away, but he tugged her back to his chest, his forearm resting firmly across her rib cage, one large hand wrapped around her waist.

"Jewel," he murmured in her ear, the husky bass sending shivers dancing down her spine.

His body hugged hers from his chest to his thighs, her hair brushed his face, his masculine scent tickled her nose, and his mouth was poised at the sensitive lobe of her ear, as if ready to demand surrender.

Should she give in to her feelings at last?

Heath was promised to another…

But right now, after saving him from drowning, didn't a bit of his life, even if it was just this moment, belong to her?

They stood frozen for several long seconds, locked in the strange embrace, eyes closed, mouths slightly open, trying to breathe without movement, without sound, and growing light-headed in the attempt. Jewel's hands had risen to Heath's arm when he pulled her to him, and she stood motionless against him, her hands gripping the hard limb holding her. She didn't dare say his name, didn't dare utter a sound. Surely it would break the spell. Then she felt his lips move ever so softly against the lobe of her ear, skim the uppermost edge of her jaw, then travel back again.

Jewel resisted the sweet shudder sliding down her spine, but Heath must have felt the tremor as his lips left her skin. He didn't pull away or loosen his hold, though. Was she about to have her first kiss? It felt as unstoppable as the weather, a seismic shift cracking open her heart. She wanted Heath to be her first…

Her only?

Opening her eyes, Jewel slowly angled her head back, feeling his breath mark a path across her cheek as she raised her face and lifted her chin. Then it was her breath tickling his cheek and warming his lips. Again, they paused, muscles tensed, straining to feel everything, to miss nothing, and still not cross the line. Heath's eyes remained closed and hers followed suit as they approached that line, stood at its edge and then tumbled over it, into each other.

She turned, and his arms went around her, holding her tight. She liked the feel of his embrace, sheltering her, when she'd never craved a man's protection before. It was oddly empowering. Exhilarating. Their bodies melded as he buried his head in her neck, dragging in a deep breath. Her pulse pounded, and her hands trembled. A deep shudder rose through him and he shook in her arms, and then he moved.

Clasping her cheeks in his large hands, he said something too low and too quick for her to make out as he tilted her head back and kissed her. There was nothing soft about it, like in fairy tales or her girlhood imaginings. This was a man's kiss, firm, real, ardent, full of the same yearning clamoring inside her. He tasted of something sweet; the cold tang of rainwater was still on his tongue. Little shivers raced through her body as she lost herself in the kiss. Her hands slid up to his shoulders and her fingers dug into the fabric covering his firm skin. The kiss was doing crazy stuff to her senses, warming her through while making her shake.

She'd never felt this before. How could such sweet wildness come from a single kiss? The release and freedom of finally letting go, of complete and utter acceptance, of having what you wanted, what you yearned for without worrying about being weak. Open. Vulnerable. The immediate and absolute rush of longing was so potent it clouded her thoughts, elation springing from tasting Heath on the tip of her tongue. Nothing compared to *this.* Why had she guarded herself from her feelings for so long? What she'd missed…

Heath broke the kiss, breathing heavily as he cradled her face. "Jewel. We need to think about this—"

She could barely catch her breath. "We will." She dragged her hands up his neck, smoothing her thumbs along his jaw. "But not now. I deserve now. We both do."

Heath didn't move, and she wasn't even sure he breathed. A lock of wet black hair clung to his face and when he finally lifted his chin, the vulnerability in his gaze seized her heart. His handsomeness was almost too perfect, but in that moment, he looked utterly human and the slightest bit lost.

I'm here, she wanted to scream. *Stop searching.*

Her heart pounded fast, but her blood felt sluggish. Was he going to stop worrying about others and live in the moment with her…just this once?

HEATH'S RESISTANCE MELTED as he stared into Jewel's expressive eyes. Mouths touched. Pressed, sought, then slid away. And his lids lowered. The intense moment defied reality, and he wanted to live in that dark limbo without his bearings.

Jewel snuggled closer as Heath shifted and the kiss began again, the angle different, more direct, less testing. *Bold. Fervent. Natural.* The words slipped through Heath's mind, and he nodded slightly. Yes. That was it. *Natural.*

Right.

With his mouth pressed against Jewel's, Heath explored the space between them with a slight touch of his tongue. Her ardent response was instantaneous.

And that heady combination of vulnerability and unvarnished passion pulled him under with the unstoppable force of the flash flood. It was like nothing he'd ever experienced before, and she cradled his face, letting him lose himself in the flavor, the texture, the heat of her mouth on his.

Then he opened his eyes. *What am I doing?*

Their eyes met, and Heath ached to lower his lids again, even as he lifted his mouth and dropped his hands from her body.

"Jewel," he whispered.

"Don't stop," she pleaded, and her eyes begged.

"We have to," he said more firmly.

He forced himself away, and his hands fell to his sides, guilt swamping him as he thought of Kelsey.

When her lashed lifted, the confusion in her eyes flayed him. She reached out, but he shook his head and stepped backward. "I'm sorry."

Jewel's face was pale, and Heath could see her pulse hammering in her throat. His own pulse pounded in his head, and a bead of sweat trickled down his spine under the shirt he wore beneath his plaid coat.

"You're a beautiful woman. Headstrong, passionate, stubborn and challenging."

Jewel's eyes snapped to Heath's, and he saw a flash of joy in their dark brown depths before it flickered out with the realization that there was more. He wasn't finished.

"But I'm with Kelsey. Engaged to marry her..."

Jewel didn't respond. Not at all. Not a glance. Not a word.

"Jewel?" The question was soft. But he knew. He could feel the connection between them, dark, slippery. Dangerous.

She turned and lifted her eyes to his. Eyes filled with the same longing drumming inside him. His breath caught in his throat as he stepped away. He had to move away from her.

What had he done?

She wasn't just flirting, testing an attraction. She cared about him. And he was unable to give himself to her. The truth he'd been avoiding rose in his chest like an oil spill. It coated everything, stopping his heart.

"I can't," he whispered.

"You can." She closed the distance to meet him. Her eyes shone, and her lips trembled.

For a moment, he let the possibility pull at him again. Could he? He shut his eyes and tried to imagine walking away from Kelsey. Daryl's words echoed in his head. Choose wisely. There are no takebacks for Lovelands.

He had a responsibility to safeguard Kelsey, and Jewel, until he settled his heart.

"I can't, Jewel," he said more firmly. "I won't." He would be strong and not lose the battle in this moment. Not even for Jewel.

"You already have." Her voice was mild, but the pain was sharp, making her mouth twist. The agony on her face echoed in his chest. She was reflected in him and he in her. When she was in front of him, she was the only thing he could see. But he needed to view the bigger picture, his life, his future. Hard to do when she filled his vision.

He closed his eyes briefly and took a deep breath. When he opened them again, only resolve remained.

"It was wrong, Jewel. On so many levels. We both know it. Neither of us can afford to let it happen again. It *won't* happen again." He kept his hands clenched at his sides, holding firm. "We're only as good as the promises we keep. And I've made a promise. You don't want a man who doesn't keep his promises."

"I don't want a man who doesn't know his heart—or follow it, either."

A muscle in his jaw jumped, and his lips firmed. "Even if I weren't engaged to Kelsey, our loyalties lie with our families. Would you choose me over your brothers? Your ranch?"

After a long moment, her head dropped, and the din of the rain slowed to a patter, then ceased. "I guess we'll never know."

Without a word, he held out his hand.

"Please just go, Heath. Just go," she whispered.

"I don't want to leave you like this."

"I need you to leave me now." Her voice grew stronger.

"I won't do that," he insisted, willing her to yield.

"You already have," she said again. And when her eyes rose to his, the tender, vulnerable woman was gone, replaced by the tough cowgirl. "Go, Heath."

It was his turn to give way. "I'll be outside, checking the herd. Join me when you're ready." With a heavy heart, he turned and opened the door. Outside, the storm had abated, welcoming a rainbow of soft pastels reflected in silvery puddles.

"Heath."

Her voice stopped him before he shut the door.

She held up four fingers on both hands, silently telling him he'd won another point…but kissing her wasn't a game, and whatever the score, he knew, deep down, he'd just lost.

CHAPTER ELEVEN

JEWEL HALF LISTENED to the Flower Gala committee's debate about centerpiece flower choices, her mind returning to her explosive kiss with Heath. Almost a week had passed, and they hadn't talked about it…or talked at all. In fact, despite working closely, driving cattle from one bad pasture to worse, they'd kept their distance, rarely meeting each other's eyes.

What would they see if they looked?

The rightness of his arms around her, his lips pressed to hers, still lingered. First kisses were supposed to be awkward, but with Heath, it'd felt natural, instinctual. For once, she'd let down her guard and become free and open.

And his rejection came back to bite her. Hard. While the kiss had felt right, what they'd done to Kelsey was wrong, even if she wasn't that nice.

Jewel mashed her eyes shut, wishing she could blot out the moment he'd pushed her away, told her they were wrong, and he was promised to another.

"Mrs. Grover-Woodhouse, perhaps we should lower our voices since Jewel's trying to sleep."

Jewel opened her eyes to an innocent-faced Kelsey and, just like that, her guilt over kissing another woman's man evaporated. Kelsey might be pretty on the outside, but she had a bit of a mean streak, too, no matter how many "good deeds" she did around town. Why didn't Heath see through her? Were looks all that mattered to him?

Although, he had called Jewel beautiful…

She bit her lip, berating herself for being naive. He must have been caught up in the moment, the storm, the near-death experience. As for her, it'd all been real. More fool her.

Clearly, he preferred someone domestic, refined, wife

material, like Kelsey. To win Heath's affection, would she have to change, or could he accept her for who she was?

Then again, did she even want to win his heart? With their families feuding and her focus on career, not relationships, it was odd to consider it, especially since his rejection at the shack still stung.

"Are we boring you, Ms. Cade?" From her seat at the head of the committee's table, Mrs. Grover-Woodhouse stared down the length of her impressive nose at Jewel.

"No, ma'am."

Beneath the table, Sierra lightly nudged Jewel's foot in sympathy.

"Then would you share your thoughts about flower selections?" Mrs. Grover-Woodhouse's pen hovered over her notepad.

"She probably thinks skunkweed's a flower," whispered Kelsey's best friend, Lara, behind a raised hand, loud enough to catch Jewel's ear and make Kelsey and her gang snicker.

"You're the skunk!" Sierra hissed. Her outflung hand knocked over her tea, sending the tepid fluid racing across the table, straight at Lara's designer dress.

Lara shot out of her chair. "You did that on purpose!"

"Calm down. We're grown women. No one is tossing tea at each other," Mrs. Grover-Woodhouse said repressively.

"Or putting down other people, or laughing at them like playground bullies," asserted Sierra, staring a blustering Lara and a sober-faced Kelsey in the eye while she wiped up the mess.

Jewel dabbed up the last of the tea and tossed the napkins.

"Although skunks are actually really sweet," Sierra whispered in Jewel's ear at the trash bin. "You should come to my practice and see the abandoned baby I'm raising. You can bottle-feed him."

Jewel nodded, returning Sierra's smile, then lowered her voice. "Thanks for defending me back there."

Sierra's ponytail swung as she shrugged. "We're sisters now. We'll always have each other's back."

"You bet."

Jewel's heart swelled as they took their seats. A sister. When her mother married Boyd Loveland, she'd thought only of what her family would lose. Now she saw all they stood to gain. The Lovelands were good people. She adored little Noah and Emma, worried about Daryl's teetering marriage and Cole's broken heart, enjoyed Sierra's company and Heath…well…that was another level of emotion altogether.

"Back to flowers. Ms. Cade—your thoughts?"

Jewel gnashed her teeth at Mrs. Grover-Woodhouse's persistence. Her former principal had never been one to concede a point. Jewel's hands clenched on her lap. Skunkweed her butt… Then an unconventional idea struck her. "The Flower Gala is to celebrate flowers, right?"

Several of the women exchanged long looks, but Jewel refused to be intimidated, to be run off to hide on the ranch.

She had worth, even in the outside world.

"Are you making a joke at our expense, Ms. Cade?" Mrs. Grover-Woodhouse's penciled eyebrows rose nearly to her hairline.

"No," Jewel rushed to say. "It's just, I was thinking that all kinds of flowers should be celebrated, not just the fancy ones like roses."

"Last year we created an entire bower of white roses donated from my family's garden," Kelsey said. "Many considered it the most beautiful gala ever."

Jewel spied a few of the women rolling their eyes, and

the sight bolstered her. "I was thinking that this year, we could celebrate local wildflowers."

"Roadside weeds?" sneered Lara.

"This function's raising money for wildlife conservation. What better way to honor it than by putting a spotlight on the everyday beauty we rarely take time to notice?" Jewel asserted.

An excited murmur broke out. Sierra turned to Jewel, her blue eyes bright. "We've never done anything like this, and I'm all for celebrating what's in the wild."

Jewel smiled. "You like it?"

Sierra grinned back. "I love it! Leave it to you to shake things up."

At last the conversations died down and Mrs. Grover-Woodhouse tapped her pen to bring them to attention. "Your idea has merit, Ms. Cade. I suggest we vote. Mind you, if we go with this theme, we'll also need to rethink our previously agreed upon tea rose garlands. All in favor of using local wildflowers to decorate the gala, raise your hands."

Jewel peered beneath lowered lashes, holding her breath. Would the women approve of her idea? Of her? To her amazement, all but Kelsey, her two minions and Mrs. Grover-Woodhouse's hands lifted. Air rushed from Jewel's lungs.

"Tied!" Lara crowed. "Now let me explain why wildflowers would be the worst—"

"Ahem. I haven't voted yet." Mrs. Grover-Woodhouse raised her hand. "Wildflowers it is."

Sierra whooped, and several women shot Jewel approving nods. One reached across the table and patted her arm, saying, "Your mother would be proud."

Jewel smiled back at Judge James, her sister-in-law Amberley's mother. "I hope so."

"I know so," Judge James vowed, her certainty filling

Jewel so full of pride she thought she'd float right to the ceiling. For the first time, she belonged somewhere besides the ranch. And she sat in a chair, not a saddle, in the dressy slacks Sierra lent her, not Wranglers, and it wasn't terrible. Or scary. Or demoralizing.

In fact, it felt great.

She was more than just a ranch hand, more than the girl who'd felt "less than" because of her-father's lack of attention. What's more, she earned respect by being herself, not by how well she roped or rode.

"Moving on to our previously tabled discussion about punch," Mrs. Grover-Woodhouse announced.

Jewel raised her hand. She'd found her voice in the real world and wouldn't lose it again. Besides, she really wanted a "tacky" Mountain Dew sherbet punch and what's more, she suspected she wasn't alone…

In fact, she didn't feel alone at all.

The rest of the meeting sped by and before she knew it, Jewel lounged in her family's living room, regaling James and Sofia with her triumphs.

"Javi's going to love the Mountain Dew sherbet punch." Sofia, stretched out on the sofa, tipped her head back and closed her eyes in bliss as James massaged her swollen feet. "Though he'll be up all night with the caffeine."

"We're using caffeine-free. I came up with that one, too." Jewel's chest puffed ever so slightly as she fidgeted with the parenting magazines on the wagon-wheel coffee table.

"Sounds like you had a lot of good ideas." James's fingers kneaded Sofia's arch.

"Heath would agree. He asked for my herd health report."

James's hands stilled. "You didn't give it to him, did you?"

Jewel shrugged. "Why not? Someone might as well read it after I went to the bother of writing it."

"That information belongs to the Cades." James slid out from under Sofia's feet and paced to the fireplace, where he stared at a wedding picture of their mother and father. "Nothing's changed just because Ma's married a Loveland."

"Don't be silly, James." Sofia sat up and slid her feet into fuzzy pink slippers. "We're a family now. Haven't you learned you can't keep things from changing?"

"Doesn't mean I'll stop trying." He strode to the kitchen counter and returned with a postcard he dropped in Jewel's lap.

"Have you even read my report yet?" She eyed the picture of a lit-up Eiffel Tower.

James ducked his head. "I've been busy."

"How? The cousins are here…you have lots of help."

"He's not delegating," Sofia interjected, wagging a finger at him in a silent *tsk tsk tsk*.

"You're kidding, right?"

At Jewel's question, James frowned. "Justin's doing an excellent job, but he's needed at Fresh Start, too. I can't turn everything over to him."

"How about me? Will you be able to give up control if you name me range boss?"

Jewel's heart sank when James cleared his throat and pointed at the postcard instead of answering. "Read it."

"Yes, boss," she grumbled, then skimmed her mother's handwriting on the back. "Sounds like they're having a good time," she mused aloud, then stopped on the last sentence and reread it. Her eyes flew to James. "What's this about an arbitration hearing?"

James dropped a thick cream-colored envelope in her lap. Their attorney's name appeared in the return address. When she pulled out the missive, her hands shook slightly as she read.

"Before the trial, Ma and Boyd want us to try to settle

the water access dispute with the Lovelands in arbitration." James took the letter from her, refolded it and slipped it back inside the envelope. "It's scheduled for this Friday."

Jewel's mind raced as she considered the ramifications of the Brahmans gaining access to the Crystal River. Their gut-fill looked worse, despite the recent deluge, the watering spots as dry as ever. If they could cross the easement, her cattle would be saved.

Her cattle.

The thought brought her up short.

The Brahmans belonged to Heath and the rest of the Lovelands, not her. Striving alongside them through this miserable, dry summer, however, bonded her with the gentle gray beasts. Despite everything she and Heath were trying to avoid, their worlds were subconsciously colliding on every level. A traffic accident in slow motion, destined and inescapable.

The door opened, and Justin sauntered inside. He carried with him the faint scent of leather and exhaust from one of his motorcycle rides.

"What are the chances we'll settle with the Lovelands?" Jewel asked.

"Nil." An easy chair creaked when Justin sat and bent down to pull off his boots. "Their cattle used to destroy our property, trample our forage and crossbreed with our herd, to name a few of the reasons why we won't give them back the easement. The main one, though, is that they're Lovelands."

"The feud is over." Jewel slapped her hand on her thigh for emphasis.

"Just because we know who really started it doesn't excuse the decades of strife in between," James said with his annoying calm. "Remember the year they dammed up the Crystal River and nearly wiped out our herd?"

"Rotten Lovelands," Justin muttered.

"That's all in the past." Jewel turned the postcard over in her hands. "We should hear their side."

"The only side that counts is ours." James gestured to Justin. "Keep your boots on. I've got something to show my range boss outside."

The moment the door closed behind them, Jewel stormed to the kitchen, flicked on the faucet and filled a glass with cold water. She was so tense there was a good chance parts of her body would start breaking. "Bossy, controlling older brother!"

How dare he? She'd spent her whole life proving she was worthy of the range boss position and James all but threw it in her face that he was giving the job to Justin.

"Would you mind grabbing me a glass, too?" called Sofia.

When Jewel returned and passed it over, Sofia gave her a grateful smile. "Sorry to put you out. My doctor wants me off my feet as much as possible."

"It's no trouble." The cool water did little to lower Jewel's temperature. James wanted to get her goat by calling Justin his range boss and it worked. He'd promised to make the formal announcement at the end of the summer. Would he honestly consider her for the job over Justin?

"I thought James was controlling before," Sofia said, and sighed. Her large brown eyes, so like Javi's, met Jewel's. "But this—" she gestured to the pillows he'd heaped around her, cocooning her "—is prison. He doesn't even want me attending the Flower Gala."

"Are you going to listen to him?"

Sofia snorted. "I'll listen to the doctor. If I'm cleared, you'll be seeing me boot scootin' with the best of 'em—or waltzing…guess that's more like a gala, right?"

Jewel shrugged. She'd never attended it or any dance. "How do you deal with him? He's such a control freak."

Sofia laughed. "Can't disagree. But I know it comes

from love…and fear. He doesn't want anything to happen to the family after losing Jesse."

Jewel's heart throbbed painfully at her deceased brother's name. "I thought he was getting better."

Sofia waved her free hand. "Baby steps."

"I'm glad you have patience. I don't."

"I also love him. He's not perfect and neither am I. Mostly I just don't take him seriously. Usually, I nod and then do what I want anyway."

"You two seem so different," Jewel observed, thinking of her and Heath. He had a sensitive side Jewel lacked…or at least, hid, whereas she had an aggressive side he only seemed to reveal when arguing with her.

"We're alike where it counts." Sofia tapped her heart. "We both value and want the same things."

Jewel sipped her water, considering what she wanted in life. Before, it was only the range boss position. Independence. Respect. Now she found herself considering a bigger future, one with a husband, children. Heath's influence? "When did you know James was 'the one'?"

"He drove me crazy at first." Sofia's lips twisted wryly, and her eyes took on a dreamy expression. "But then, when we took Javi to cut down a Christmas tree, James sang the wrong words to 'O Tannenbaum' and admitted he forgot to bring the marshmallows for the hot chocolate. He wasn't as in control as he pretended and wanted to change. Falling in love isn't really falling, it's more like two people bending until they meet in the middle."

Jewel nodded. These past few weeks, she and Heath had made concessions on the range, learning to give and take, trust and support. Could their bending extend to their personal lives, too? "You believe people can change?"

Sofia nodded vigorously. "Even you Cades."

Jewel laughed. It did seem a tall order.

"So…are you talking about someone special?" Sofia's

voice rose at the end, teasing, and warmth flooded Jewel's cheeks. "Someone you've been working with perhaps?"

"Me? That's crazy talk." Jewel stood, trying, and failing, to look indignant.

Sofia swatted Jewel's leg as she passed by. "Your secret is safe with me. Though your brother may have already guessed. Why do you think James is so worried about you working over there?"

Jewel gaped at her. "James is worried about me?"

"He doesn't want to lose you to the Lovelands. He wouldn't know how to manage without you."

Fussing baby noises emerged from the monitor beside Sofia. She heaved herself to her feet. "Duty calls." She caught Jewel in a hug and whispered, "Remember. It's your life, not your brothers'. And if you want to change, don't be afraid to try."

Jewel watched Sofia disappear upstairs, then strode outside. Leaning against the porch banister, she stared at the stars, noting the constellations. Depending on the seasons, they changed positions. And the moon, it waxed and waned, but it was always the moon. Could she change, become more vulnerable and open, without losing her strength? Her independence?

Sofia said falling in love was more like bending to meet in the middle, but if Heath didn't bend, too, she'd fall flat on her face.

CHAPTER TWELVE

"ARE YOU TWO all set for the night?"

At Daryl's question, Heath dropped another log on the fire, turned and followed his brother's gaze to Jewel. A brisk scraping sound rose as she scrubbed the cast-iron skillet in the trickling stream. The sweet scent of their dessert, a berry cobbler, lingered in the twilight while the bulky shapes of the cattle meandered in the purpling gloom.

"Fine." Heath brushed the dirt from his jeans, his movements jerky, stiff. For the past week, he'd been confused and furious with himself for kissing Jewel and betraying Kelsey. Tough as it was, he'd done his best to distance himself from Jewel, until now…

Daryl lifted one thick eyebrow. "Fine, huh?"

Heath nodded fast.

"So why are you acting funny?"

"I'm not." As he and Jewel had wandered deeper into backcountry, laboring to save the herd and ranch, it'd been nearly impossible to avoid her. Try as he might, he thought of their kiss nonstop, his wish to repeat it followed by a full lashing of guilt. He'd betrayed Kelsey and trifled with Jewel's heart—an unforgivable act. For a person who considered himself a peacekeeper, he'd done his share of stirring up trouble.

"You're wearing one of your Sunday shirts."

Heath glanced down, astonished. "Must have grabbed it in a hurry."

"Um-hum." Daryl's eyes narrowed. "And you're smelling like you used one of those shower gels instead of plain bar soap."

"Gets pretty odorous up here."

"Ain't heard you complain about it before."

Heath shoved his hands in his pockets. "What are you getting at, dude?"

"Are you okay being alone with Jewel tonight? Those coyotes might have moved off, or I could ask Jewel to sit with the kids if LeAnne's gone out while I stay here with you instead."

"I'm fine being alone with her. She's just a ranch hand."

Daryl's piercing blue eyes called Heath out for a liar. Jewel was much more than that. They'd grown closer as they'd worked together, traversing the property to higher ground in search of a consistent, elusive water supply.

Too close.

And now they'd spend an entire night alone together—something he'd managed to avoid since their kiss.

"Just a ranch hand," Daryl echoed before swinging himself into his saddle. "Now how come I don't believe that?"

"Overactive imagination?"

"Nah." Daryl retrieved his flask, drank a long gulp, then tucked it back in his saddlebag. "All I need is these." He pointed at his eyes, then swung his fingers between Heath and an approaching Jewel. "Night, Jewel."

"Night, Daryl," she called. When Daryl trotted away, she turned to Heath. "What was up with the eye pointing?"

"Nervous tic." Heath shook out his bedroll and laid it on the soft, grassy soil. It'd been a relief to discover this still-green pasture. While not lush, it had enough water and forage to keep the herd going for a few days if they stretched it. After that, things only got tougher. The next watering spot was a steady four-hour climb the weaker cattle might not make.

"Never saw him do it before." Jewel unrolled her bedding, then sat, cross-legged, on the shiny outer material. "What's he nervous about?"

"The coyotes," Heath blurted. There. Lie number two.

Jewel was turning him into a dishonest person in more ways than one.

Jewel pointed to the rifle she'd retrieved with her sleep gear. "If we didn't scare them enough earlier, we'll give 'em a good reminder tonight."

"Their pack's been following us for weeks." Heath grabbed the guitar case strapped to Destiny's saddle, opened it and pulled out his acoustic. "And growing bolder."

"They see some easy pickings. The cattle are getting weaker." Jewel yanked out the elastic bands on the ends of her braids and loosened her plaits.

Heath sat and strummed a D chord. "Not much we can do about it unless we reach an agreement at Friday's arbitration."

Jewel snorted. "Those mosquitoes have a better chance." She pointed to the bats swooping through the sky, gulping down the insects stirring the warm air. They'd appeared after the rainfall and seemed to be making up for lost time by swarming anything that moved.

"Or we could just drive the herd to the Crystal River ourselves."

"Is that why you kissed me?"

Heath's fingers froze on the strings. When he lifted his eyes, Jewel's stricken expression pierced him through. "I kissed you because I wanted to, not to get something."

"You said it was wrong."

"It was, but it doesn't change how much I wanted to kiss you."

"Do you still?"

"So, we're going there, huh?"

"Pretty much."

He began playing Darius Rucker's "Don't Think I Don't Think About It." The notes floated on the still, dry air, his music speaking for him.

"Guess that's my answer?" Jewel asked when he finished the song.

"This isn't easy for me."

"You think it's easy for me?" Jewel jumped to her feet and pointed down at him. Her loose hair flamed around her face as bright as the fire. "You're the last person I want to care about!"

His mouth dropped open. "You care about me?"

She whirled around, her back hunched. "Forget it."

"I will not!" He laid down his guitar and stalked toward her. Irritating cowgirl. She never quit trying to call the shots.

He stepped in front of her, angling his head left, then right, until he caught her eye. "Talk to me, Jewel."

"I got nothing more to say."

"Maybe I do."

"Whatever it is, I don't want to hear it." She began to walk off again, her momentum checked when he dodged in front of her.

"You darn well will hear it!" he shouted, surprising himself. "Maybe I care about you, too!"

Instead of looking happy about his declaration, Jewel shoved him hard in the chest, catching him off guard so he tumbled backward and landed on the seat of his Wranglers. "What was that for?"

One side of her tense mouth lifted. "The 'maybe' part."

"Fine." He extended his hand and she tugged him to his feet. He was amused at her cheek and determination to drag the truth from him. "There is no 'maybe' part. I do care. I just can't do anything about it."

Jewel's shoulders drooped. "Because of Kelsey."

"Because of lots of things." He stared into Jewel's heart-shaped face, smudged from the days' work, the circles under her eyes from lack of sleep, and marveled. How had he won the affection of such a tough, tenacious big-hearted cowgirl? They argued more than they got along, and he hadn't kept the peace with her the way he did with other women. In fact, he'd been downright antagonistic at times. Maybe that was a truer, more honest side of him. Jewel made him see himself, and his relationships, in a whole new light.

Before now, he'd always considered love a conditional emotion. A transaction. If he made someone's life easy, they'd care about him. It'd never occurred to him someone might have feelings for him based on who he was, not what he did for them...and considering he was a broke range boss on a nearly bankrupt ranch, he wasn't much.

What could he offer Jewel, even if she was the one?

"Besides." He rubbed the back of his tense neck. "You never want to settle down. Unless that's changed?"

Jewel's mouth worked before she shook her head. "I don't know what I want anymore." The cresting moon illuminated the high color in her cheeks. Sympathy for her welled. She was turned inside out, just like him. "Guess we're a pair."

"Guess so." But what kind of a pair? Work partners or more? Were their feelings born of proximity or rooted in something deeper?

Heath laced his fingers in hers. "Come back to the fire. We'll talk about anything else and forget about—" he gestured between them "—this." Although he knew *he* wouldn't forget. Jewel cared about him and he cared for her, another complication to his already-difficult summer...but darned if it felt like a negative even if it was confusing as all get-out.

"Anything?"

He nodded, a sinking sensation settling heavy in his gut.

They wandered back to the sleeping bags and scooched to the ends closest to the crackling fire. When Jewel didn't speak, he picked up his guitar and played one of his originals, a tune about the roads he'd never know, the paths he'd never follow. As his fingers slid and pressed, he glanced up and met Jewel's eyes, her expression as rapt and fierce as the night he'd spied her in the Silver Spurs crowd.

When he finished, she asked, "What was the opportunity Clint chastised you for not taking?"

Heath shrugged, picking chords.

"You can say anything out here," Jewel persisted. "No one'll hear but me, and I won't repeat it." She crossed her heart. "Scout's honor."

Heath studied Jewel, wondering if he dared open up and trust her. Something in her steady brown eyes assured him.

"A Nashville producer offered me a tryout a couple weeks ago, but I had to turn it down when Cole hurt his arm. Otherwise Pa would have canceled his honeymoon."

"Did you ask them to reschedule?"

"Nah. Kelsey gave me until the end of the summer to set a date and begin planning the wedding. There wouldn't be enough time to give Nashville a real try before that to prove we could make a life there together."

"Tell Kelsey to wait. You have a gift, Heath. You're a darn fool if you don't take risks or put yourself first."

"That's selfish."

"It's honest." A lock of Jewel's hair swung forward with the force of her answer, and he couldn't resist slipping it back behind her ear, his fingers lingering on the silky tress. "You have to chase your dreams." Her voice trembled slightly.

If only it were that easy. He lost himself in Jewel's eyes for a moment, glimpsing another path, other dreams, then yanked his thoughts to a halt. If he kept going, who knew where he or Jewel would end up? He respected her too much to lead her astray. "Okay. My turn."

"Huh?"

"To ask you anything."

She sucked on her bottom lip. "I don't know about *anything*."

"That was the deal."

She drew in a deep breath, and he held his. "Okay. Fine."

"Back when we were ten, at the 4-H exhibit, why were you crying?"

A log popped in the silence while bullfrogs in the brush called to one another. Jewel didn't speak, but a tortured, pinched look crept across her face.

"It had something to do with your father," Heath prompted.

She turned away and spoke to the mountainside. "He didn't congratulate me on my blue ribbon."

"Maybe he was busy. Didn't notice."

"That's the point. He never noticed me." Her hair slid over her cheeks as she angled her head his way again and large eyes were as dark as the sky…darker as they lacked the glimmering stars. "All he cared about were his sons. No matter how well I rode or roped or shot, he never saw me. Growing up, I kept thinking if I could be as big and tall and tough as them, then my father would love me like he did my brothers…but no matter how hard I tried, I was like the shrub in the forest—he couldn't see me for the trees."

A band tightened around Heath's chest as understanding dawned. "So that's why."

"Why what?"

"Why you pretend you don't care what others think."

"I'm not pretending!"

"Yes, you are, because if you weren't, you wouldn't be trying to prove you're as good as or better than everyone all the time—to me, to your brothers, maybe even to a father who's passed on…but what about living life as if you've got nothing to prove except to yourself?"

"I am." Her half shout startled a pair of doves from

some nearby brush. They winged to a nearby tree in a panicked flap.

"You're not. Are you acting like you don't care what others think because you're independent? Or are you wanting to be independent because of what others made you believe about yourself?"

"I'm the only one I can depend on," she said, speaking the words so quietly he wasn't sure she'd said them at first.

"Why's that?"

There was another long stretch of silence, and then she said, "I won't be weak. My father hated weak people."

"Depending on others isn't a weakness." He cupped her shoulders, then slid his hands down the length of her arms, stopping to twine his fingers in hers. "I wish you'd trust me—depend on me—more."

She jerked back. "Why should I? You're about to marry Kelsey."

"Even though I haven't settled things with Kelsey, you and I can still be friends." "

Her eyes rounded, brightening slightly. "Oh, really?"

"Yes."

"Either way—" she lay down and stared skyward "—I'll never rely on anyone."

"Because they'll let you down like your father?"

She squeezed her eyes shut, and her chest stilled as if she held her breath.

"I'm sure he loved you."

"The day he died, he asked to speak to each of his children." Her voice was soft, almost inaudible.

"What did he say to you?"

"Nothing." Tears seeped from beneath her lashes, and he ached, knowing how much those tears, her confessions, cost her.

"Were you too late?"

"No." When she opened her glittering eyes, they swam

with pain. “He never asked for me. Even then, I didn’t matter.”

“Jewel.” Heath’s heart turned over heavily for the forsaken daughter, the girl who’d fought and failed to win her father’s affection. He set down his guitar, stretched out beside her and pressed his forehead to hers.

“It doesn’t matter.”

She started to look away, but he placed his fingers on her cheeks, stopping her. “It matters. You felt rejected.”

“Don’t tell me how I felt.”

He lifted his hand and pushed her long hair away from her face so he could see her better. “Then tell me how you felt.”

“I felt unworthy. Unlovable!” she cried, and he gathered her close, pressing her cheek to his thudding heart.

“You’re anything but unlovable.” He moved his hand to her chin and gently raised her head to kiss her forehead. Never had he spoken truer words. They poured from his heart without filter. Like a tornado, Jewel uprooted his life and twisted his emotions, sending him in a disorienting spiral.

He was falling for Jewel. Did he love her?

“The only person who ever really loved me was Jesse.” Her body tensed up and a sad quietness overcame her, thick like fog.

He moved one hand to the back of her head, guiding her face to his chest, and wrapped his other around her hand. “He was the closest to you in age?”

“Justin was three minutes older than Jesse, but age didn’t have much to do with it. Jesse was like me…an outsider. He wasn’t much for cowboying, though, so Pa didn’t pay him much mind, either. He was my best friend.” Her voice caught, and he brushed the damp from her cheek. “After he died, I was lost. Once I heard you singing, my heart beat again.”

Heath's arms tightened around Jewel. Her words struck him like the first press of a finger to a keyboard, sending a pulse, a vibration, through him.

"That's why you shouldn't give up singing." She leaned her forehead against him for a moment and then looked up again. "You touch people's lives…like mine."

"I learned that young. Playing music with my mother kept her calm." His heart tossed in his chest, caught in the storm of his emotions. "She had mental health and addiction issues. I was the only one who could distract her."

"You were her favorite."

"It wasn't a good thing." Heath's cheek slid over the side of Jewel's head as he inhaled the faint remnants of her shampoo. "My childhood was all about keeping the peace. Soothing her, catering to her."

"No wonder."

"No wonder what?"

"You never learned it's okay to put yourself first sometimes."

"I did once. At Cole's sixteenth birthday. He asked Ma to stay away because he was afraid she'd embarrass him in front of his friends. It set her off. I'd never seen her so bad. Crying, ranting, then she got quiet. Too quiet. She just lay down and looked up at the ceiling. She wouldn't talk to me. Look at me." He paused as the words, the memory, echoed in his mind. They bounced off his brain before falling down the hole into his heart to slowly leak into his gut, eating at him. "I should have stayed with her, but I really wanted to go to the party."

"I don't blame you." Jewel pulled back and peered up at him. "You were a kid."

"While I was having fun at the bonfire, she left her room and walked to the pool." His throat felt as if it was closing off. "And drowned herself."

Jewel's hand lifted, and her fingers sifted through his hair. "That's horrible."

Not trusting himself to speak again, he nodded. His head swam, and dark spots clouded his vision. In the distance, a lone coyote yipped while the cattle rustled through the tall grass, seeking a resting spot.

"It was horrible of *me*," he whispered, then leaned his cheek into her palm, comforted, somehow, by the strength of her hands, the calluses that bore witness to a hard life, one tested like his. "I could have prevented it."

"Maybe you could have stopped her that time...but she wanted to kill herself." Jewel's lashes fluttered shut briefly, then reopened. "If not that night, then another. You can't blame yourself for someone else's actions."

"Putting myself first led to tragedy." He exhaled deeply, rubbing a hand along his jaw.

"That was a fluke."

"It was confirmation." His voice cracked. "Always put others' needs ahead of my own."

"That's crazy." She thumped him hard in the chest, as if performing CPR. Was she trying to save his life? "You love music. If you only did it for your mother, you would have stopped playing long ago."

"After her suicide, music was how I coped. It held me together when my family fell apart." His eyes drifted from hers to stare into the gloom. "When I sing it sends every trouble and worry I have to the wind."

"Which is why you can't just give it up to please Kelsey or anyone else." She turned her hand under his, so their palms touched, and their eyes shifted from their joined hands to slowly meeting each other in the dim light. "In the end, you only regret the chances you didn't take. Someone wise told me to live my life as if I only had to prove it to myself."

"Wise, huh?" One side of his mouth lifted as he considered the advice he'd given her.

"Very wise," she said through a yawn.

In the silence, her body gradually relaxed against his, her breathing growing regular. In a moment, he'd let her go, but not yet. Not when it felt too good, too right, to keep her close.

He rested his chin atop her head, feeling as though he held the most precious thing in the world. A truth-speaking, tough-talking cowgirl with a heart as big as Mount Sopris. It shone right out of her like a spotlight.

Jewel.

He couldn't deny the bond between them anymore. Unlike Kelsey, who'd always shut down his music ambitions, Jewel had taken a keen interest from the start. She stopped chattering when he played, listened closely, her eyes glistening, her tough outer shell gone. She was the first person in his life to see how much music really meant to him.

Should he consider her advice and travel to Nashville when things quieted down on the ranch? If he did, that'd mean postponing setting the wedding date and planning it as Kelsey expected, and delay starting the secure, lucrative job that'd also save his family's ranch. It'd also mean leaving Jewel, a complicated woman he had no right to care about. If they got together, it'd throw everyone's life in disarray, upsetting Kelsey, his family and her family.

The advice Jewel had thrown back in his face, to live his life for himself, returned to him. She had a point…

And possibly, his heart.

Did his life belong to him or was it a selfish thought destined to lead down another dark road?

You only regret the chances you didn't take, Jewel had said.

Was Jewel a chance he'd regret not taking?

CHAPTER THIRTEEN

"SILENCE!" THUNDERED THE ARBITRATOR, Wilhelmina Gaynor, momentarily quieting the rising Loveland and Cade voices for the third time in twenty minutes.

Jewel lifted her hair from her neck in the humid conference room and shot Heath a quick look across the table. He shrugged his broad shoulders, as if to say *this is pointless.* They should be herding cattle to another water source this morning, not wasting time trying to budge each other on century-old positions. Their parents had demanded this last-ditch effort to settle the water access rights before next week's trial, though, leaving everyone with no choice but to attend.

Pointless indeed.

They'd begun quarrelling from the moment they sat in rigid molded plastic chairs that didn't fit Jewel's body shape in any way. In fact, the divide only seemed to widen. She shifted to ease her stiff back.

"We must proceed in an orderly fashion," decreed Mrs. Gaynor with a pompous air. She was eccentric-looking, with too-short bangs and frizzy gray hair that puffed over her ears. Yet she also had a stately, delicate face, and implacable gray eyes that could look right through you or pin you to a wall as she was doing. Her gaze swiveled between the Lovelands, clumped on one side of the table, and the Cades, on the other. "I believe James Cade was speaking last."

James lifted his chin. "Thank you, Mrs. Gaynor. As I was saying, no proof exists that our ancestor's brother, the judge who rescinded the Lovelands' easement to the Crystal River, acted with corrupt or malicious intent."

"Bank records show a ten-thousand-dollar deposit in his

account a week after the trial," drawled Maverick, who'd withdrawn from a major rodeo event to attend today.

"Could be for anything." Jared tore the plastic lid off a creamer and dumped its contents into his coffee cup. "Besides, he was our relative. Why would we need to bribe him? Makes no sense."

"Or it was a thank-you to him for giving our family payback since they blamed us for Cora's Tear's disappearance," Sierra countered. "And Maggie Cade's death."

"Our family had good reason for those beliefs." James leaned forward and flattened his palms on the table. The skin around his knuckles blanched. "Everett Loveland was found beside Maggie's body. No one knew of their secret love or the baby on the way. Since my family assumed Maggie was happily betrothed to Clyde, and her brooch was gone, it seemed likely Everett, who'd left his railroad job without explanation, had come upon her and murdered her for Cora's Tear."

"What you believe is different from what you know, and what you know is different from what you can prove." Travis straightened one of the stars on his county sheriff's uniform collar. "Your ancestors strung up Everett Loveland even though he didn't have the jewel on him. No questions. No trial. Vigilante justice at its worst. We ought to demand restitution for his cold-blooded murder, too."

The noise in the room swelled again in a swift crescendo, all shouting a chorus of—

"Hotheaded Cades."

"Stubborn Lovelands."

The adjudicator pounded on the table. "Name-calling gets us nowhere. Katlynn Brennan and her team on her show *Scandalous History* proved Maggie buried Cora's Tear on Loveland property and was murdered by her betrothed, Clyde Farthington. The unwarranted hanging of Everett Loveland is certainly worth our consideration."

"Not to mention the Cades broke their family members out of jail before they could be tried for Everett's killing." Travis's heavy boots stomped across the floor as he headed for a water cooler, grabbed a paper cup and filled it. "The pair became outlaws, harassing our ranch, vandalizing it for decades, and never faced punishment for their crimes."

"Indeed." Mrs. Gaynor eyed the Cades long and hard while Jewel mulled Travis's points.

She'd always believed her family was wronged by the Lovelands. Seeing it from their perspective, though, shifted the balance of blame and challenged her loyalty. Their family had suffered as much as her own. While she wasn't the make-peace-not-war type like Heath, the time had come to lay down their arms. The Lovelands weren't their enemies, especially Heath.

Her heart stumbled as she pictured his fervent expression when he'd confessed he cared about her. Did he mean it romantically or in a more general way, like a stepbrother?

And how did this factor into his relationship with Kelsey? He'd sworn nothing was settled between them.

"Did these offenses enter into your restitution calculations?" Mrs. Gaynor asked the Lovelands. "Or should more damages be added?"

"Five million is already too much." James's foot began to tap a swift staccato on the floor. "It's based on unreliable profit projections. And we don't have that much fluid equity. We'd have to sell off our land."

"You could sell Cora's Tear." When Cole leaned forward, his head brushed the domed light fixture dangling over the table, sending it swinging. "The auction house Christie's sold a thirty-five-carat sapphire for seven million, and it wasn't even a brooch made by famous German jewelers or historical."

"Cora's Tear belongs to Jewel!" Justin rose slightly in

his seat, knuckles planted on the table. "It's her to use and pass down to her daughter."

"Jewel told me she's never marrying." Travis crumpled his empty paper cup, paced to the trash bin and chucked it inside.

She flushed as Heath's deep blue eyes probed hers, the same eyes she'd woken to on the range. He'd been lying on his side, up on an elbow staring down at her, his chagrined smile when she'd caught him endearing.

She'd stare at him all day herself if he weren't already bound to Kelsey. *If* he was bound to Kelsey…

Did she dare let go of her independence and become more vulnerable, show her softer side, to be with him?

"A lady has a right to change her mind," Heath said, his gaze locked with hers.

"Who's a lady?" snorted Jared, earning him a hard elbow to his side. He doubled over with an "oof" then gasped, "See!"

"Mess with the bull…" Jewel curled in all but her index and pinkie fingers to form horns, waved them at him, then shoved her hand below the table when she caught Heath's mouth drop. Shoot. She no longer wanted to be just a rough-riding cowgirl, but a woman who could act like a lady, too. If only it weren't so darn hard…

"Cora's Tear would still be lost if Katie-Lynn and I hadn't found it," Cole asserted, using Katlynn's original name before she'd changed it as part of her transformation from country mouse to Hollywood star. The sadness accompanying any mention of his ex tugged down the corners of his mouth. "We deserve a finders' fee."

"I can agree to that." James nodded stiffly.

The arbitrator's sudden smile revealed child-sized teeth. "What do you believe is a fair amount?"

James reached in his pocket, then tossed a dollar bill at Cole. "How's that?"

Instantly, the room exploded in shouts with Cole accusing James of being a cheap so-and-so and Justin swearing Travis was no kind of lawman to be a part of this gang of thieves.

"Quiet!" hollered the unlikeliest of voices.

Mouths snapped shut and all eyes swerved to Heath. Gone was the easygoing family peacekeeper. In his place stood an avenging angel. With his black hair falling over his lowered brow, his symmetrical, fine-featured face set, he was imposing and otherworldly handsome. His blue eyes glinted with hellfire, intense and captivating. He looked ready to wield Saint Michael's sword into battle. "We haven't heard Jewel's thoughts."

"We know her thoughts." James brushed a hand over his thick hair, dismissive. "We're family."

"You don't know everything about her." Heath's gaze lingered on Jewel, and she stuffed her fidgeting hands in her pockets, willing the heat creeping up her neck to stop. Heath, who never fought anyone *but* her, was now fighting *for* her.

"You keeping secrets from us, Jewel?" Jared asked.

She shrugged. "Not all my business is yours."

"The heck it's not," James rejoined, his confidence in his right to know and control everything on clear display.

Aggravating brother.

"The heck it is." Jewel shifted inside her stiff dress shirt. "I don't have to think and act and speak just like all of you because I'm a Cade."

"What would Pa say?"

Jewel flinched at James's reminder. "Since it's me," she murmured, low so only her brothers could hear, "he probably wouldn't notice."

Justin reached across Jared to squeeze her rigid arm. "Don't say that, honey."

"You know it's true!" she said beneath her breath. "He

only paid you boys any attention. As for me, I just needed to mind my manners and wear a dress on Sunday."

"That's not how we feel." Jared added his hand to Jewel's arm, which, given both of her brothers' tight grip, was starting to lose sensation.

"Isn't it?" she asked, then raised her voice loud enough for the table to hear. "You want me to keep Cora's Tear for a dowry, like you think I need to pay off someone to marry me. Like nobody would take me otherwise."

If she sold the brooch, she'd settle the restitution part of the dispute and save the Loveland ranch…either making her the most naive woman west of the Mississippi for letting Heath and the Lovelands charm her, or possibly putting right an old wrong.

"The man who gets you would be the luckiest fella in the world, darlin'," James vowed so fervently, Jewel nearly forgave him his overbearing, brotherly ways.

Nearly.

"Well. It'll never happen." Heath flinched, slightly, at Jewel's declaration. "Sell Cora's Tear. Pay the Lovelands for being denied their easement these past hundred-plus years."

Gasped circled the table.

"You don't know what you're saying," James practically fire-breathed.

"You're the one who doesn't listen to her," Heath interjected, rising to Jewel's defense once more. "Have you even read her herd health report?"

James stared at Heath hard and, to give Heath credit, he didn't back down an inch. No easy feat when a Cade had his dander up.

"If you haven't, you're making a big mistake." Heath's eyes glinted, bright and hard as steel. "She knows more about cattle husbandry than all of us put together. Because of her, we haven't lost any livestock yet. Dismissing her is a mistake."

Jewel's insecurities about Heath melted away at his praise. He believed in her when her own family didn't.

"I know your game."

Heath's jaw clamped at James's accusation. "What game?"

"You're flattering Jewel to win her over to your side. You're playing her."

Jewel shot to her feet. "No one plays me. I've a mind, and heart, of my own." Her gaze flickered to Heath and then she fled.

She stormed from the room, down the hall, then burst outside into the bright sunshine of a cloudless noon. Was Heath playing her as her brother suggested? The other night he'd seemed sincere. Her judgment couldn't be that far off…on the other hand, he had a fiancée and shouldn't have held her so tenderly, kissed her so passionately and told her he cared. She swallowed back a groan, her head aching along with her tortured heart.

"Jewel!" Heath caught up to her in the parking lot and drew her to a stop, forcing her to turn around and see him. His normally tan skin had lost color and his eyes burned navy blue. "Your brother's wrong."

"Is he?" She tugged her hand free.

"I'd never lie to you."

"Why'd you hold me last night?"

Heath lowered his head and scuffed the road grit with his boot. "I couldn't let you go."

Jewel's heart added an extra beat. "Are you planning on telling Kelsey about our kiss? She deserves to know."

He nodded, and his eyes rose to meet hers. "I'll tell her everything."

"Good."

"Can I drive you back to the ranch?" Jewel nodded. They'd ridden together since her truck refused to start this morning. "I can take you to the Flower Gala, too, if you like."

Jewel considered Heath's earnest face. Should she accept? It wasn't a date by any stretch, especially since he'd most likely be bringing Kelsey, who might or might not know by then about their kiss. Awkward as heck. And if Jewel tuned up her truck, ordered a new battery, she'd probably have it working in time for the party.

On the other hand, maybe she'd like to depend on Heath a little…

Today's fiasco proved what happened when neither side gave a little. Sofia said loving someone meant bending to meet in the middle. Unless Jewel let down her guard and tried, she'd never know if she and Heath had a future, even if it meant falling…tumbling to the ground on her own, breaking her heart in the process.

CHAPTER FOURTEEN

"Hurry up, Jewel! We're going to be…"

Heath's mouth dropped open as Jewel glided down her front porch steps. In a vintage rose-colored dress that cinched in her tiny waist and belled around her shapely legs, her red hair caught up in a high ponytail that bounced around her bare, lightly freckled shoulders, she looked as though she stepped from a time machine…

Or one of his dreams.

"Catching flies?" Her brown eyes sparkled as she waltzed by, leaving a mouthwatering citrus scent in her wake.

He snapped his mouth shut and grinned. No amount of "pretty" would erase Jewel's brash manner. And he'd never want it to. "You look beautiful." Somehow, she'd even managed to pin down her cowlicks.

Yet, while she looked elegant, he preferred the natural, country-girl side of her. Strange how he'd always been more attracted to women who dressed up and wore makeup before.

Her cheeks pinkened. "This was my grandmother's prom dress."

"You've done her proud." He reached around her to pull open the door, reining in the urge put his arms around her.

"You look quite handsome yourself." When she brushed a bit of pollen from his navy coat, he spied the rose-colored polish on her short nails. She'd put in a lot of effort tonight. Was it for him? He had no right to wish it, but he hoped she'd thought of him when she'd applied the same color shining on her smiling lips. Lips he ached to kiss.

He held her hand, soft from lotion he suspected, and helped her into the cab. She didn't need assistance, yet she didn't refuse it, either. Their fingers tangled for a protracted moment before someone, male and angry-sounding, cleared his throat behind them.

"I could still drive you, Jewel."

"Hello, James." Heath turned, stuck out his hand, and James shook it stiffly. Since the failed adjudication, neither family had spoken except through their lawyers. The trial date loomed, closer than ever.

"You could ride with me." Justin sauntered up wearing a motorcycle helmet. He planted his feet apart and stared hard at Heath through his open visor. "I just have to stop by Fresh Start first."

Heath eyed him back. Whatever they might think, his intentions with Jewel were honorable. And he'd do everything in his power to keep it that way.

"I'm fine. Good grief. Can't a girl get a ride without all this fuss? Besides, I need to get there early to set up." Jewel shook her head, and her ponytail swung. "I hope *you're* not all Neanderthal protective over Sierra like this, Heath."

"Guilty." He grinned with an unrepentant shrug. "Guess all big brothers have that in common." Justin and James gave him grudging nods.

Justin closed the gap between them and cracked his knuckles. "Take care of my sister or I'll knock you into next week."

"I'll send you into next year," James added, low, joining the huddle. "Heck. You'll time-travel."

"What are you hens cackling about?" Jewel called behind them.

"Your brothers and I are just coming to an understanding," Heath said evenly, his eyes locked on James and Justin, willing them to understand he cared for Jewel.

Maybe even loved her.

Was it possible to love two women at once?

"As long as we understand each other." James stepped

away, dragging Justin back a pace. Justin shook off his brother's arm and shoved his hands in his leather jacket.

Heath nodded. "See you at the gala." He closed Jewel's door, jogged around the pickup's hood and jumped behind the wheel before the hotheaded Cades changed their minds.

"What'd they say?" Jewel flipped down the visor and peered in the small mirror as they sped down Cade Ranch's gravel drive.

"How happy they were that someone as nice as me was taking you to the gala."

"Yeah, right," she scoffed.

They stopped at the driveway's end, and he reached across to unlock the glove box with the magnetic key he kept under the dashboard. "There's tissues if you need to fix your makeup."

Jewel snorted. "I hardly know half the stuff I'm wearing. This is Sofia's doing." She waved a hand around her face, then shut the box. "And can you imagine if this were a real date?"

"They would have strung me up."

"After they'd drawn and quartered you."

Their laughter mingled with the Anne Murray country tune crooning through Heath's speakers. When they quieted, Heath sang along, asking if he could have this dance for the rest of his life.

He tore his eyes from the road to briefly glance at Jewel's delicate profile. The wind whipped through the cracked-open window, fluttering strands of hair around her freckled face. Funny how he'd thought them unattractive before. Now he wished he could kiss each one.

Maybe one day, when he'd gotten everything sorted, he'd do just that. "Will you save a dance for me, Jewel?"

He sensed her eyes on him and wondered what expression they held. Surprise? Pleasure? Annoyance? They hadn't spoken about anything deeper than their worries over the cattle recently, and he appreciated the space she gave him. He knew what he had to do but struggled to take an action that'd disappoint everyone…especially Kelsey on her big night overseeing the gala.

"Wouldn't dancing with me make Kelsey mad?"

"Yes." A herd of longhorns picked up their heads as they whizzed by. "Forget I asked."

"Asked what?" She cranked up the radio, then flopped back in her seat, arms folded across her chest.

"I'm sorry, Jewel," he said at last.

"Sorry for what exactly?"

"Not having my head on straight."

"Sounds like a *you* problem."

He laughed, a short, bitter sound. "It is, and I shouldn't make it yours."

"Appreciated."

His cell phone buzzed when they reached the main highway. "Would you mind?"

Jewel grabbed it from the console and hit the speaker button.

"Hello?" He sprayed his windshield and flipped on the wipers when they drove through a swarm of gnats.

"Heath? Can you pick me up after all? Mama wrecked her car and took mine without asking. I know I said I'd meet you, but I can't get a hold of Daddy and I need to get there early to oversee the setup. How fast can you be on the road?"

From the corner of his eye, he glimpsed Jewel kick off her heels, plant her feet on the seat and throw her arms around her raised knees. She rested her cheek atop them and turned away.

"Heath? You there?"

"Sure. Jewel and I are already on our way."

"Jewel?" Kelsey's voice rose. "Why are you driving *her*?"

"Her truck broke down, and she needed to get there early like you."

"Doesn't she have a gazillion brothers who could have driven her?"

"Am I picking you up at home?" he asked wearily, dodging the question since he had no good answer. Deep down, he'd wanted to take Jewel to the gala, wrong as it was on every level.

"Yes, and hurry. I should have been there ages ago."

Kelsey hung up, and Jewel clicked off the phone.

"Jewel, I—"

"Don't say anything."

Fifteen tense minutes later they pulled in front of Kelsey's large house. He rang the bell, then staggered backward when she opened the door and flung herself into his arms, kissing him so hard their teeth crashed together.

"Ow!" He untangled her death grip around his neck.

Kelsey peered over his shoulder at his pickup, then planted another kiss on him. "You look so handsome. I'm glad the suit I sent over fits."

"That wasn't necessary of you, though it was appreciated."

"You know how I like to spoil you." She slid her hand in his and squeezed, before nearly yanking him off his feet to sashay to the truck. Kelsey was generous to a fault, yet somehow it always seemed to come at a price.

"Hey, girl!" she crowed as Jewel scrambled into the back seat. "Don't you look pretty?" Kelsey buckled her seat belt. "The pink is gorgeous with your complexion and red hair."

Heath briefly met Jewel's eyes in the rearview mirror, then started up the engine. Funny how he hadn't even noticed Kelsey's hair, outfit or makeup, or any of the tiny details he'd quickly noted about Jewel. When had he stopped "seeing" Kelsey? Or was it that, with Jewel around, he couldn't see anyone else?

"Where'd you buy your dress? It's so retro." Kelsey leaned over and changed the radio to a Top 40 station.

"My grandmother wore it to her prom."

"You cowgirls don't care much for dresses or dances, do you?" Kelsey glanced into the back seat, then continued without waiting for an answer. "You didn't go to prom, did you, Jewel?"

"I had a horse show that weekend."

"Right. Horses. Cows. Those were always your priorities." Kelsey dropped her hand on Heath's lap, her signal for him to hold it. The color leached from his knuckles as he gripped the wheel harder. "You were always different from other girls."

"I guess," Jewel said, terse.

"That's a good thing," Heath cut in, protective and defensive of Jewel.

"Of course it is." Kelsey pulled down the visor and touched up her lipstick. "I'm sure the livestock are very appreciative."

"Kelsey," Heath growled lightly.

She looked up at the ceiling a long moment, then said, "I'm sorry, Jewel. I'm acting insecure when you haven't done one thing to make me jealous. Will you accept my apology?"

Jewel gave a strangled "yes," feeling as guilty as he did, no doubt, since they'd both given Kelsey plenty to be jealous of…

Heath spotted an enormous sedan driven by what appeared to be just a pair of knuckles. He tapped the brakes before signaling and passing it.

Kelsey twisted around in her seat. "Heath can be sooo sensitive."

"It's one of his finest qualities."

Kelsey shook her head. “Oh, Jewel. You are the queen of sarcasm.”

“That was the truth, not sarcasm.”

Heath glanced in the rearview mirror and met Jewel’s eyes again before they fled his.

“I had my ring cleaned at the jeweler.” Kelsey held up her left hand and waggled her ring finger. “Doesn’t Heath have amazing taste, Jewel?” Then, without waiting for an answer. “I can’t wait for the matching wedding band. We already have it picked out. Mine is a circle of tasteful diamonds in platinum and Heath—Heath’s is a simple, but elegant gold band. Isn’t that right, Heath?”

He made a noncommittal sound, having been shown dozens of wedding band options Kelsey cut out of bridal magazines, and stopped the car behind a sixteen-wheeler idling at a red light.

“Oh, I can’t wait until our wedding day!” Kelsey sighed. “Of course, we’ll be inviting you, Jewel, seeing as you’ve been so kind to help my sweetie this summer.”

Behind him, Jewel made a choking sound. His heart plummeted. He spied her turning away, fast, but not before he glimpsed her crushed expression.

Understanding socked him across the jaw. Hard. Jewel cared about him—romantically—feelings he didn’t deserve while beholden to Kelsey. And why was Kelsey going on like they’d set a wedding date or something? His temples throbbed.

He fought the urge to reassure Jewel…that he couldn’t marry Kelsey, not when he had feelings for her. But it’d be cruel to correct Kelsey in front of Jewel. He’d take her aside once they got inside and set the record straight.

Besides, Jewel still refused to set aside their family differences and grant his cattle passage through her property. She’d offered to sell Cora’s Tear, but her priorities lay with her family, not him.

The moment they arrived at the gala, Jewel flung open the rear door of his extended cab and stomped inside the town hall. He hopped out to open the door for Kelsey, but she hustled to a group of her squealing friends to show off her dress before he could get her alone.

The walls seemed to close in on him, fun-house style, as they stepped into the town hall. Wildflowers spilled from earthen-colored containers spaced around the hardwood floor, filled mason jars set in the center of each table and covered the entrance's lattice bower. It resembled a Garden of Eden, wild and beautiful, just like Jewel.

Wicker chairs were everywhere, and they weren't empty. Volunteers of all ages were scattered about, sitting alone or toiling in groups, talking and laughing as they worked. He dragged in a deep breath of floral scented air, grabbed a cup of sherbet punch and drained the sweet concoction in a single gulp. Beneath his dress shirt, his body grew sticky.

"Hey, you two." One of Kelsey's friends from out of town stopped by to hug them both. "Have you set a wedding date yet?"

"We have some things to settle." Heath stiffened as Jewel passed by, face averted, carrying a box of napkins.

"Christmas Eve is my preference." Kelsey waved her left hand, and her engagement ring sparkled beneath the overhead lights. "You know how I love red. And we could do white spider mums and..."

Beads of perspiration broke out across Heath's brow. He tuned out the chatter, his thoughts turning in circles faster than a twister. He needed to confront Kelsey and tell her the truth. He didn't want to marry her, but was worried about the consequences of breaking off their engagement.

Kelsey aimed a brilliant smile at him he struggled to return. The more she spoke about possible wedding dates, the deeper a hole she dug for him. He had to stop her, but how? He wouldn't shame Kelsey in front of her friends and he didn't want to hurt her.

On the other hand, he felt cornered. Herded. Trapped. Yes, he'd been headed in this direction all summer. Except his confused feelings for Jewel complicated everything, along with her advice to live his life for himself and not others. He couldn't marry Kelsey when he cared for Jewel as well—a woman who'd never have him, even if he were free, he reminded himself.

"My fiancé will help you!" Kelsey said to a man passing by with a ladder. She kissed Heath's cheek. "Now be a dear and help hang the daisy chains, will you?"

"We need to talk. Now."

Kelsey nodded, distracted, her attention on volunteers hauling in supplies. "Of course. And I'm sorry for suggesting Christmas Eve when we haven't firmed up our date yet. I guess I'm just getting excited for summer to end so we can start planning. Forgive me?"

"Let's clear some things up first."

Her eyes closed, and she breathed deep. When she opened them, they were bright with unshed tears. "I'm turning into a bridezilla already. Oh, Lord, I never want to be one of those." She squeezed his arm. "We're going to make everyone so happy. I'm thinking we plan on marrying December 12, my grandma's birthday."

She dashed away to direct the influx of supplies before he could respond, leaving Heath to follow the crew hanging the ceiling decorations. Kelsey was right. Their marriage would make lots of people happy…but what about *his* happiness? Jewel insisted he had a right to it, in whatever form it took.

A couple hours later, Heath stood with one shoulder propped against the wall. Out on the dance floor, yet another cowboy led Jewel through a two-step. The plastic sides of Heath's cup dented as the man slid an arm up her back and drew her closer. Impotent jealousy torched his chest, yet he held himself in check. He had no right to intervene, to claim Jewel as he longed to. Watching her with other men, however, was killing him.

The song ended, and with a winsome smile, Jewel slipped outside alone. He tossed his cup, pivoted and strode through the open French doors after her. The darkness obscured his view. Then a slight breeze swept clouds from the moon and he caught sight of her fluttering rose dress as she stood alone, down by the pond. She pulled her hair loose from her ponytail.

The sound of the fountain grew louder as he approached. It must have muffled his footfalls because she jumped when he called her name.

She whipped around, the same anger spewing from her he'd seen the first day she'd come to work with him. She brushed at her cheeks and glared up at him. "What are you doing here?"

"Looking for you."

Her slender white neck moved as she swallowed. "Shouldn't you be with your fiancée discussing your wedding plans?"

He took a deep, pride-eating breath. "I'm not setting a wedding date with Kelsey and we haven't picked out wedding rings." One red lock clung to her tearstained cheek. He reached out to free it, but he hesitated a mere heartbeat away from her skin.

"No?" Her eyes widened.

He swore she quit breathing…quit blinking, and for a second, so did he. In a deliberate movement, he freed the curl. "She's shown me dozens of pictures of wedding bands, but we've never gone to a jeweler."

She exhaled a shaky breath, and he slid his right hand down her arm, cradled her hand against his chest and swayed them from side to side. "Dance with me."

A little tension eased off her face. "To what music? I don't hear anything but the fountain."

"Slow drumbeat." With one finger he tapped the beat into the small of her back. "Acoustic guitar." He leaned down and hummed his favorite song in her ear. Her fresh scent intoxicated him.

She relaxed slightly, fitting perfectly into his body. In the soft, warm August air, they swayed together, moving to their own personal beat. His pounding heart kept time.

Craving more of her touch, he shifted and pressed his cheek to hers. Somehow it seemed like he floated above the ground, his blood ran warm in his veins, and he felt at peace—no, not just peaceful, invincible. For a moment, they escaped their troubles. No lawsuits, no feuding families, no struggling cattle, no fiancée—just the two of them dancing.

His song ended, his finger stopped tapping the beat, and they ceased moving from side to side. Jewel held perfectly still, keeping her hand in his, her head resting on his shoulder. He nuzzled into the warmth of her silky hair, tightening his hold. Jewel was becoming essential, like air.

He lowered his head and inhaled her scent at the nape of her neck, allowing his nose to skim along her inviting skin. Her chest rose and fell at a faster pace. His hand melted on the curve of her hip. He reeled with the force of his emotions.

"Heath," she breathed out.

Forgetting every ounce of sense he should have in this moment, his hands wandered up her back, twining in her hair, bringing her nearer still. He closed his eyes to regain some control over himself. He wanted Jewel. He needed Jewel, but he had to figure out how to handle his situation with Kelsey without hurting those he loved first.

A car door slammed shut in the parking lot, startling them. Jewel swiftly pulled back and turned toward the rumble of the engine. They watched as the red taillights glowed toward them, then away when the car accelerated onto the main road.

Her eyes met his again. "What does this mean for us?"

He lowered his head to hers. "I don't know."

The moment the words flew out of his mouth, he regretted them. Sometimes when you see the line, you think it's a good idea to cross it and be honest—until you do.

Jewel looked as if he'd slapped her. "You're such a jerk!" She whirled on her heel and stalked off. "I'll get a ride home with Justin."

Darn it. Just darn it. "Jewel!" He ran after her. "Jewel, wait."

But she didn't. He caught up to her, grabbed her arm and turned her toward him. Darn it all to heck, tears poured down her face. What was he supposed to do now?

She sniffed and wiped the tears with the back of her hand. "Are you breaking things off with Kelsey at least?"

I want to, but I can't."

The truth stuck in his throat. He wanted to tell her he would, but he couldn't. Not yet. He hadn't had a chance to process everything. The summer meant to bring him clarity, had only confused him more.

She ran a hand over her hair. The pain in her eyes knifed him in the gut. "You're a coward, you know that? I thought you were a nice guy. Sensitive. But really, you're just clueless. You're trying so hard…so hard to appease everyone that you're making everyone miserable—me, you, Kelsey." She gestured with her hands between them. "You can't make anyone happy, not even Kelsey, until you've made yourself happy, too."

Jewel brushed past him, bringing him to life. "Wait."

She glanced over her shoulder. Pink rimmed her eyes, and her shoulders slumped forward. How come he'd never seen her exhausted before? Broken.

Jewel never tired. Or bent. At least, not before now.

His conflicted heart was wearing her down and messing her up, and she deserved better. Her father had dismissed her—and Heath wasn't treating her any better by playing with her emotions while he figured himself out.

When he said nothing, the best thing that'd ever happened to him in his entire life up and left.

His heart clenched in pain as he trudged back up to the gala alone. Bad timing or not, he had to talk to Kelsey.

"Anyone seen Kelsey?" he asked a couple of the volunteers ladling punch. One pointed him to a group of high-backed chairs facing away from him.

"You're one lucky girl," Lara, one of Kelsey's friends, said as he neared. "I never thought you'd lock down that gorgeous cowboy."

"It's not luck, it's persistence," Kelsey responded, her voice gleeful. "Once you've got them on the hook, you don't quit until you reel them in."

"Kelsey?"

At her name, she leaped to her feet, turned and twirled her pearl necklace into a twist. "Heath! You're as quiet as a cat. How long have you been lurking behind me?"

"Long enough," he said grimly, cupping her elbow. "Mind if I steal you away?"

"Now why would I mind that?" She waggled her fingers at her ashen-faced friends. "See how crazy Heath is about me? Can't stay away one minute."

Once they reached the empty rear hall, he jerked to a stop. "Did you make up that stuff about our wedding bands? I don't recall picking any out officially."

Kelsey's lower lip trembled, and her wet lashes swept down to her cheeks. "What are you accusing me of?"

"Yes or no, Kelsey?"

She dried her tears and planted her hands on her hips, akimbo. "Fine. You forced this issue because you never want to talk about the wedding with me. I thought I'd jump start things to get you thinking about setting the date."

"Why'd you have to bring it up in front of Jewel?"

One of her shoulders lifted in a shrug. "Who cares? Jewel needs to know where she stands so she'll quit mooning over you and meet some nice cowboy tonight. It's only fair to her."

Fury howled between his ears. "Fair?"

"She's not your fiancée, *I* am. Like you said, she's nothing more than a ranch hand."

"She's much more than that." He pinched the bridge of his nose, bracing. "I—I kissed her."

"You what?" Kelsey whispered.

"I'm sorry for betraying you, Kelsey. A snake couldn't get any lower."

"I warned you about spending so much time together." Kelsey's eyes sparked before she lowered her lids and sighed. "As long as it was just physical…a momentary weakness…"

"I've got feelings for Jewel."

Kelsey gasped. "And what about me?"

"You know I care about you, but she's opened my eyes to a lot of things."

"If you want her, then why aren't you with her?"

"Because I'm conflicted," Heath admitted, his eyes imploring her to understand. "And even if I weren't, she'd never give up her independence for me."

"Then what's the conflict?" Kelsey flung both hands in the air, as if warding off a stinging insect. "She doesn't need a partner like I do. Daddy won't give me the business unless I'm married."

Heath stared into Kelsey's flushed face, stunned. She cared more about gaining control of her family business than she did about him kissing another woman…about admitting he had feelings for someone else…

What's more, the relief he felt meant he didn't care about her, either. He didn't love Kelsey. Just as Jewel said, by always doing what was expected of him, like staying with Kelsey and not chasing his own dreams, he'd done more harm than good. "This is all just a business proposition for you, isn't it?"

Kelsey nodded before catching herself and shaking her head instead. "I—I need you, Heath."

"Your father thinks you need me, but I disagree. I think deep down, you do, too. Tell him what a creep I turned out to be and how you're ready to take over the business on your own."

She flipped her eyes to the ceiling and released a jagged sigh. "I'd be telling the truth."

"We both deserve to chase our dreams. I'm not your dream, Kelsey."

She stared at him a long time, then slowly pulled off her engagement ring and passed it back. "I've loved you for a long time, Heath."

"I loved you, too."

"But you care about Jewel more."

His shoulders rounded. "It doesn't matter, since she'll never have me or any man."

"Then what's next?"

"There's someone else I should get to know better."

Kelsey's nostrils flared. "Is there any girl in Carbondale you *haven't* been kissing?"

"Not a girl…me. I need to figure myself out."

He'd lost two women in one night, but maybe he needed to be on his own for a change. Like Jewel said, he'd never make anyone happy until he started with himself.

"Good luck, Heath." Kelsey rose on her toes and pressed a kiss to his cheek. "When I'm through shredding your reputation, you won't be able to hold your head up in Carbondale."

"I expect nothing less." He hugged her briefly, then stepped back. "I'd wish you luck, but you don't need it. Those good old boys in the ranching supply world better watch out."

Kelsey's eyebrows quirked, and the corners of her mouth curled. "They won't know what hit them, including my father. Should I go with the jilted, brokenhearted fiancée angle for sympathy points, or just tell him straight out that I'm taking over on my own?"

"Are you brokenhearted?"

She seemed to consider his question, then shook her head. "No. I—I actually feel free. No offense."

"None taken. I'm happy for you."

"Thanks." With a bittersweet smile, she briefly touched his arm, then turned away. "Bye, Heath."

After searching for Jewel and learning James drove her home, Heath hopped in his pickup. He scrolled through his contacts, dialed a number and waited for the voice mail signal to end before leaving a message that might change his life forever.

"Mr. Parsons. Heath Loveland here. I'd like to come down to Nashville in a couple weeks if the offer's still available."

CHAPTER FIFTEEN

"THE CATTLE WON'T get up."

Daryl's grim observation as they rode among the exhausted Brahmans shot panic through Jewel like an IV drug. It pushed through arteries, veins, and capillaries until it nearly incapacitated her. Black dots danced at the edges of her vision.

It was early dawn, the transient quality of the morning light casting just enough of a glow to reveal the listless Brahmans lying on the ground. Their tails remained motionless despite the swarming flies. Others stood with drooping heads, their breathing labored, movements sluggish and ribs visible. They'd nibbled the forage down to the roots and only a trickle of water wound along the streambed.

"Is there still water at Fresco Outlook?"

Daryl nodded. "I rode to it last night, but it's a four-hour climb. Steep, too."

Jewel gnawed on her bottom lip as her eyes traveled up the slopes of the surrounding mountains to the cresting sun. Sunrises usually filled her with hope. Instead, dread clenched her gut. Another hot, dry day. "They're too weak. We'll lose some in the attempt."

Daryl leaned forward and braced himself on his saddle horn. "Their gut fill's worse. So's the eye and ear discharge."

"And they're coughing. They're getting sick." Blood streaks appeared in some of the excrement littering the field. How to save the precarious herd?

She glanced over her shoulder and spied Heath directing the dogs to harry cattle into standing again. Since the gala, she'd rebuffed his attempts to talk to her. Now he kept his distance, saying little to anyone, even his brothers.

He was getting married soon. Shouldn't he be happy?

As for her, she was as dispirited as the Brahmans. If she didn't have a job to do, she'd lie right down with them. Stupid her for being vulnerable. Instead of meeting her halfway when she'd "bent" like Sofia advised, Heath withdrew and shattered her exposed heart.

At least Kelsey hadn't come around flashing her stupid ring and rubbing her impending marriage in Jewel's face. Kelsey had what she wanted—a ring, a fiancé, a wedding date. What did Jewel have? Before Heath, she'd only imagined working Cade Ranch as range boss. Respect, attention, power. Now she envisioned more. A family. A partner. A home of her own where love, not power, meant respect. Problem was, she could only picture that life with Heath.

He rode up and his eyes connected with hers before swerving to Daryl. "Not much luck keeping them on their feet."

Daryl yanked his brim against the first slanting sunrays. "If they can barely stand, how're they going to climb?"

"There are no other watering spots closer?" Jewel asked. It was mostly a rhetorical question. She'd studied the Loveland Hills maps so many times, she could ride the land in her sleep.

"Only the Crystal River." Bitterness colored Heath's voice a dark, heavy gray. The only access to it was across Cade land, through the old Loveland easement.

"Dude. Stop harassing Jewel." Daryl shooed a fly from his horse's neck. "She's loyal to her family, just like us."

Jewel studied the fragile cattle. How many more would she lose today? Three had succumbed yesterday and two the day before that. An ugly fear grew in her like a tumor; it was an idea she hadn't wanted to contemplate until now. When she'd agreed to take this job, she did so with the same attitude she approached every task. Never do anything halfway. Always put the livestock first. She'd been charged with keeping them safe, and driving the beleaguered cattle up the mountain would be a flat-out dereliction of duty.

On the other hand, if she drove them onto Cade land, she'd betray her family. *Her unreasonable family.* At the arbitration hearing, they hadn't budged when the Lovelands aired their valid grievances. But she had. They weren't the bad guys. James would say Heath caused her change of heart.

And he'd be wrong.

Heath broke her heart, but fair was fair. She needed to stop wallowing like the cattle. No more thinking of herself or trying to prove she was the best, the toughest, most loyal Cade. She was done pledging allegiance to a father who never fully loved or appreciated her.

Heath preferred Kelsey just as her father had loved her brothers more, but neither her parent nor Heath defined her worth anymore. She did, along with her actions. One of the Brahmans lifted its head and let out a rattling breath before dropping it to the ground again. The various textures of Jewel's fear sifted through her: shivery, visceral, tight, pounding, in turn or all at once. The time for talking was over.

"Heath's right." His gaze snapped to hers. "Our only choice is to drive them straight to the Crystal River. It's two hours on a downward slope. We might not lose any head if we hurry."

"What about your brothers?" Heath's forehead bunched. "Your chances of being named range boss?"

"The herd comes first," she said firmly.

Heath shot her an inscrutable look; approval, gratitude and something unidentifiable swirled in those blue depths. "Agreed. To the Crystal River."

They wheeled their horses around and began working the cattle as a cohesive team, driving the animals to their feet, to move, to walk. Remaining motionless meant death.

The sound of barking dogs, shouting cowboys and bellowing cattle filled the warming air. The bond between her and Heath, their connection, felt stronger than ever. With looks, nods and gestures, they drove the herd mercilessly, never letting them quit as they crossed onto Cade land.

When Jewel's brothers and cousins appeared to block the way, her fingers tightened on the reins. Bear snorted and shook his head. He sensed her tension as she braced for a standoff.

"I'll ride ahead and talk to them," Heath said. "I'll tell James we forced you to drive the herd here. You had no choice…"

"I'm no liar. And I'm not afraid." She squeezed Bear into a trot, canter then gallop until she reached her family.

"What are you doing?" James's eyebrows were so far up his face they disappeared under his hat. Disbelief and irritation fought to dominate his expression.

"Using the Loveland access." She flipped up her brim and stared him dead in the eye. The tread of Destiny's hooves striking bedrock signaled Heath's approach.

"That ain't been settled in court," Justin growled. With his black hat, shirt and jeans, he resembled an outlaw, full of dark menace.

"Since when has your family ever worried about following the law?" Heath scoffed, his jaw hard.

"Heath's right." Jewel cast her eye around the group. She had everybody's attention. "Our family killed Everett Loveland without the facts. We broke Cades out of jail and helped them hide out to ambush the Lovelands." She paused, making sure her siblings were taking it all in. "And we rewarded a judge to take away their easement."

James tore off his hat and scratched the back of his red neck. Patches of sweat had appeared under his armpits, staining his shirt. "That's not proven."

"Everett didn't hang himself," Heath said, grim. "And

we didn't rustle our own cattle, set fire to our buildings or bribe the judge to rule against us."

"No arguing with that logic." Jared squinted at Heath, then Jewel, his expression not exactly unfriendly. She took heart.

"Whose side are you on?" Frustration crackled in James's voice.

Jared shrugged. "Just stating a fact."

In the distance, the faint lowing of the straggling herd, driven by Daryl, reached her ear. She wanted to howl with fear, or to rage, but she did neither, because her hands shook and her stomach turned, threatening to upend the coffee she'd sipped earlier, the bites of jerky she'd forced herself to swallow. She had fifteen minutes, tops, to make her brothers give way before the cattle caught up to them.

In her mind's eye, she pictured a wall-mounted fire-hose case and the words Do Not Break Unless Emergency.

She braced herself and mentally swung. The faint tinkling of glass reverberated in her ear. "Here's another fact. Ma's wish is for us to become a real family. She wants that more than anything. And family doesn't stand in the way of one another."

"Aunt Jewel is right!" Javi shouted. He was seated atop Milly, a horse her oldest brother Jack had brought home and Javi and James rehabilitated. Javi flicked the reins and crossed to Jewel's side.

"Javi, get over here," James ordered.

"Heroes stand on the side of justice," Javi said stoutly.

Jewel patted the top of his helmet in approval. What a kid. Eight years old, and he was wiser than all the adults. "Also, when Cole returned Cora's Tear, he did the right thing." She blotted the perspiration dripping in her eyes. "We should, too."

"Fair is fair, Pa!" Javi called.

"Our longhorns are miles away." Jared plucked his

shirt's damp fabric from his chest. "No chance of the cattle mingling." He tapped his horse and joined Jewel, Javi and Heath. When he shot her a smile, her lips wobbled up in return.

"And we demolished the old barns out here." Justin inserted a toothpick in his mouth and chewed before adding, "No chance of the Brahmans doing any structural damage." With a cluck, he hustled his horse across the space and lined up beside Jared.

Jewel blinked back the sting in her eyes. Her brothers' support meant everything. She'd been so focused on competing with them for her father's affection she'd failed to fully value the love they gave her. And the respect.

"You'll have to go through me, then," James declared, his jaw clamped, his features set.

"Good luck with that," Jared scoffed. "I'll try not to trample your hat."

"I won't be so careful," Justin bit out. "Enough, James. Look at those cattle."

Their collective gazes followed his arm sweep. The herd trudged closer, heads bowed, bloated guts bouncing, bones protruding, and eyes and noses running. James's expression softened. No respectable rancher tolerated animal suffering.

"If they don't drink in the next couple of hours, they'll start dying." Heath's voice rang out, loud and clear. "We're out of options, but if you want us gone, we'd better turn 'em now."

"Don't kill them, Pa!" Javi yelled.

"The heck we'll turn them!" Jewel pounded her thigh with the side of her fist, willing James to hear her. "We're coming through, so step aside or be run over." Her cousins Hayden and Graham exchanged worried looks.

"I'll call the sheriff."

Heath chuckled at James's threat. "You mean my brother Travis?"

There was absolute silence, as if the mountain range were holding its breath, then James's eyes flickered from Jewel to the nearing Brahmans. At last, his chest lowered in a long exhale. "Fine. We'll grant them passage."

"Forever." Jewel jutted her chin, determined to settle this once and for all. "We're drawing up a new map and returning the easement to the Lovelands."

"That's for the courts to—"

"We're deciding!" Justin growled, cutting off James. "We don't need fancy lawyers. We know what's just and you do, too. Not wanting change ain't any reason to deny what's right."

James's lips twisted in a wry smile. "I think I've heard that before."

"Only from Sofia a hundred times." Jewel rolled her eyes. "Things can't always stay the same. Accept it." At his slow nod, euphoria nearly lifted her from the saddle.

"All right then," James said. "We return the easement, and the Lovelands drop the restitution demand."

Heath nodded. "If any of my brothers or Pa disagree, then the deal's off the table."

James rode close enough to shake Heath's hand. "Let's drive these cattle." He turned to the cousins. "You boys and Javi head up to our herd and keep an eye on them. We're not moving them until tomorrow." Then, with a loud "yip" he tore off, galloping down the side of the stumbling herd to join Daryl. Jared and Justin lit out after him.

"Are they going to die, Aunt Jewel?" Javi's large brown eyes swung between her and the cattle.

"We won't let them," she promised through an encouraging smile. "You go on with Hayden and Graham now. Okay?"

"Okay."

She watched until Javi caught up to the young men, then gathered her reins.

"Hold up, Jewel."

She steeled herself, then slowly raised her head to meet Heath's eyes. Sweat rolled down his flushed, handsome face. His eyes were a clear blue, and his lips were parted in a smile so genuine it'd break her heart if he hadn't already done so already. "I don't deserve you siding with me, not after what happened at the gala, but thank you."

She tipped her chin, torn between leaning closer and skirting away. Every muscle screamed to drag him off his horse and fall into him. Her brain told her to keep her distance. With a sigh, she followed her head. "It wasn't for you."

"Then who?" He lifted an inquiring eyebrow.

"Me." She galloped off to join her brothers and Daryl.

As the Cades and Lovelands worked together to hustle the cattle to lifesaving water, dust clouds rose. The animals were on their last legs. Many stopped and knelt, preparing to lie down and quit until one of the dogs or riders came along, urging them to move. Move. Move. Too frightened to resist, they thankfully kept up the painstakingly slow pace.

An hour later, Jewel smelled the Crystal River before she saw it. The fresh scent of flowing water over moss-covered rocks brought tears to her eyes. As if sensing it, too, the cattle picked up their heads. Their bellows grew louder, urgent. Heath flashed by with a dehydrated calf secured across the front of his saddle. Justin harried a couple of drowsy heifers to pick up the pace while Daryl and James zoomed back and forth in the rear, applying steady pressure.

"Almost there," Jared called as he cantered by, his faithful cattle dogs racing beside him.

"Almost," she whispered to herself. Faintness made her head lurch and spin. They'd make it. They had to.

Gradually, the dirt gave way to grass and then grass to reeds. The herd practically stampeded to the water and splashed into its shallow end while others lined up along the bank to drink their fill.

James approached. He clamped his jaw so tight, she swore he'd break it himself.

She held up a hand. "Don't even start. I'm in too much of a good mood."

"I've made a decision about the range boss position."

She groaned. "Forget it. I don't even want it anymore."

James's serious expression relaxed, and a glint of humor lightened his dark eyes. "That's too bad."

"Why? I denied you the pleasure of telling me I didn't get it? That I'm too soft on the Lovelands to be a tough Cade range boss?"

James shook his head, then wheeled his horse around. "You took away the pleasure of me offering it to you," he called over his shoulder, then trotted away.

"Wait! What?" Giddiness bubbled in her veins like a New Year's toast as she rode after him. "I—I'm Cade Ranch's range boss?"

James slowed, then reined his horse to a stop beneath a weeping willow. It leaned over the bank, trailing leafy ropes into the swirling water. "You just said you didn't want it."

"Only a fool would say that." She might not need the range boss position to prove herself anymore, but she'd worked for it her entire life. She wanted it with all her heart.

"And fool you're not." James grinned, then sobered. "You impressed me today. It took guts leading the herd over here. And heart. You need both to be good range boss. And I read your herd health report."

She sucked in a quick, surprised breath. "You did?"

He nodded. "Heath was right. You have a lot of good ideas, ideas I'd like you to implement as range boss."

"What about Justin?"

"I just told him. He wasn't broken up about it. Seems they're expanding the ranching skills program at Fresh Start so he's got enough on his plate."

"And I've got nothing else," she murmured to herself once James moved off, her eyes on Heath as he encouraged the rescued calf to drink. Her earlier euphoria disappeared. It was a fizzled-out firework, a limp balloon.

She'd won the job of her dreams, but she'd lost the man she loved.

The old Jewel would have been content with her promotion and wouldn't moon over a man. She'd followed her heart and failed. But she wouldn't quit putting herself out there and letting others see her softer side, as Ma advised.

She hopped off Bear, tied him up and began checking the herd. Her vision blurred as she studied the drinking cattle.

It was her strength, not a weakness after all.

CHAPTER SIXTEEN

HEATH TRUDGED UP the ranch's porch steps in the deepening twilight, his body sore, but his spirits high. They'd saved the herd. No. Jewel—brave, bold, beautiful Jewel—saved the herd. The Brahmans now had access to the Crystal River, virtually guaranteeing a high enough head count going into the beef auctions to stave off bankruptcy. Better still, his family avoided a costly trial. In one simple, courageous act, Jewel resolved the last of their families' differences and ended their 130-year feud.

Now he and Jewel needed to resolve their issues, too.

But that required talking and privacy, two things she'd avoided around him since the gala. She wanted her space, and he respected that. Respected her.

Loved her.

Yes, that, too.

He'd known his heart fully when she'd stood up to her brothers, a gutsy and selfless act. She'd jeopardized her dream of being Cade Ranch's range boss by angering James, but she'd put the cattle first. It proved her strength and character. She was authentic, driven and independent. She didn't want anything from anyone except their love and respect. And now he was free to give it, especially since Andrew Parsons never called back. He'd lost the opportunity of a lifetime, but if Jewel would forgive him, he might not regret it.

"Heath! Phone!" Sierra held out the receiver as he opened the screen door and plodded inside.

When he reached for the receiver, she clamped a hand over the mouthpiece and whispered, "What'd you do to Jewel?"

"Nothing."

Everything. Guilt swamped him. Toying with her feelings before resolving things with Kelsey had been selfish and hurtful, everything he'd apologize for if she'd just let him.

"She's upstairs packing her gear. Says she's leaving since Pa and Joy come home tomorrow and Cole got his cast off. What's the rush?"

Heath squeezed his sister's shoulder. "Will you stall her till I get off the phone?"

She brushed her blond bangs from her eyes and peered up at him. "Only if you promise not to hurt her. She's not as tough as she looks."

"I know."

Sierra released the phone and stomped upstairs.

"Heath Loveland here," he said, one eye on the stairwell.

"This is Andrew Parsons."

Heath's heart kicked up a gear. "Yes, sir."

"Got your message. Have to say, I was surprised when you turned down my tryout invitation last month. And I don't give second chances."

Heath's throat constricted. After clearing it, he said, "I understand, sir. Thank you for—"

"Don't thank me. I haven't heard your audition…yet."

"Excuse me?"

"I've decided it's worth giving you one more shot. After you left your message, I had one of my staffers share your video on our blog. It's got over a hundred thousand likes so far. Those are mighty persuasive numbers."

Heath's breath quickened. "A hundred thousand?"

"And that's just in the past week. You've got potential I'd like to explore. It's a once-in-a-lifetime opportunity. What do you say?"

Jewel's voice caught his ear and grew louder, mingling with Sierra's as their boots clattered down the stair treads.

"I—I'll have to call you back, sir."

"But—but—"

"Promise," he vowed, then hung up on the sputtering

music producer. A possible recording contract was his dream, but Jewel had become just as important. He needed to know where things stood before committing himself.

She stalked by, saddlebag slung over her shoulder.

"Wait!" Emma and Noah raced from the kitchen table, where they'd been coloring with Daryl and flung their arms around Jewel. "Ain't you gonna say goodbye?"

"*Aren't* you and *going* to," Sierra corrected, ruffling Noah's hair.

Jewel's mouth relaxed into a smile. "Of course I was. I just didn't see you there."

"How come you gotta…?" Emma paused at Sierra's headshake. "*Got to* go tonight? We were going to play Monopoly."

Noah nodded. "You promised."

Jewel's eyes swerved to Heath's. "It's better if I leave now. Y'all got everything in hand, and your pa, uncle Heath and aunt Sierra can play with you."

"But they don't always lose like you do," Emma insisted.

"Except Pa!" Noah giggled. "He never wins."

Daryl shot them a comical hangdog look. "Guess I'm just a born loser."

Heath guffawed at Daryl's exaggeration. Growing up, he'd been a wily competitor. Most likely he "lost" to make up for the real loss of the children's mostly absentee mother. Like Heath, Daryl knew the pain an unhappy parent inflicted, doubly so since his real parents had abandoned him at Loveland Hills when he was only five. Perhaps because he was adopted, he took extra care to bend over backward to keep his little ones happy. If Heath was even half the dad Daryl was someday, he'd know he'd done right by his own kids.

Jewel chucked the children gently under the chin. "You'll have to up your game. Just remember. Uncle Heath is a sucker for the railroad properties. He'll pay anything to get them all. And Aunt Sierra always had extra money hidden under the board."

"Hey!" protested Sierra with a grin. "You can't give out all my secrets." She hugged Jewel. "I'll drive Bear over to you in the morning."

Jewel thanked her and headed for the door. Sierra turned to the kids. "Let's set up the board."

"We need to talk before you go," Heath said, following Jewel outside.

She paused on the top step. "It's not necessary. I'm sure you and Kelsey will be very happy."

He caught her hand with his. "Kelsey and I broke up."

In the deepening gloom, he struggled to make out the expression in her enormous eyes. "When? Why? I thought—"

"At the gala. I overheard her talking about— Well, it doesn't matter. But I realized she didn't love me."

"What about you?"

"I knew I didn't love her either…hadn't in a long time. She was safe, predictable, and all wrong for me." He led Jewel to the porch swing and tugged her down onto the seat beside him.

"But she's beautiful, smart, classy."

"I care about someone else. Apparently, I have a predilection for bossy redheads with hair-trigger tempers."

"She sounds like a handful." Her tone of voice was attempting to be jokey, but her bottom lip wobbled.

"She's impossible." Heath gave an exaggerated sigh. "But I only want her." He cupped her chin. *"You."*

"Heath," she breathed.

"I tried to tell you before, but you kept pushing me away."

"I was angry. Needed my space."

"Understandable. I've been a jerk and I'm sorry."

"And clueless. You forgot that one."

He chuckled. Jewel. She was a button-pusher, one of the

traits he liked most about her. *Loved* about her. He'd heard opposites attracted, but he never would have believed it until now. "I thought pleasing others was selfless, but it was selfish. I wanted to be the good guy. The hero who saves the day, rather than just me, because deep down, I thought it was all I had to offer."

Jewel flung her arms around him, crossing her wrists behind his neck. "How could you think that? You have so much to give. The thing is with me, I don't ever want to take, to depend on anyone, but I'm learning, Heath. My brothers used to tease me about having a crush on you for years, but it's because they never thought I'd be soft on someone—or soft at all. You bring that out in me. I—I forgive you."

"What would they say if they saw us right now?" he teased. The moon broke through cloud coverage, illuminating an expression on her face that was so horrified he almost laughed. When she began to withdraw, he placed his hands atop hers, locking them in place before spanning her slender waist. "You're not afraid of what they think anymore, are you?"

"No..." she said and followed that with a little outtake of air, a puff of distress that dispersed into the night. "But maybe we should keep us a secret for a little while, just until the season's over and things quiet down."

"Not sure if that's going to be possible because there's something I want to ask you."

"Okay." She recoiled slightly and stretched out the word.

"Don't worry—it's not what you think it is." He dug his feet into the porch floor and shoved off, gently rocking the swing. "I know you don't ever want to get married."

She laughed, a shaky, uncertain sound. "I might have had a change of heart about that."

The revelation stitched the frayed crack in his heart after her rejection the past week. "How about going to Nashville with me, then?"

"What do you mean?" She arched a brow. "Like on a trip?"

"After the gala, I called that music producer for another shot." The porch swing creaked beneath them as he pushed it forward then back, swifter now.

"Was that who you were just speaking to?"

"He still wants me to try out, but I told him I'd have to phone him back." He skimmed his thumbs over the thin T-shirt covering her taut stomach.

"Are you insane? Guys like that don't wait around!"

"I needed to ask you first."

Jewel's eyes bulged. "Why?"

"Because I wanted to hear your thoughts and see if you'd go with me."

"Oh, Heath." She shook her head slowly, her voice low and full of sorrow. "There you go again."

"What do you mean?"

"What's it matter what *I* think?" She dropped her hands from his neck and poked his chest with her index finger. "You're trying to please me, and you know what? I won't let you." She pressed her lips in a firm line.

"What do you mean?"

"James offered me the range boss position."

He caught her in a tight hug. "About darn time."

"If I said I wanted you to stay here, what would your answer be?"

"I'd tell Parsons no." He ignored the slight pang in his chest accompanying his vow.

She drew back. "And you'd be fine never knowing if your dream would have come true?"

"I'd have another dream." His right knee jiggled up and down. "You."

"But you'd still never know."

For a second or two there was silence, an emptiness, which neither wanted to fill with words, because they were both thinking about what that might mean for their potential relationship, and how bad that could be.

"I want you in my life, Heath. I do," Jewel implored. He heard the drag of grief in her voice, as if she were already mourning him. Them. What could have been. "But I don't want you to look at me one day and regret the chance you never took. You saw how your mother suffered, stuck in a life she felt trapped in, unable to explore her own music career. You need to go to Nashville and stay there until you make it. Music is what got you through in life, long before I ever came around."

He inhaled the familiar horse scent that clung to her clothes, the soapy aroma of her skin. He was losing her. Yet staying behind, giving up his music for marriage and kids for the person he loved, was no different from what his mom had done. Eventually he'd come to resent Jewel, and she was the last person in the world he ever wanted to resent because he loved her. But if she would go with him, then he could have the best of both worlds "Then come with me."

"And do what?" Her eyes shut as her face tensed. "I'd be a concrete cowgirl spinning my wheels in Nashville. What would I do? Waitressing? Driving Ubers? My life can't revolve around yours, either. Is that what you'd want for me?"

"You should have your dream, too." Emotion clawed at his insides, raking him raw. He couldn't walk his mother's path, and neither should he expect Jewel to. "I never want you to change for me."

Despite her glistening eyes, her expression remained stoic. "We'd only end up hating each other if we did." The swing rocked back on its chain as she stood. "We want different things."

He nodded, unable to push words past the softball-sized lump in his throat. Until their dreams converged, they had to part ways. As much as it hurt, they owed it to each other to pursue their own futures.

He followed her down to her truck. "Thank you, Jewel. For everything. For—"

"Not necessary." They were words of reassurance, but Jewel's eyes told a different story. He read in them a quality and depth of despair that matched his own, and that pained him even more. "We both got what we wanted, didn't we?"

He snorted at the irony, a quick, off-pitched sound, a fish gulping air. She pressed a kiss to his cheek, hopped in her truck and drove off without waiting for his answer.

Had they gotten what they wanted?

As her pickup disappeared around a bend, his heart rode shotgun beside her. It'd left his chest, if the gaping, hollow sensation was any indication. Part of him wanted to chase after her like a cattle dog until she slowed and let him inside. But he had to follow his own road, as did she.

Would his be a dead end? One that never led him to the happiness Jewel gave him?

There was only one way to find out.

He forced himself up the stairs, inside the house and dragged the rotary phone to the kitchen table.

"You've made the right decision, son," the producer crowed a couple minutes later.

"I hope so. Thank you, sir." Heath placed the phone on its receiver.

Emma rolled the dice, then moved her game piece. "What are you hoping for, Uncle Heath? Did you make a wish?"

Dropping his elbows on the table, he planted his face in his hands. His insides twisted and burned. He'd just made the most important and possibly worst decision of his life. "I don't know, darlin'. Maybe I need a couple shooting stars."

"You can only make one wish at a time." Noah shook the dice in his fist. "Or it won't come true."

Heath nodded. Only one wish.

That was exactly the whole darn problem.

CHAPTER SEVENTEEN

HEATH SHIFTED RESTLESSLY in a straight-backed chair as he awaited Andrew Parsons. His eyes roamed over the framed platinum records hanging in the producer's office. Legendary names and iconic songs jumped out at him. Would he find a place on that wall someday? It'd been three months since his failed tryout with Freedom Records, ninety-two nights of nonstop gigging, 2,208 hours of missing Jewel so bad his body felt like a bruise, beaten; his heart, broken. His only relief had been writing songs and recording demos in hopes of securing a contract with another company. He used to sing his troubles to the wind. Now he sang to Jewel, hoping she'd hear them someday and think of him.

Morning rain tapped on the floor-to-ceiling windows. It turned downtown Nashville into an impressionistic painting of itself, blurred lines and colors running into each other. When he'd first arrived, he'd been intent on making his mark on this city. Instead, he spun his wheels like a stuck pickup. Why had Parsons summoned him today? Had he changed his mind and decided to sign Heath after listening to the new demo he'd sent?

The thought didn't excite him like it once had. His eagerness had given way to loneliness. Sure, the crowds were bigger, the paychecks, too. Yet he enjoyed performing for the friends and familiar faces at Carbondale's honky-tonks more.

He pulled up the collar of his jean jacket against the damp chill seeping through one of the cracked-open windows.

Here, folks looked out for themselves, grinding to get discovered, thousands chasing one dream. After singing every night and staying mute all day to save his voice, he hadn't had a decent conversation in weeks. Months.

He gigged with down-to-earth guys, but they didn't compare to his Outlaw Cowboys bandmates. The groupies hitting on him didn't hold a candle to Jewel. Her memory burned brighter than the city lights. How long since he'd seen the way her eyes flashed a deep brown and narrowed like a wild animal when he riled her, the way her freckled cheeks filled with color and her eyes lit like sparklers when she laughed, the way her soft lips responded beneath his…?

A vision of Jewel pressed softly against him at the gala rose in his mind's eye, and an extraordinary sense of warmth spread through him. His heart lurched, and his pulse throbbed in his fingertips.

Too darn long.

Living without her felt like existing in a coma—his life support, his music.

Was he happy?

No.

But if he went home, he'd abandon the road to a music career. He'd never expected it to feel so empty, though. What happened when reality didn't live up to your dreams?

The door behind him whisked open and Parsons strode in with his customary speed. In five steps, the tall, slender man reached his desk chair and sat. He had dark hair that circled a significant bald patch, and wore jeans, a pressed shirt in country checks under an old-fashioned blazer, and polished cowboy boots no real rancher would be caught dead wearing except—of course—at his own funeral.

Parsons thrust out a hand. "Keith. Good to see you."

Heath opened his mouth to correct him, then shut it and pumped the music producer's hand instead. Who cared what the guy called him so long as he earned a contract in the end?

Parson leafed through pages inside a folder. Heath stiffened when he recognized his song title on one of the sheets. "Got the new demo you sent. No denying, you're a talented singer and the ladies love you."

Heath braced for the silent *but* he sensed.

He forced his breathing to slow and his muscles to relax. Mediocre steaks and rejection were two things he'd become familiar with in Nashville. If Parsons didn't like his new material, why call this meeting?

"And you've made progress from our initial tryout." Parsons pressed a button and ordered a couple of coffees from his receptionist.

Heath realized that he clenched his fists and opened them. "Glad to hear it, sir." He rubbed his palms against his legs. He'd worked hard to pay for studio time to record, writing lyrics about his messed-up heart on sleepless nights.

"I'm not offering you a recording contract. Yet. Your voice is too much of a throwback." Parsons studied the records crowding his wall. "Like a young Johnny Cash or Hank Williams."

"I appreciate the comparison. Grew up listening to them." A ghost of a smile curved his lips as he recalled singing "It Ain't Me, Babe" with his mother. It was a happy memory from one of her good days. One he treasured. She'd loved the oldies. He'd thought he'd only sung them to please her...yet he'd grown to love them, too, and music, because of her.

Heath nodded his thanks to the receptionist when she passed him a warm mug. Steam curled off the dark surface. The smell of roasted beans was sharp as he breathed it in, waiting for Parsons's next critique. What others thought of him wasn't more important than his reality, he'd come to understand these past few months. He wasn't the negligent, selfish son whose abandonment caused his mother's suicide. Pursuing what he wanted didn't automatically lead to disaster. His mother chose her path, and he'd needed to as well that tragic night. He hoped she understood. Deep down, he believed she did.

In fact, she might even be proud of him.

"Milk? Sugar?" Parsons held up packets.

Heath shook his head, then burned his tongue when he sipped the black brew.

"I like the classics, too. Don't get me wrong." Parsons dumped sugar into his coffee and stirred. When he dropped the small plastic stick on the empty packet, a wet brown stain spread. "But country fans aren't listening to them now. Brett Young, Luke Combs, Midland…that's where it's at. I'd like to hear more traditional voices like yours on the radio, but it doesn't translate. Performance, appearance—you've got it. Singing, too, but the style won't sell enough records."

Heath took a deep breath, ordering his thoughts. "Why'd you call me in then, sir?"

"I've regretted turning you down." Parsons stared hard into Heath's eyes and the lines of his face cut deep. "Hearing your new demo made me realize why. I should have had you work with our vocal coach to retrain your voice. In a couple of months, we could have you sounding just like Luke Bryan."

Heath clamped a hand on his knee to stop it from shaking up and down. If he learned a modern country sound he'd change who he was, putting himself aside to appease someone else again.

"Let me get Jim Este up here to see what he thinks." Parsons picked up the phone and requested his secretary connect him to the renowned Freedom Records vocal coach.

While Parsons relayed his wishes, Heath stared out at the umbrella-carrying pedestrians scurrying across the Cumberland River bridge. They hustled back and forth, eager to escape the driving rain, but were they really going anywhere? Was anyone?

Heath's own thoughts were a jumble, veering from anticipation and curiosity at the thought of working with a legend like Jim Este to concern at losing touch with the sound, the storytelling that'd drawn him to country music in the first place. He hadn't left behind the woman and life he loved to become someone else. He didn't need cheering crowds or a contract to be a musician. Just as Jewel had been right not to let him become a full-time rancher for her sake, he'd be wrong to transform into a different singer to fit the country music industry. *He* defined his career, not anyone else.

"Jim's on his way," Parsons said. "He's pleased at the idea of molding the next big country star."

Pleased.

The word struck Heath in the pit of the stomach, like a rock from a sling. His whole life had been about pleasing others.

Heath set down his half-finished coffee and stood. "I appreciate the offer, sir, but I won't change who I am."

"Just your sound." Mr. Parsons waved a dismissive hand. "When we first tried out one of our top female recording artists, cats in heat were less pitchy."

"My sound is who I am," Heath said mildly, hoping that the sudden lurch of his heart didn't show. "Thank you. I'll show myself out."

A knock shook the door's wooden panels and a tall, well-built man with stubbled cheeks, spiky, highlighted blond hair and hazel eyes strode inside. He wore skinny jeans, a loose sweater and trendy sneakers that looked too young for him. "How can I help?"

"Convince this young man not to walk away from the greatest opportunity in his life, one he'll regret, Jim."

Jim Estes frowned. "I've listened to your demo. If we expand your upper register, get rid of that twang and add in some falsetto, we—"

Falsetto? The word had *false* right in it.... Heath cut off Jim with a headshake. "I'm not interested."

Jim peered at Parsons, eyes wide. "Is he for real?"

Parsons scratched his bald patch. "Unfortunately for us, he's *too* real."

"He's got talent." Jim rubbed a knuckle hard across his lips and glanced at Heath. "You're one heck of a songwriter."

Heath tipped his head. "Appreciated."

"We need those songs." Jim paced. "At least half a dozen of our singers would sound great on them."

Parsons strode around his desk. "You're right." He drew a deep breath and seemed to relax a bit. "It's a shame to waste those looks, but how about becoming one of our songwriters?"

Heath felt a rushing in his ears, together with a peculiar sense of detachment that sometimes came from a draft of Daryl's moonshine after a long day in the saddle. "Meaning you'll buy some of my songs?"

Parsons clapped him on the back. "I want all of them, and first crack at the next ones you write and the ones after that, if you'll sign a contract with us."

Heath suddenly forgot how to breathe. He worked his tongue in an effort to regain enough saliva to speak and noted the names of famous songwriters on Freedom Records' platinum discs, too. He didn't need to be on stage, didn't need the attention, the adulation, for a creative outlet. Stardom wasn't his dream, after all; Jewel was. He could write songs anywhere, and he'd rather do it by her side. Where better to compose music than in his hometown beside his muse?

His love.

Parsons's cheeks puffed as he released a long stream of air at Heath's silence. "And I'll also let you sit in on the recording sessions. You can do backup vocals and instrumentations on the songs you choose," he added, then turned to Jim. "Keith drives a hard bargain."

"I accept," Heath said, achieving speech. Euphoria burst

inside him. *Flash bang.* He pumped Parsons's hand, strode to the door and paused. "And the name's Heath. Spell it right on the contract, now."

He nearly chuckled at Jim Este's and Parsons's shocked expressions. No more appeasing others. Not even music industry titans. His fast strides carried him down the hall and out into the rainy fall morning. The pavement was dark with wet and the air thick with the scent of woodsmoke. Heath settled his hat firmly, bending his head into the wind.

Rain was falling in a downpour now, crashing through the canopy of the tree-lined street, their trunks streaked from it. They arched over him, a vibrant tunnel of colors, urging him onward, making him feel as if it anything was possible at the rainbow's end. Happiness, success, even love. His breathing was ragged and fast, his heart thumping, his boots splashing through puddles, never moving fast enough.

With every step he was soaked some more, but with every step he cared less. This was a baptism. A rebirth. He rounded a bend in the sidewalk and headed onto the Cumberland River bridge. He wiped the rain from his face, felt his sodden clothing cling coldly to him, impervious. Leaning over the railing, he watched the water swirl, driving in one direction.

He knew the direction he needed to go in, too.

West.

To Jewel…

If she'd still have him.

She valued her independence, and he'd never want her to lose it.

As for him, he couldn't live without her. Not anymore. Not ever again. It was what he wanted; what pleased *him* was Jewel.

CHAPTER EIGHTEEN

"HAVE TO SAY, the new fall feeding system isn't bad."

"Not *bad*?" Jewel cast James a sideways glance and assessed him to be tantalizingly out of range for a much-needed shoulder jab. She contented herself with an exasperated huff. It plumed the November air with white as she fastened her heavy overcoat's top button against the growing chill. "It's Thanksgiving and we've barely touched our hay because of the winter forage planting and the new fencing and padlock system I installed."

"*We* installed," James grumbled, with his typical mix of superiority and amusement.

"On *my* orders."

James grunted something indiscriminate, which Jewel chose to interpret as, "You're the best range boss *ever*." They watched closely as the fenced-in area's Batt-Latch opened with a *clang*. Snow flurries cascaded from the gray sky and swirled around the grazing cattle. They picked up their heads at the sound Jewel had trained them to recognize and hustled through the now-open gate toward the thicker forage on the other side of the fence.

"They're learning," Jewel observed with pride. As soon as the last longhorn left the old grazing area for the next cell, the gate shut behind it to prevent any from returning.

"I am, too." James blew on his bare fingers, then pulled gloves from his pocket and shoved his hands inside them. "Never heard of this mob thing before, but it's working."

"It's mob grazing." When Jewel shook her head, a shower of white flew from her hat brim. "Rotation, rest and better distribution of manure reinvigorates the soil. It improves forage quantity and quality and provides drought resistance."

James nodded, his cheeks stained red from the cold wind. He edged closer. “It’s saving us time and money.”

“More importantly,” Jewel cut in, “it’s less stress on the cattle, which improves the quality of the herd.”

James slung an arm around Jewel and pulled her tight to his side. “You’ve done well, sis. Now let’s get some turkey.”

For some reason, his praise brought tears to her eyes. Not happy ones, but shameful, weak salty wetness that splashed down her freezing cheeks.

“Hey. What’s this about?” James caught her in a tight hug. Her hat tipped back and fell to the ground. “What’s wrong?”

“Nothing.” The instant she shoved at his brick wall of a chest, he released her. She whirled and furiously wiped her eyes. Her feelings kept bouncing back and forth between pride at her hard-won accomplishments and loss at what she’d given up achieving them.

Heath.

A family.

Love.

“It isn’t nothing. I haven’t seen you cry since—since Jesse passed.” James strode around to face her, then followed in every direction she spun until she quit and glared up at him.

“I didn’t cry then, and I’m not crying now.”

James brushed his thumbs over her damp lashes. “Then how about ‘your eyes are leaking’?”

She half sobbed, half laughed. “Just forget it.”

“The heck I will. I thought you’d be happy as range boss.”

She sniffled. “I am,” then she burst into humiliating tears again.

James slung his arms around her again, alternating, “Shhhhhhh” with “It’s going to be okay” as he brushed back the damp strands clinging to her cheeks.

When her eyes dried up and her body stopped its shameful convulsing, she sagged in his arms. What was the point of trying to be tough when your traitorous heart gave you away every time? You couldn't fight nature. Especially the human kind.

"Is it Heath?"

She stiffened and jerked away at James's question. "W-why would you say that?"

"Because you love him. You've never missed one of his shows and you defend him as hard as you defend anyone you love."

"I don't..." She groaned when she caught her brother's knowing look. "James. How do I make it stop?"

He chuckled, long and deep. "You can't. Trust me on that."

"Then how do I stand it? I've got everything I ever wanted, but I'm miserable."

"Everything but *Heath*."

She nodded glumly. She missed Heath like crazy, although she was happy to hear he was gigging in Nashville, chasing a recording contract. He wanted music and, despite wanting to prove herself as range boss, all she'd really proved was she was miserable alone. There was no better place to heal a broken heart than on the back of a horse, some said, a theory she'd just disproven. "I never thought I'd need a man to be happy."

"You don't." James kept his voice neutral, soft, like he was trying to calm a fussing child. But she wasn't a child, as James was well aware. "You need Heath."

She swooped down, grabbed her hat and jammed it on her head again. "Well, I can't have him."

"Why not?" James vaulted into the saddle and wheeled his stallion around as she did the same. They trotted down the trail home in the intensifying storm. Snowflakes rained down from the heavy-bellied clouds now, rushing toward her, never-ending, uncountable. Too many thoughts swirled through her brain, endless and confusing as the snowflakes.

"I'm not the fiancée type." Jewel straightened her slouch, despite the weight of her emotions, and rode straight-backed and strong. "He's going to be a country star who needs a glammed-up gal on his arm. That's not the kind of world cowgirls like me are a part of."

"Who told you that?"

Jewel reached forward and brushed some of the gathering snow from Bear's mane. "Let's face it. I've never been good at the girlie stuff."

James swayed easily in the saddle and shrugged. "Who cares?"

"Pa did! I embarrassed him so much he could hardly look at me because of my ragged nails and tangled hair." Her fingers curled inside her gloves. "All he ever saw was you boys."

James snorted a little; his breath purled white in the winter air. "He loved you best."

"No, he didn't." The old hurt was still intense, tasting like bitter grapes in the back of her mouth. "He didn't even ask for me when he was dying."

"Yes, he did."

Jewel stiffened, and Bear's gait faltered, sensing the tension flowing from her hands through the reins. "He didn't. He called in each of you boys and spoke to you last."

"Almost right." James tugged his bandanna to cover the tip of his pink nose against the bitter wind. His next words were muffled, and Jewel strained to hear them. "He asked me to send you in next. Said he was saving the best for last."

Jewel swallowed back the feelings in her throat and tried to speak. With an unsteady inhale, she drew the freezing air deep into her lungs. Her voice was low, barely a whisper, when she finally responded. "Is that what he called me? The best?"

James's eyes clung to hers briefly. "Yes."

"Why didn't you ever tell me?" The emotion swelled again, and her thoughts were so loud, so insistent, that she pressed a trembling hand to her forehead so they wouldn't escape. "I thought he just forgot me."

Their horses forged on at a trot, their heads wreathed in white steam from their panting breaths.

"I'm the one who forgot." James ducked his head. "Pa started having trouble breathing, and I ran to get Ma. It slipped my mind because—because..."

"He passed away," Jewel finished for him, marveling, her feelings careering among anger, grief and wonder. All this time, she'd been furious with her father, when he'd asked for her after all. She had been worthy to him. She'd mattered.

Just over the next ridgeline a trail of chimney smoke rose, signaling they neared their ranch house.

"We were trying not to think about losing Pa since we were right in the middle of the season and couldn't stop driving the cattle." James's head lifted, and he blew out a long white breath over his slipping bandanna. "I must have pushed those last moments with him out of my mind... I'm sorry, Jewel." He transferred his reins to his right hand and reached for hers. "Forgive me."

"There's nothing to forgive." The last of her defensive anger chilled, leaving her cold. She squeezed his fingers awkwardly through their thick gloves, then let go. "It's not your fault. I could have insisted on seeing him instead of waiting my turn. Deep down, I didn't think he'd care."

"He cared. Pa wasn't one for showing emotion, but he loved you."

The new thought turned in Jewel's mind, spinning faster

and faster until she grew slightly light-headed. "I should have checked to see if he asked for me."

"I should have remembered," James insisted.

"But the thing is, I was too proud to let you see how much it hurt me, to show you how I felt. If I'd opened up, you would have remembered, and I wouldn't have spent all these years feeling like I wasn't good enough."

"You're more than good enough. Like I said before. You're the best range boss. *Ever.*"

Despite the somber moment, she laughed. So, she had heard James right earlier. James joined in, and their guffaws filled the stable once they reached it and began untacking the horses. They worked side by side in silence, each alone with their thoughts. When she finished, she stroked Bear's silky nose and breathed in the sweet, familiar molasses scent of his feed. She'd been around horses and cattle all her life and took pride in her skill and knowledge. In a way, though, they'd allowed her to avoid people, people she'd assumed would judge her harshly without giving them a chance. The Flower Gala committee, Heath, and James's revelations proved how wrong she'd been.

"What are you going to do about Heath?" James asked once they trudged up the small slope to the ranch house. It glowed like a pearl in the swirling snow. Their feet slipped and slid beneath them. Pickups lined the drive since this year's first ever Cade-Loveland Thanksgiving was being held at Cade Ranch. A new tradition…

She walked toward her home, heedless of the clinging snow, her heated blood in tumult. She was thankful for her amazing blended family, but she wanted more. A family of her own. "What *can* I do? We're miles apart," she finally responded. "I wish he could have come home for Thanksgiving." According to Boyd, he had last-minute work and wasn't sure if he'd make it home in time.

"Are you going to hang around like you did for Pa, waiting to see if he'll ask for you?"

"I can't just leave my job."

James shrugged. "The cattle are in the last grazing cell. After this, we'll put them in the winter pasture and then it's just hay feeding. We can spare you for a few months."

Her heart faltered. "But—but what if he doesn't want me?"

"Then he's an idiot and I'll kill him," James said, infusing a deadly promise in the last part of that statement.

"Over my dead body," Jewel rejoined, just as fierce.

Nothing was more important to her than Heath, even her pride. Being vulnerable didn't equal weakness. She could still be strong and access her softer side.

Of course, she'd already figured those facts out, or she thought she had. Apparently, she had about as much self-awareness as James did about his controlling ways. Maybe less. She groaned. Definitely less.

She should have fully revealed her feelings to Heath and insisted they remain a couple, even long-distance. She'd let her insecurities undermine her happiness—a mistake she would not repeat.

"I'm actually more afraid of you than Heath," James confided with a chuckle.

"You should be," Jewel growled, giving him the shoulder jab he'd earned earlier. When they burst inside the house, the din of voices momentarily quieted.

"Happy Thanksgiving!" Ma called, wiping her hands on the turkey-patterned apron matching her burnt-orange dress. She hurried to give both Jewel and James hugs. She beamed up at them, her eyes shining though her glasses. "You need to get out of those coats and boots. You're wet and freezing."

As she hung James's coat, her face whitened. She grabbed hold of the windowsill and swayed slightly.

"Ma?" Jewel anxiously studied the droplets of perspiration appearing on her mother's brow. James caught her firmly around the waist, steadying her. Since her trip overseas, she tired easier than usual. At first, she'd blamed it on jet lag, but the fatigue never seemed to go away.

"I'm fine." Ma waved them both off and hastily gulped the water Boyd rushed to offer her. "I don't know what you're all fussing about." A timer shrilled in the kitchen. "Oh, now look. There's goes the pies, and I forgot to put the pie shields on them. The crusts will be black!"

Jewel sniffed the air but was unable to detect any telltale scent of burned pastry above the waft of roasted turkey, coffee and buttery mashed potatoes drifting from the kitchen. As Ma hustled away, Jewel, James and Boyd swapped concerned looks. "Has she seen the doctor yet?" she asked Boyd.

"She's fighting me on it." The skin around Boyd's mouth tightened. "Thinks seeing a doctor will make her sick."

"She's always been stubborn." Jewel hung her coat on a peg.

"I see where you get it from." Boyd gave Jewel a one-armed hug. "She promised she'd go in for a checkup after the holiday as long as I won't worry."

"How are you doing keeping up your end of the bargain?"

Boyd's lips twisted in a sad, rueful smile. "Not well. Plus, we've got a new issue with the ranch. Some fella's filed a claim to it. Says he's a brother I never knew about."

"The only thing he's getting is a butt-whooping if he so much as sniffs in our direction." Maverick clapped James on the back, then hugged Jewel.

"We're family now. We'll fight like one. Cades and Lovelands always stick together," James vowed, and the four of them exchanged firm nods. They'd been formidable enemies before but together…whoever this guy was wouldn't stand a chance.

Jewel gnawed on her lower lip as she sauntered into the large, vaulted, two-story living room. Emma, Javi and Noah played hide-and-seek among the furniture while her oldest brother Jack added a log to the flagstone hearth.

"It's nasty out there and getting worse." The flicker of the fire danced across Jack's scarred face. "Wouldn't want to be traveling in it."

Jewel extended her stiff hands toward the dancing flames, soaking in the warmth. "When did you and Dani get in?"

Jack grabbed the poker and thrust it into the fire, stirring it so that sparks flew up the chimney like a swarm of fiery bees. "Around three. We had to stop on account of her getting sick a few times."

Jewel glanced over at Dani, who hauled out a pink ambrosia salad from the fridge, her cheeks just as colorful. In fact, she seemed to glow. Jewel swung narrowed eyes back on her brother. "What kind of sickness?"

Jack stepped closer and lowered his voice. "Morning sickness, though the doctor says the worst should pass when she's out of her first trimester next month." Jack's face, scary to some because of the gash marring his cheek, creaked into an astonished and fiercely proud smile.

She wrapped her arms around his barrel chest and squeezed. "Congratulations! Does everyone know?"

He ran a hand over his thick brush of hair. "We're going to announce it at dinner, but I wanted to tell the baby's godmother first."

Jewel jaw went slack. "Me? A godmother?"

"There's all kinds of mothers, and Dani and I agree you'd make the best kind…if you'll agree?"

"Yes," she choked out, then watched her brother stride away to help his wife.

Jewel dashed the tears from her eyes. Would she make a good mother? She cared about her cattle, worried about every living thing in her charge for that matter. And she'd enjoyed helping at Emma's fairy princess birthday party. Why had she thought having her own children would be different? Stupid her for even thinking she wasn't cut out for motherhood or marriage.

"Is that you, Jewel?"

She glanced up and spotted Amberley, her brother Jared's wife, approaching with her guide dog, Petey. "How's the barrel racing going?"

"I had to pull out of my last competition."

Jewel peered at Amberley's serene face. Funny how the ultracompetitive pro didn't seem the least bit upset about it. "You did? Why?"

Jared ambled close, laid his chin on Amberley's head and reached around to caress the small round of her belly. "It's a secret."

Jewel clutched the top of the rocking chair beside her, reeling. "You're pregnant."

Amberley gasped. "How did you know?" she whispered.

"Just a hunch…and congratulations." The shock wore off and freed her to move. She hugged Amberley. "How far along?"

"About two months." Jared flashed his traffic-stopping smile. "Don't tell anyone. We're going to announce it at dinner."

"You might have to take a number," Jewel muttered, biting back a grin.

"What?" Amberley tilted her head, and her golden hair spilled over one shoulder.

"This is going to be one exciting Thanksgiving." Jewel smiled at the couple and willed her own loneliness away. This was the last holiday she'd spend without a love of her own, she vowed…as long as Heath hadn't rethought his feelings while away or met someone else…

Jared shoved his thick brown hair from his brow. "Who'd have thought we'd be sitting down to a meal with the Lovelands?"

"Better than in a jail cell like we did after the last Christmas party," Jewel quipped.

Jared chuckled. "But look at us now." He brushed Amberley's cheek with a kiss, then led her back to the couch, where a dozing Sofia sat with her feet propped on the wagon-wheel coffee table. Baby Jesse snoozed nearby in a swing.

Something crashed in the kitchen and Jewel raced to help Brielle pick up bits of glass and cranberry sauce. "Clumsy fingers." When Brielle straightened, a thick square of paper fell from her pocket.

"'The honor of your presence is requested at the wedding of Brielle Thompson and Justin Cade.'" Jewel's eyes lifted to meet Brielle's. "Did you two finally set a date?"

Brielle snatched the wedding invitation and thrust it back in her pocket, her normally composed face contorted with emotion. "Yes. But don't tell anyone. Justin's planning to announce it at dinner."

"Wow." Jewel held in a laugh. "Can't wait for things to get started."

"Hey, Jewel." Katlynn, Cole's new wife, passed by bearing water pitchers.

Jewel scooped up a couple of butter dishes and followed her into the dining area. The table was set beautifully with tasteful autumn decorations, a mum-filled cornucopia perfuming the room while light from the overhead fixture reflected in the crystal of the glasses. "How was the honeymoon?"

To everyone's shock but hers, Cole had followed Jewel's advice a couple of months ago and flown to LA to tell Katlynn he shouldn't have let her go. His proposal on national TV and their mountaintop wedding, officiated by Brielle, a former army chaplain, had been beautiful.

"Great." Katlynn flashed the high-wattage smile that made her one of America's most popular television hosts. "We had enough supplies to last us the entire week in the cabin." She set down pitchers at either end of the table.

"You didn't leave it?"

"Nope. Cole's turning me into a hermit, too, I guess." Katlynn pressed a hand to the back of her neck, then her forehead, as if testing her temperature. "It's a nice break from Hollywood."

"I bet."

Katlynn grimaced. "Although, I haven't been able to shake this bug I caught."

Jewel squinted at her fitted sheath dress, a suspicion rising. "You're not pregnant, are you?"

Katlynn's surprised laugh petered out, and her eyes rounded. "You don't think..."

Jewel set a small knife beside the last butter tray. "At this point, nothing about today would surprise me."

"I need to talk to Cole." Katlynn hurried away, leaving Jewel shaking her head and smiling.

And missing Heath.

If she'd followed the advice she'd given Cole, taken a chance and accompanied Heath the Nashville, they'd be together today, too.

After James carved the turkey and platters of food were set out, the Cades and Lovelands finally sat at the long family table. It was extended by two rectangular fold-up tables and a card table to fit the entire clan.

"Let's join hands and pray," Brielle instructed from her seat beside Justin.

James's hand slid in Jewel's, and Javi's laced with the other while they bowed their heads.

"...And we thank you for the love that carries us home and the blessing of your grace," Brielle concluded a moment later.

Amens circled the table, and the group fell on the heaping platters of turkey and fixings like a pack of ravenous animals.

"That was beautiful, Brielle." A puff of steam rose from the roll Boyd split apart.

"Such a beautiful message about opening our hearts to love and family," gushed Ma, spooning mashed potatoes onto Noah's extended plate.

Love that will carry us home...

Jewel, who had been buttering her roll, paused open-mouthed, knife in midair. Brielle's words ran through her mind again. She'd told Heath she was soft on him when he said he cared for her, but hadn't told him she loved him, fearful—deep down—that he might not say it back, just as she'd been too afraid to encounter rejection by asking to see her pa.

What kind of cowgirl was she?

No kind at all if she let her fear get the better of her. No more hiding her feelings, she thought, watching the snow come down outside. Ice crystals coated the glass beside her like clouded lace, but Jewel barely noticed the cold seeping through the panes; she was burning.

She drew a long breath, then pushed back from the table in sudden decision. "I'm heading out."

"What? Where?" James demanded around a mouthful of turkey.

"Not in this weather." Ma twisted her napkin.

"It's important."

Justin's black eyes pierced hers. "What could be important enough to risk your neck in an accident?"

Oh. That was rich coming from daredevil Justin, though he'd certainly settled-down some after his engagement.

Jewel took a deep breath. "I'm going to tell Heath I love him."

The group exploded into laughter.

"Good one, Jewel!"

"She's the most sarcastic of all the Cades put together."

James's eyes met hers, the only look of understanding, empathy, coming from the otherwise incredulous crowd.

"I mean it!" she shouted, then burst into tears, letting go of her thick-skinned facade at last. If they didn't believe her, how would Heath?

A movement in the doorway drew her eye, and she glanced up to see a tall, impossibly handsome cowboy standing there, hand braced against the jamb. Heath. Her head jerked as she did a double take. The sudden leap of her heart at the sight of him was like spotting the first shooting star, a brief and silent streak of light before her eyes. Startling. Wondrous. The universe shifted around her.

Concern darkened Heath's brow and deepened his blue eyes as he strode toward her. He shocked the rowdy group silent by gathering her in his arms. Coldness seeped from his jacket into her shirt, but she didn't shiver. Warmth glowed inside her instead, his touch setting her aglow.

"I love Jewel," Heath proclaimed, staring everyone dead in the eye in a decidedly un-peacemaker way.

Her gaze flitted from her openmouthed family to Heath. Was this going to be complicated? Maybe. But the words doing cartwheels in her head were these: *open yourself to love.*

Love.

She'd never have it if she didn't lower her defenses.

"You really love me?" she asked.

When he nodded, she pulled his face down to hers and kissed him with all the love in her heart, unafraid to show her sentimental side just as Heath was now no longer following anyone else's path but his…or theirs…

A collective gasp rocked the room followed by Javi's, Emma's, and Noah's ewwwwwwwws. Heath drew back. "Jewel and I have some talking to do." Without another word, he grabbed her coat from the hook and ushered her through the door onto the porch.

Outside, the storm had stopped, but the dark sky hung low and heavy, and there was a sense of stillness in the air, the earth awaiting more snow.

Jewel thrust her arms in her jacket and zipped it closed. "What are you doing here?"

"Coming home." Heath twined his fingers in Jewel's and tucked their laced hands into his pockets, pulling her closer. "To you."

"I don't understand. Boyd said you were gigging..."

"We finished the set at midnight, and I hopped the first flight home."

She stared up at him, stunned. The night was still and cold, and yet seemed full of the same restless movement twisting her stomach into knots. "I was planning to do the same thing. I wanted to come home to you, too."

"To Nashville?"

She closed her eyes the moment he released her to circle his arms around her waist. She slid her hands up over his broad shoulders and reveled in his familiar strength. For months she'd felt like a puzzle with missing pieces. Their bodies fit perfectly together, making her feel whole again. "Wherever you are *is* home. I was acting insecure when I let you go. I should have told you how I really felt."

"Which is?" A warmth spread in her belly at the husky note in his voice. He ran his fingers through her hair.

"I'm not happy without you in my life. It doesn't matter how far apart we are. I need you, and I'm not afraid to admit it or to depend on you. I—I love you, too."

His face exploded in a smile. Happiness seemed to pulse

out of him, a flipped switch setting his eyes alight. He smiled all the way from his boot tips. “Of course you do.”

Her dreamy state dissipated, and she shoved him in the chest. It was like shoving a mountain. “Humble? Sensitive? I’d say egotistical fits you better,” she huffed.

“I didn’t mean it like that. It’s just I know you, Jewel. I can’t explain it, especially because we’re so different.” His lips touched hers, tenderly. “But your heart speaks to mine—it always has. Always will.”

Her breath caught as his lips took control over hers. She wrapped her arms around him, holding him close. His tongue swept over hers, and the taste of him drove her crazy. She kissed him back, wrapping her arms around him again. His fingers gently massaged her neck, releasing the tension, erasing the last of her doubts. The kiss became a drug and she craved more with every touch. Their bodies pressed so tightly to each other she had no idea where she began or he ended.

Heath felt strong and warm and muscular and safe and he smelled, oh Lord, delicious. She couldn’t stop kissing him if her life depended upon it: his lips, his jaw, his ear, and Heath seemed as hungry as her. He kissed the corner of her lips and then started a line of tiny kisses that trailed down her throat.

They gasped for air in rapid, synchronized bursts of white. His heart thundered against hers. His lips skated over her cheek toward her ear and he whispered words that made her cheeks burn. At last he drew back slightly, and she rested against him, her muscles loosening, enjoying the relaxing pull of his hand through her hair. His lips whispered across her face.

“What are you doing?”

He pressed a kiss to her forehead. “Indulging a fantasy.”

“Are you kissing my freckles?”

“Maybe.”

"That's your fantasy?"

"One of them."

She shook her head. "You're one twisted cowboy."

He lifted an eyebrow. "And you're just discovering this now?"

She laughed. "Maybe I need to rethink all this. And… I'm sorry things haven't worked out in Nashville yet."

"Things turned out exactly as they should." Heath withdrew his cell phone from his pocket and tapped its music icon.

A female singer Jewel recognized but couldn't name crooned a power ballad with a familiar hook. "Is that…? Did you…? Is she singing one of your songs?"

Heath nodded, and his eyes gleamed with fierce pride. "Freedom Records bought it from me along with eight others. They gave me a songwriting contract."

"Not a singing one?"

Heath shrugged, tucking a lock of her hair behind her ear.

"You don't look upset about it."

"It's the best compromise. I can be a songwriter *and* a rancher. I want to spend most of my time in Colorado, with you, if you'll have me." He trailed a line of blazing kisses along her jaw confusing her brain. Part of her responded to him, clung to him, held him tight again. The other part stiffened, worried about him giving up his dream for her. "But what about being famous? A star?"

His warm breath tickled her ear. "I couldn't care less about that. I only want to love you and make you happy because it makes me happy, too."

She squeezed her eyes tight and squeezed him harder. This man owned her soul and stole her heart. "Then you'll be my star."

"I'll take that…and return it, darlin'. I know what I want most." His hands framed her face and his tone was edged with husky authority mixed with tenderness. "I only want to love you, cherish and protect you for the rest of my life, if you'll have me."

Have him?

As in marriage?

Shock jolted her, and she inched away to make sure she understood. "Before I answer that question, I'd better warn you. I don't believe in quiet, civilized divorces. The only way you'd get out of being married to me would be in a casket."

"Let's remember to put that in our vows." One side of his mouth lifted in an amused, gorgeous smile.

"Not too morbid?"

He held up his thumb and index finger then lowered them. "Nah. So…?"

"I don't need the protecting part, but I'll take every other thing about you for the rest of my life." He'd opened himself to her, giving her love and never asking for anything in return. She rose on her toes to kiss him, the words *I love you* stuck in her mind.

"What about a ring?" A moment later, he pressed his forehead to hers and gazed down at her steadily. "Too soon?"

Her eyes stung. Darn if her entire world wasn't changing. "I'd say right in the nick of time. Let's tell the family."

Heath angled his head at their rubbernecking kin. Lovelands and Cades crowded every window, their fingers and noses pressed to the panes, their breaths fogging the glass. "I think they've got the gist."

"That's the thing about big families, no privacy."

"Ain't it great?"

"Yeah." She laughed softly. "The last person I expected to make news today was me."

"What's that mean?"

"You'll see." She grabbed his hand and nearly dragged

him off his feet. "In fact, we'd better hurry up and share our news to beat the rush."

"What rush?"

"Wait till you hear the bombshells our brothers are about to drop." She wrenched open the door. "We've got to be first."

"Still competitive?" He waved a hand, ushering her inside ahead of him.

"No." She huffed out a breath. "I just think I deserve to be heard first for once."

"I agree." He pressed a kiss to the tip of her nose.

"Oh, and Heath." Jewel held up both hands and waved all her fingers once she stepped inside. "Cades five, Lovelands five. Guess we both won."

Heath lowered her face and captured her lips in a searing kiss. "No guessing about it. Happy Thanksgiving, darlin'."

* * * * *

MILLS & BOON

Coming next month

FROM HEIRESS TO MUM
Therese Beharrie

'Still can't get used to this view,' Hunter said quietly as she stopped next to him.

Autumn followed his gaze onto the city of Cape Town. When she'd moved out of her family home—the Bishop mansion, as some people liked to call it—she hadn't tried to find somewhere outside the city she'd grown up in to live. She'd merely been drawn to the Bouw Estate.

It had green fields that exploded with wildflowers; rolling hills beyond the fields; a river that surrounded the estate. The old manor and barn on the property had been renovated into what were now her home and her bakery, respectively.

'You didn't come here at eleven at night to talk about this view.'

His eyes slid over to her, the brown of them a well of emotion, before his head dipped in a curt nod. 'You're right.'

She gestured to the outdoor table she'd lovingly selected when she'd furnished her house. 'Shall we?'

He nodded, pulled a chair out and stepped back. With a sigh, she sat down, thanking him when he pushed it back in. She waited as he sat down opposite her. A long silence followed. She used it to study him. To watch the emotions play over his face.

When his eyes met hers, she caught her breath, and wished she had something to drink to distract herself from how vulnerable all of this made her feel.

'I don't know how to say this,' he admitted eventually.

She let air into her lungs slowly. 'Just…get it out.'

He angled his head, as if accepting her suggestion, but didn't speak.

'Hunter.' She paused. 'Are you in trouble?'

He opened his mouth, and Autumn could almost see his lips forming no, but then he closed it again. Rubbed a hand over his face; took a deep breath.

'I am.'

She straightened. 'Yeah? You're in trouble?'

His eyes shone with an emotion she couldn't quite define. It disturbed her. She'd dated him for two years; they'd been friends for one more. She should be able to tell what he was feeling.

'Yes.'

After a brief moment of hesitation, she laid a hand on the one he'd rested on the table. 'What's going on?'

He took a breath, then exhaled sharply, his gaze lowering.

'I'm a father.'

Continue reading
FROM HEIRESS TO MUM
Therese Beharrie

Available next month
www.millsandboon.co.uk